Copyright © 2024 by Adrian R. Hale

All rights reserved.

Cover design by Sarah Kill Creative Studio

https://www.SarahKillCreativeStudio.com

Edited by Indie Proofreading

https://www.indieproofreading.com

THE
BOURBON
Bargain

ADRIAN R. HALE

Also by Adrian R. Hale

A Taste of Bliss

Drift Series

Drift Heat

Broken Drift

Southern Gods Series

The Bourbon Bride

The Bourbon Bargain

The Southern Thirst Trap

The Southern Submission

For my people-pleasing, words of affirmation love language girlies realizing you have a praise kink… that's my good girl.

Playlist

Come Back...Be Here (Taylor's Version) – Taylor Swift
I Need My Girl – The National
Make You Miss Me – Sam Hunt
Empire State Of Mind – JAY-Z, Alicia Keys
Follow You – Bring Me The Horizon
Sorry – Aquilo
It's Not Living If It's Not With You – The 1975
Delicate – Taylor Swift
You Still Get To Me – Teddy Swims
Unsteady – X Ambassadors
White Flag – Bishop Briggs
Older – Isabel LaRosa
Stand And Deliver – Patrick Droney
Run This Town – JAY-Z
This Love (Taylor's Version) – Taylor Swift
Golden Hour – Rain Paris
Wildest Dreams – Duomo
The Exit – Conan Gray
Money Ain't A Thang – JAY-Z, JD Surabaya

This story contains explicit sexual content, profanity, may contain mild violence, and topics that may be sensitive to some readers. This story is best suited for readers 18+.

One

Hayes

"You really fucked up this time, big brother. Your Savannah exodus and the fact Paige stayed behind is all over the Atlanta Haute List. Whatever you're trying to do here isn't staying under the radar."

I turn toward the annoyingly chipper voice and see Payton standing in the doorway to my office. It's barely nine in the morning and already he's giving me shit. My shoulders bunch into tight knots of tension and rage, and I give him a stare I'm sure he's familiar with by now.

"You've mentioned it. Do you have anything useful to say, or do you just want to fucking waste time that's better spent working on the roll-out plans?" I stand from my desk and take the few strides to face him in the doorway. I'm ready to bodily remove him from my office.

"Why the fuck are you even here?" Payton crosses his arms and returns my hard stare. "You piss and moan about work stuff that doesn't even matter when you have more important things to take care of."

"Unlike you, I actually care about what happens next with phase two, so I'm working." I grip the heavy door of my office and start to push him out when it's stopped by a more solid and imposing force than just one brother.

"Can't you see, he's hiding from his lady problems, Pay."

Fuck, now they're both starting in on me.

"I'm not hiding. I'm busy." I give up on closing the door and let it bang back into the open position as I stalk back to my chair. Payton and Zander crowd into the office after me and make themselves comfortable on the chairs opposite my desk when they should just turn the fuck around and get out of my sight before I throw my laptop at them.

"I'm no relationship expert, but even I know you need to get your ass on a plane to Savannah and win your girl back."

"Really, Zander, it's that simple?" I scoff. "You have a new woman on your arm every week and never do repeats. I think you're the last person I would take advice from and the least qualified to be dishing out any suggestions right now, anyway."

"Which is why you should really listen to this piece of sage advice that makes complete sense."

I roll my eyes at him.

"Paige seems different. *You* were different with her. She may hate your guts for buying out her company, but that doesn't mean she doesn't still love you. Let me tell you, hate fucking is even better than happy fucking, so it's worth your time and effort just to experience that side of a fight at the very least."

Payton holds out his hand to stop Zander. "Slow your roll, little bro. Hayes may have married her on a whim for his own gain, but there's no way he's in love with a girl he's known less than a month." He turns his attention back to me. "Or would you like to correct my assumption that you only married her for access to her daddy's hotels? Was she actually different and responsible for changing your view on relationships? Did you fall for her, even when you were focused on buying out the very company she was set to inherit?"

I glare at them both and stay silent. Of course I love Paige. There was very little that could have stopped that from happening after just a few days with her beautiful soul and kindhearted ways, despite my penchant for being the very opposite. A now familiar wave of dread passes through me as I think of Paige. I may have fucked this up, but she is the one that fucking left. That was a dagger to the heart of any feelings I could have fallen into. Now I'm trying to stay removed from any of the desires to believe in love she may have kindled in me.

"He doesn't even have to answer. Look at that dorky expression on his face as he thinks about her now. He's head over heels, and he knows he's fucked up big time."

I turn the force of my glare on Zander and wish they would just fucking leave.

"If you care that much about her, I repeat, what the fuck are you doing here? We have everything under control and plenty of teams working on phase two. You're not needed here, but I'm sure there's a feisty girl who actually needs you right now." Payton tips his head toward the open door.

I am done with their patronizing. They don't understand the situation in the least. I slam my palm down on the desk so hard it shudders. "There's nothing to do about it. She walked out on me." My words come out harsh, my tone meant to stop them from their conjecture and mockery.

"Ah, it all makes sense now. His pride is bruised," Zander says in a mock whisper to Payton. "He's never been rejected, even when he deserved it."

Payton leans his chin onto his fist, his elbow propped on his knee. "You could have warned her, you know. Told her about your plans for the future that included her hotels. Maybe she would have warmed to the idea, or at least not left when she found out."

I clench my fist until my knuckles crack. "Well, I didn't, so stop telling me what I should have done and get the fuck out."

"Why don't you just put her in charge of the eastern contingent of hotels? She's young, but from what I've heard, she was born and bred to run the hotels anyway, so she could be a good fit."

I snap my gaze to Zander, who leans back comfortably in the leather chair.

"Don't you think I've considered that option?" I grind out. "Paige was set to inherit the hotels, not just run them. They would have been hers, rather than a small group she oversaw for someone else. The consolation prize would be a slap in the face to her lost legacy."

"It's better than nothing. Or you could give her an entirely new legacy. You've got plenty of companies under your personal enterprise to have something that would suit her. Time to pony up the big gifts, Hater." His use of the childhood nickname ruffles the feathers he was just smoothing with the potentially plausible idea.

She could rule the Underworld Spirits brand without breaking a sweat. I don't even have to give it a second thought. I pick up my phone and dial legal. It might be an act of desperation, and who knows if she'll accept, but it may just be what she needs. But could it make what I have done less egregious? I fucking hope so. I will do anything to get my wife back and reverse some of the damage I have inflicted.

"Draw up contracts for the transfer of Underworld Spirits. Put it in Paige's name and give her controlling interest, too. Yes, I know that means my share would decrease. No, I don't want any stipulations for how she wants to run the business. It'll be up to her." It takes a few moments to start the process and I hang up, satisfied I can have this well in hand just as easily.

"And that is why I'm the CEO. I come up with brilliant ideas. You really should listen to me more," Zander quips to Payton.

"Yeah, Zand, I'll take your advice when I want a sexually transmitted disease or a broken bone from an extreme sport." Payton rolls his eyes in an exaggerated way and I almost smile. Almost.

"One fucking time I crash from a skiing accident, and you think it happens every time. I'm all healed up and not pushing the sharp bone ends of a compound fracture out of my arm, thank you for asking."

"You refute the broken bone comment but not the STD? Telling." Payton says.

"I'm clean, so there was no need to even deem it worthy of comment."

"I've started the big gesture, so you can both fuck off now." I wave my fingers along with my words and hope they just go. They can continue their bickering elsewhere for all I care. I feel the headache building and just want to make things right with Paige if she'll even let me.

"That's only the beginning, Hayes. Sure, the big gesture is nice and may soothe her hurt feelings over losing the future she was groomed for, but now you gotta figure out how to make right all the shit that likely came with it. Betrayal! Underhanded business dealings! Lies!" He animates his words with jacking off hand gestures.

"Zand is right, and I don't admit that easily, but I will when it's you who has fucked up and needs to hear it."

Payton inclines his head my way and I'm back to hating my brothers. I cross my arms over my chest and glare at him. He levels me with his own surly look before he continues.

"You're in luck. We're on the case of returning your balls to Paige because she's the only one who deserves to carry them in her Chanel purse."

I bristle and I'm about to once again demand they get the fuck out when Zander speaks.

"If you want to keep that beautiful wife of yours and avoid the annulment, or worse, the divorce I'm sure her daddy is itching to file—taking half of everything you have—you better take notes." He holds up one finger. "First, you need to admit that what you did was wrong, even if you managed to get the outcome you wanted from the situation. Second, you need to apologize for putting your shit first, instead of her. Third, you need to get on your knees and eat that pussy like it's your favorite ice cream."

"Bravo, Zand. You managed to make what was a half-decent apology vulgar," Payton says as his eyes roll toward the ceiling.

"Listen, I may not do relationships, but even I know an apology is best served with a side of cunnilingus, vulgar or not." Zander brings his hand to his mouth, splitting his fingers into a V and flicking his tongue through the opening.

"You're a fucking idiot," I growl and swat at him across my desk to make him stop.

"You most definitely need to fight to get her to forgive you, but no one said you have to fight fair. Now get your ass out of this office and don't show your stupid face again until you have your bride back." Zander stands and rounds the desk, grabs the laptop out of my protesting hands, and shoves it into my briefcase.

"He has a point. Use whatever means necessary if she's really that important to you. Otherwise, you might as well just let her go and move on because you got what you wanted. Either way, you need to ease the fuck up on everyone here and get on with it." Payton comes around the opposite side of the desk, palming my shoulders and forcing me out of my chair before pulling my suit jacket from the hook on the wall and folding it over my arm.

"I can't believe I'm actually listening to you two fools," I grumble, now standing between my two irritatingly stupid, but loyal, brothers.

"I already called the pilot. He's on standby to fly you to Savannah whenever you're ready."

I tilt my head and appraise Payton.

"You were that confident you could convince me that you arranged for the pilot to be on standby?" I cross my arms over my chest and wonder at the ruthless manipulation skills of my brothers. I've seen them in action many times, but I never realized they could work so well on me.

"You were getting on that plane of your own free will or with us throwing you on it, so yeah, I made the arrangements in advance."

"You shifty motherfucker."

"Oh, shut the fuck up and go get your girl already. Jesus, it's like you prefer being here, giving us shit, to fucking your hot wife. If you're that ambivalent about it, I'll take it from here."

My hand is on Zander's throat before I realize I've moved. He's pinned to the door and struggling to breathe, his hands clawing at mine.

"Don't you ever talk about fucking my wife. I don't care if it's a joke, you say one word that even insinuates you're thinking about her that way and I will end you, brother or not." My voice is a low growl of rage and Zander's eyes widen when he takes it in.

"Hayes, let him go."

Payton places his hands on my shoulders, but he doesn't force me away, likely knowing I would smash my elbow into his face if he even tried. I have murderous intent on my mind, and he'd be my next victim.

"He fucking asked for it, but you can't choke out your own brother for a misspoken and crass joke."

I release my hold on Zander and back up a step, fully expecting him to throw a punch and turn this office into the sparring ring of our youth. He rubs his neck and sends me a dark stare that crackles with electricity.

"You get one pass for being in a fucked up headspace over your girl, but if you ever touch me like that again, I'll bust that perfect nose of yours in a way no surgeon will be able to fix." He reaches out and flicks the tip of my nose with his finger. "Boop."

I knock his hand away and lunge for him, but Payton grabs me by the arms and stops me.

"That's enough, you fuckheads. Zander, get out of the fucking way and quit antagonizing him. Hayes, get your ass out of this office and try to salvage what's left of your marriage before it's too late." He shoves me past Zander and hands me my briefcase, physically separating me from going back in to knock out my asshole of a brother.

"I swear to God, if you put half of the aggression you're displaying into fighting for your wife, maybe you wouldn't be in this position." Zander's grumbling is low and fed up, but I hear him loud and clear as I spin on my heel and leave the office.

I crack my neck and shove a hand through my hair as I stalk through the building to the elevator and punch the garage button hard enough to crack it. It kills me that he's fucking right. I should have fought harder for Paige. If I had transferred the energy I spent this week being irritated by my brothers to mending my relationship, I wouldn't be in this shitty place. *Unless it's too late and there's no mending what I broke.*

Fuck.

I didn't stop her from walking out on me because it hurt. Yeah, emotionally it devastated me, but it was my ego that suffered most realizing that she would even consider it. It fucking tore me apart watching her walk away, but I couldn't comprehend her not even *wanting* to listen to me. I let her go, thinking she should have given me the chance to explain myself. That she owed me the opportunity to explain, which would have made it so easy for me to turn things around.

It's taken me a few days to realize that maybe Paige was *never* beholden to my right to an explanation, though she deserved to hear the truth from my lips. It was still selfish of me to expect her to sit quietly and let me validate my actions when every step to that point hurt her in some way. She was justified in her anger whereas I wasn't, and that's a tough pill to swallow when you're used to getting your way and having people bow and scrape to keep you happy.

It's my turn to bow and scrape. I owe that much to her. I owe her everything.

Two

Paige

I'm going stir-crazy, holed up in my apartment, pacing like a caged tiger at the zoo after turning my phone off. It was ringing and pinging nonstop with calls and messages from Mama, her friends, and people I've never even met trying to get me to comment on the state of my marriage. I can't stay here like this anymore. I pull on a baseball cap and set out on a walk to a nearby park just to get a little reprieve from nearly climbing the walls. I need fresh air and exercise to sate the anxious energy rippling through me like a roadside puddle disturbed by passing cars.

"Where's your new beau, sugar? I wouldn't let a handsome man like that out of my sight," a woman I've never met says as I pass her on the street.

I guess I won't be able to even walk around Savannah for a while without someone stopping me to ask about what should be my private affairs, either. I don't know when my life became so interesting, but I'd like to go back to being relatively unknown. I've kept a low profile for years hoping to keep myself out of the Savannah gossip mill, yet here I am, right in the middle of it anyway, getting crushed for the amusement of others. Is this what my life would be like if I stay with Hayes? A spectacle for others to comment on and my reputation forever to be known as the girl who was too young, too foolish, and too hasty to marry a billionaire after knowing him for a week. It doesn't look good, even from my own vantage point. It's no wonder people are voicing their concerns and opinions openly to me on the street. I look like the biggest idiot, and of course Hayes gets away with his own reputation unblemished.

The most infuriating part is that everyone seems to think *I* was the one to mess this up, and for whatever reason—maybe because Hayes is rich, or older, or a high-profile businessman—it's somehow my fault. Newsflash: Money and age don't make you impervious to making mistakes that you need to own up to, and Hayes has a lot of responsibility to accept for his part in whatever this is. A fight for the ages, I would imagine. *Or the end of everything we had together.*

While it was once a delight, right now I hate that I live off Broughton Street, a busy shopping area, with people out in droves this afternoon. *What day is it, again?* I look around at the shoppers with bags on their arms and see the holiday displays in the windows as I pass each store. *Oh.* Christmas must be less than two weeks away by now. A fresh wave of sadness and pain pierces my chest. I was going to spend my first Christmas with Hayes, and now I'm thinking I will spend it perfectly alone, since I'm not on speaking terms with Mama and Daddy, either.

As I'm passing a boutique I usually love to pop into, Liliana Bailey and Amber Cramer, two girls I went to school with, exit together with shopping bags in hand. They turn directly into my path, and I have a moment of panic, instantly trying to avert my face so they don't recognize me. I just want to get past them quickly and avoid any kind of conversation.

Liliana snags my arm, so I have to stop, and turns me toward them. "Oh, Paige, we were *just* talking about you," she says sweetly, though her smile is vicious.

"Hello, Liliana, Amber," I say with begrudging politeness. My practiced manners are the only things keeping me from being rude and snubbing them completely, even if I'm not yet ready to engage with her on whatever she is speaking about.

Of course, they would be talking about me. As the reigning mean girls at our high school and members of the social circles that keep Savannah afloat, I was always subject to Liliana's tortuous attention and Amber's willingness to go along with whatever cruel plot Liliana came up with. I thought I had managed to escape the worst of it as an adult. Who knows what Liliana's jealous of this time, or if she really is just that mean.

"We were wondering how you could be separated from your billionaire husband so quickly. I mean, that's the rumor going around, and you look like shit, so it must be true. What happened?" Liliana asks, her voice dripping with sarcastic concern.

"You had it good, why'd you let that man get away?" Amber adds with mock sincerity as she comes up on my other side, trapping me between them.

"I'm sorry, I really have to go," I say as I duck my head. I wish I had turned in the opposite direction when I left my apartment. It's just my luck to actually see someone I know at exactly the worst time. I try to remove my arm from Liliana's clutches, but she clamps down harder and keeps me in place.

"How did someone like *you* get the attention of someone like Hayes Olsen in the first place? He is way out of your league, and I just don't know what he saw in you." Liliana's gaze rakes me from head to toe, taking in my jeans, chunky sweater, and the hat I threw on over my lank, unwashed hair before leaving. Her lip curls in distaste as she flicks her silky auburn hair over her shoulder.

I silently meet her cold brown eyes briefly and fidget uncomfortably. I've asked myself that very question. What could Hayes have seen in me?

"Oh, wait, it must have been because he wanted to buy your daddy's hotel group. What a shame that is for you," Liliana says, her bubblegum pink lips curving up into a mean smile. "Bless your heart. You must have been collateral damage for him to get what he truly wanted. There is no way he actually wanted to be with *you* of all people." She tsks. "That must be it. How sad for you, Paige. If only you had a little more experience you could have kept him interested longer. But no, he got what he wanted and dumped you like yesterday's garbage."

Tears prick my eyes, and I am frantic to leave before she can see just how badly she's hurt me with her words. "That's enough, please let me go," I plead, my eyes downcast.

"You should have stuck with Garrison Daniels when you had the chance. At least his mama and daddy would have made him stay married to you, not that he really cared about you. Gosh, you really are just a means to an end, aren't you, sweety?" Amber says, her smile just as vicious as Liliana's when I risk a glance in her direction.

A tear tracks down my cheek as I yank my arm away from Liliana and take shaky steps away from these horrible women who laugh as I flee. I turn a corner to get away from the busy street and my tormentors, feeling the tears sliding down my cheeks unchecked. Of course they know about Mama's plan to marry me off. That means all of Savannah does, too, since they are notorious gossips who relish spreading hurtful rumors and truths alike.

I turn into the park and take a trail off the main path, heading into the Spanish moss-draped oaks and magnolias to find a space that's not crowded with people so I can sob freely. I sit with my back to an ancient oak and wipe my cheeks. It's so unfair that I am cast in the villain role. This thing with Hayes didn't happen without both of us contributing to the fight, and I know the part I played. I walked out when he betrayed my trust when I probably should have stayed long enough to get the explanation I was due. Walking out after that may have still been warranted, but I'll never know for sure because I acted on emotion.

Now, pride keeps me from reaching out, especially knowing the mess that the South thinks of me. The Fairchild name is being dragged through the mud and my reputation is the lowest it's ever been, all because people make assumptions about a situation they have no business discussing. This is between Hayes and me. But... isn't he the one who needs to reach out? If he wanted to make things right, he could have just come after me at The Abyss and fought for us. He chose not to do that and here we are, separated for nearly as long as we were together.

When I'm cried out and done feeling sorry for myself, I stand and let my hands drag over the large leaves of the bushes to my sides as I walk aimlessly through the interior of the park. Rationally, I know I had every right to be upset that he wouldn't have included me in such an important, life-altering decision that one hundred percent affects me. And if he had his head too clouded with business wheeling and dealing to see that, it's his loss.

Being in the right doesn't make it any easier to weather this storm. Hayes became all-consuming for the short amount of time he was a fixture in my life, and it absolutely sucks to be without him now. I hate the part of me that wants to call him, or even drive to Atlanta and beg him to take me back like I was in the wrong, but it's undeniable that I miss Hayes. His warmth, his big arms that make me feel so safe and protected when I'm in them, the way he could look at me and I knew I was treasured. I especially miss his demon spawn dog and even Hayes's devilish ways.

So much can change in a matter of weeks, and I'm discovering that in some cases, those changes are indelible. Like my heart. It was whole and untarnished a few weeks ago, but now it's cracked and there isn't anything that can fix the Hayes-shaped hole that's left behind.

A snapping twig catches my attention and I freeze mid-stride. I slowly set my foot down and turn to look around me. I don't see anyone in particular, so it could have been a squirrel or bird that made the noise. I resume my walk, but my steps are a little quicker and I head toward the pathways that crisscross through the park so I feel less alone.

Being this angry is also an isolating experience. I'm lonely. I've refused to speak to my parents right along with Hayes. I've come to expect ruthless dealings from

Mama, but Daddy selling the hotels without even consulting me showed a new side of his own calculation. It all comes down to money, and I'm beginning to see that it really is the root of all evil. Even if it can make you happy in a materialistic way, it can just as easily destroy you.

A few people are walking through the park when I reach the paths, and I keep my head down to avoid making eye contact with any of them as we pass. I feel my shoulder bumped and I look up to catch the eye of a man in dark clothing as he brushes past me. I mumble an apology and shiver, hugging my arms around my body as I continue walking toward home.

Despite all that she did, I find myself wanting to call Mama and ask for her to take over again. Maybe things would go back to normal, even if my normal has had a seismic shift from what I was used to. I pull my cell out of my back pocket and stare at the screen, debating if I have it in me to do it. With a big sigh, I swipe the screen open and have the phone dialing before I can overthink one more thing. I don't have to force myself to be lonely and sit in my pain all by myself. I do have people in my life who care about me, even if they are few and far between.

"Hey, sorry to call you out of the blue," I say, pressing my free hand against my eyes. "I guess I just need someone right now who gets me."

Three

Hayes

I can't find my wife.

I've searched all over Savannah and can't seem to locate where she has gone to ground. All I want to do is have my chance to grovel, but I can't even get on my knees if I can't find her. I've had my assistant scouring everywhere and providing addresses where she might be, but my list is exhausted.

Except for her parent's house, where I'm currently haunting the doorstep of the large, covered porch that spans the entire front of their historic home. It's not as grand as The Mansion that they just sold to me, but it's stately and fitting for a family like the Fairchilds.

I run a hand through my hair and mount the steps that take me to the large front door. If there is a God, I hope he's merciful, because I'm about to step into the lion's den and I am not prepared. This is not like a business deal. It's rather like facing an executioner on their day off, and I have just the head they want to chop off.

I ring the doorbell and listen to the chiming sound it makes through the door, hoping they aren't here and I can check another stop off on my list to find Paige. Instead, I see a shadow approaching through the sidelight and know I couldn't get that lucky.

"Well, if it isn't Mr. High and Mighty come to darken my doorstep. I'd say it's a pleasure, but I'd be lying." Caroline Thackery Fairchild minces no words in her displeasure at seeing me. She doesn't even give me the niceties one would expect from her social standing.

"Ma'am," I say, inclining my head in her direction and trying to keep my temper from rising through proper Southern manners alone, even if she won't. "Is Paige here?" I feel like a high school boy coming to pick up a prom date and facing down the dragon lady of a mother she has instead.

Caroline's mouth pinches and her green eyes which are so much like Paige's stare daggers at me. "Why would I tell you that? You're the worst thing to happen to this family since the Civil War."

"I beg your pardon," I sputter, knowing full well it's futile to fight with her, but I'm not *that* bad. "I just want to talk to Paige. I have a lot I need to tell her, and she won't answer my calls or texts. And she isn't anywhere I can find her in Savannah."

"Well, she's not here and I'm glad she's not giving you the time of day. You don't deserve my daughter and never will," she seethes, her hand white-knuckled around the edge of the door.

"Caroline—Mrs. Fairchild, I love Paige very much," I hold up a hand to stop her quick retort, "despite what my business dealings may look like to you. I know I messed up, and I just want to work through it with her, which is damn hard to do when I can't even find her to fight for her."

Caroline seems to defrost the tiniest bit, her pinched mouth smoothing and her eyes beginning to lose some of the zeal they had a moment before. "That filthy Atlanta gossip site had something to say about Paige again today. Another mark against you, for bringing her onto their radar and making her a target for all of Georgia to pick apart." I definitely haven't won her over, but that one admission points me in a new direction I can potentially use to find Paige.

"I appreciate you telling me that." I take a step away from the door, ready to turn and book it down the steps to the drive. I shake my head and turn back before I make it to the driveway. "She has me bent out of shape and head over heels," I say, staring at the wide porch beneath my leather Ferragamos. "I wouldn't be looking for her if I wasn't completely in love with her and wanting to ensure our future together."

"You're a calculating devil, and I don't believe a word you say," she replies, though the tone has cooled from her initial fire.

"You don't have to believe my words, I'll show you," I say as I turn and take the steps two at a time.

Four

The Atlanta Haute List

Spotted: Savannah Heiress Catching Flights, Not Feelings

Paige Fairchild, former hotel heiress and newly minted wife of Olympic International CFO Hayes Olsen, was seen boarding a commercial flight from Savannah to JFK, sans billionaire bridegroom. What, no private jet for the brand-new bride? We smell trouble in paradise. Time apart is quickly outpacing the time together column on this business deal, and we are more than wondering if our favorite billionaire brother will end up back on the market as Atlanta's most eligible bachelor. The whirlwind romance of Fairchild and Olsen did seem too good to be true, but even our Grinch hearts wanted to see them have their own Hallmark Christmas movie moment. Too soon to tell, or has the ink dried on an annulment? Click Like and Subscribe for all the Haute gossip.

Five

Paige

"Thank you for getting me out of Savannah and away from everything," I say, tucking my head into Alex's shoulder in the back of the cab. My best friend saved me, once again, from a situation I had no control over, and I am unendingly grateful to have at least one person ready to take on this hot mess express.

"It's pretty unusual for you to tell me you're hiding from your Mama, who wanted to marry you off, and the next time I hear from you it's because you actually *are* married and things aren't going well. I thought the obvious response was to get you up here just so I could hear the whole story," Alex says, wrapping an arm around my shoulders and giving me a squeeze. "Besides, it's been too long since you've been to The City to visit, and I found a really good new Korean fusion restaurant you will die for."

I smile, the movement feeling foreign on my face. "Of course you did. Does it have a Michelin star or a mouse problem?" I tease.

"I can't say for sure, but I didn't personally see any rodents," Alex says with a trace of laughter in his voice.

"Sounds like one of your winners, then." I sigh deeply and feel a weight lift off my chest. It's so nice to feel normal and to leave the mess of my life behind in Savannah. A streak of guilt passes as I think of the habit I've made of running from disasters. I'm not very good at sticking around through the hardships, it seems. Maybe I can add that to my vision board for next year—*stop running from your messes*. That'll be great.

The Manhattan skyline looms out the windows in bits and snatches between buildings as we make our way through Brooklyn to Alex's apartment. New York feels like the polar opposite of Savannah. Fast to slow and big enough to get lost in instead of being front-page news. It's a welcoming relief.

Alex's fifth-floor walk-up has a decent, if partially obstructed, view of the Williamsburg Bridge and a lot of mural art featured prominently on neighboring buildings, which of course is super inspiring for the hipster art scene that Alex loves.

"I've got a great new kombucha from the local artisan market that you have to try," Alex says, unlocking a series of deadbolts to open the door. "It's ginger, which is so warming for these cold months when everything is gray and the stupid snow sticks around too long."

I shiver in my light jacket and think a hot latte sounds better, but I'm willing to settle. "That sounds great. I could use something to warm up. I didn't anticipate the cold. Savannah was so mild, and I packed so quickly I didn't think about a winter coat. I guess I really have been away from New York too long."

"Don't worry, I have plenty of coats you can borrow if you need one." Alex pushes open the door and bows me inside the tiny one-bedroom he's lucky enough to call home without the requisite roommate situation that New York City is known for.

I execute my best curtsy and step into the vibrant apartment, decked out with deep blue-green walls in the kitchen, exposed brick in the living room, and funky mid-century light fixtures. I loved living in The City during my internships and would have considered moving here permanently had I not anticipated running the Xenios Group from Savannah. My heart squeezes involuntarily when I remember The Mansion and the hotels will be under new ownership come the new year, and I instantly spiral back into anger and frustration.

"Quick, tell me something about your life that is really fun and distract me before I start to cry," I say, flopping onto Alex's mustard yellow velvet sofa that was probably a vintage store purchase. Or maybe it came off the street. You never know with Alex's taste running so eclectic.

"I went to a warehouse party last week and ended up coming home with a drag queen's wig on and in someone else's sequined pants," Alex deadpans. "The wig is in the oven because it freaked me out so bad the next morning. Be sure to remove it before pre-heating if you plan to bake, as I'm pretty sure it's plastic and will melt." Alex hands me a cold bottle of kombucha.

I burst into laughter at the mental image. "You did not," I say on a wheeze.

"The sequined pants are actually really awesome. I felt like Harry Styles, so that was most definitely a good trade." Alex falls onto the couch next to me, reaches his hand under, and drags out the red sequined pants. "You can wear them if you need a pick me up."

"You have the strangest life," I say, holding my sides from the laughter. It feels wonderful to laugh like this again.

"I think you could probably beat me, as of late. Feel like sharing what the last few weeks have been like since I saw you at your debutante ball?" Alex settles back on the couch, tucking a leg under him and giving me his full attention.

My laughter and mirth fade but I give him a look of appreciation and comfort. Alex and I used to have plenty of heart-to-hearts back in high school before he transitioned, and I am so glad it feels just as natural to want to pour my heart out to my best friend now. Though his hair is shorter and his mama can't make him wear frilly dresses anymore, not that she had much luck when Alex was younger, either, I'm so glad it feels just as natural to want to pour my heart out to my best friend now. I take a sip of the effervescent drink and wrinkle my nose at the taste. Kombucha is not for me, but it certainly was bracing. I set the bottle down and clear my throat to begin.

"Well, let's see. I met a man, ran away to Atlanta with him, fell in love, got married, and then he bought my legacy out from under me and broke my heart," I summarize.

Alex whistles. "When you commit to something, you *really* commit. Tell me more about the man who finally swept you off your feet and got you interested enough to marry him within a week. And please say it wasn't some idealistic bullshit like you wanted to stay a virgin until you got married, because that is archaic and something the patriarchy and religion have used to control female bodies for millennia."

I brush a finger under my eyes when I feel the tears start. "Nothing so archaic as that. His name is Hayes Olsen, and he's the CFO of Olympus International. I met him at my debutante ball, right after you left and I snuck up to the rooftop garden to get away from Mama."

I sniffle and actually sit with the memory for a minute before continuing because it really was so beautiful. That first meeting will forever haunt me in the best, most romantic sense.

"Alex, it was like lightning. Finding him in the moonlit garden, wreathed in cigar smoke with a glass of bourbon in hand, it felt like I was seeing a man for the very first time. His voice literally drew goosebumps up my arms, and his eyes, wow, were they something to fall into. I knew within the hour that he was something special I wanted to know more about, so when I saw him the next day after fleeing the family dinner Mama used as the cover story for trying to marry me off, I thought my best option was to go with him to Atlanta to get away and maybe get to know him a little better."

"I cannot believe your mama tried to marry you off," Alex says, smacking a hand into a round pillow and hauling it against his chest as he becomes more involved in my story. Southerners live for juicy family drama. "Talk about archaic. That arranged marriage thing isn't for people like us. No wonder you ran off."

It's refreshing that Alex *hasn't* heard all of this second or third-hand and he's hearing it from the source. *Thank you, New York City, for not caring a lick about an insignificant Southern belle and her would-be romance gone wrong.*

I nod and pinch my lips together for a moment to staunch the hint of nausea that rises at the memory. "To

Garrison Daniels, of all people, so we could join the family businesses. I thought she had lost her mind. I ran out of dinner and straight into Hayes's arms, it turned out."

"That is insane. I always knew Caroline Thackery Fairchild was a calculating woman, but that seems beyond her normal level of overbearing pageant mom-ing."

I roll my eyes. "You're telling me. There have been many lines that she has crossed in this life, but that was too much for me."

"Not to skip over your crazy mama, but back to Hayes Olsen, because I've heard of him. He's a freaking billionaire! And isn't he, like, kind of old for you? That's so hot. Did you call him Daddy? Or maybe he's more of a Zaddy?" Alex asks, but his smile is all teasing.

"No, of course I didn't! He's only thirty-five, so it's not like he's old enough to be my actual dad. But I did say several filthy things in the span of a week and decided I really, really like sex with him," I admit, my cheeks heating as I press my hands to my face. Alex is the first person I've been able to talk with about this and I find I really want to delve into just how good it was.

"Paige Fairchild, as I live and breathe! You had sex and you *liked it.* Hussy! That means you held out for a good one, and I'm happy for you." Alex pulls me into an awkward sitting hug that I return as best I can. "But wait, I know there is so much more to this story that I am still missing. Go on," he says, releasing me and making a carry-on motion with his hand.

"Oh, goodness. Where to start on how it went badly?" I muse, sorting the days and incidents in my head. "Well, Mama wouldn't give up on me marrying Garrison. She even sent him all the way to Atlanta to retrieve me. The police had to escort him off Hayes's property, which was a moment of justice if I've ever seen one."

"He deserves that and more." Alex shakes his head, his lips pinched flat.

I feel a vindictive smile stretch my own mouth. It's a foreign expression but feels justified when thinking about Garrison Daniels and how easily he was let off the hook for what he did. And not just to me. Hayes said there were at least six other women who were his victims.

"Hayes said Mama wouldn't be able to make me marry Garrison if I was already married. I said yes because I was already in love with him and just like that we flew to Las Vegas and were married within hours, which, now that I say it out loud, actually sounds completely bananas and I would be cringing for any other girl telling this story." I drop my face into my hands, feeling my cheeks heat with embarrassment.

"I always thought you would be the marrying type rather than the casual fling type, but that's really fast for you. I think it was just a whirlwind of everything you never knew you wanted hitting you all at once and also an answer to a bad situation. What happened to get you here in New York without your new husband?"

I lift my face and tuck my hair behind my ear, making a mental note of the cracks in the brick wall across from us. "I'm pretty sure Hayes had been planning to buy Daddy's company before he ever met me. I don't know what he planned to do with me initially when I ran into him after leaving that disastrous dinner, but I certainly brought plenty of fuel to the fire he had going wanting to buy up the hotels. He must have been working on the deal the entire time I was staying with him, falling in love with him, and thinking he was just as in love with me." I shift in my seat as I realize just how naive I was. "The day after we were married we went back to Savannah, and he talked Daddy into selling my legacy along with the whole company. I'm still trying to wrap my head around how someone I thought loved me enough to marry me could buy out my legacy. I don't know all of the details, only what Mama told me over a short phone call before I left Hayes."

Gosh, it sure sounds bad when I admit that out loud. I didn't let Hayes tell me his side at all, believing Mama, who has been dead-set on controlling every facet of my life for so long. Not that there could be much in the way of reasons Hayes bought the Xenios Group that would have eased my anger over being lied to and manipulated, but I didn't even give him the opportunity.

"I guess the silver lining is that he stuck to a plan he had before ever meeting you, rather than seeing an opportunity and wanting to exploit it, ya know? It's still pretty messed up either way." Alex reaches out and squeezes my shoulder. "What do you want to do now?"

I sigh and stare up at the ceiling that has a faint, yet ominous, water stain. Everything around me spells disaster.

"I don't know if there is a simple answer. I really rushed into this, so there's the logical side of me that wants to downplay the feelings and write it off as a fluke, maybe just wash it all away with an annulment."

It wouldn't be the first time I let a bad situation direct the course of my life. I managed to keep my head down and stay away from men and dating entirely for seven years after Garrison tried to have his way with me, so why shouldn't I become a hermit and remove myself from society for the rest of my life after this particular patch of bad luck?

"I hear a huge *but* in that statement, so out with the rest of your thoughts," Alex coaxes.

"Fast or not... my feelings were real, and I so badly want them to be true for us. It's just... really hard to align the falling in love with this incredible man part and also knowing how calculating and underhanded he is. I told him how important running the hotels was to me, and how that's the only thing I've ever wanted to do, and he never even hinted at his plans to take away what I wanted so much." I feel so stupid about this whole situation. Distance really gives a new perspective, whether I want it or not.

"Just playing the devil's advocate here, but if you were in Hayes's position, would you have said a thing about the acquisition? Don't those brothers have a reputation for ruthlessly acquiring whatever they want to expand their empire, then they strip the businesses down to the small portion that makes all of the profits while disposing of the rest? It's probably ingrained in him now to think about what they are taking over next, without a thought for the people who get the short end of the stick in the process. To him, it's probably just business." When I look up at Alex, he has an apologetic expression plastered on his face.

Ugh. That's a gut punch. "So I was cannon fodder for the takeover blowback and he gets a free pass?"

Alex rolls to his knees and leans forward to squeeze my cheeks between his hands. "Of course not, you nut! In my mind, he's one hundred percent a bad man for taking away something you loved. However, there are"—he pauses and settles back on the couch—"layers, I guess. I'm totally on your side, but I've had too many years of therapy to just ignore that relationships are complicated, and people have many perfectly valid, and sometimes not so great, reasons for why they do what they do."

"Can I stay petty and mad about this situation while you look at it from your healthy mindset from therapy, or do I have to be rational and accept everything you say?"

"Honey, we are Southern. We get to be petty even when we rationalize. We just do a great job of making people guess about the motives because we smile and play nice with them despite it."

I laugh and feel another layer lighter. Maybe I can get through this, after all.

"Why do you have to live so far away? I need you nearby all the time so I can get through my own junk without completely ruining everything. Come back to Georgia, please."

"Georgia tends to deny all of my human rights because I'm a transgender person, so I don't think I'll be calling it home anytime soon," Alex says nonchalantly, despite the roller coaster the last few years have been. There was a huge strain on him to live in a state that dislikes people who have chosen a different path than the one those in power think is right.

What a reality check it is, listening to his quick summarization of the harrowing experience he had, when I thought my life was hard. Confusing, yes, but hard? Not by a long shot. I am privileged beyond belief, and my problems are small, though still important to me. It's very hard not to get caught up in them, in the moment.

"Be straight with me, should I try to make things work with Hayes, or do I give up and concede maybe my mama was right?"

"Well, I haven't been straight a day in my life, so that's a tough ask," he deadpans, and we both laugh. "I think the question you need to answer is if you *want* to make it work, no matter what else comes with it. Also, we both know your mama is never right when it comes to you, so stop allowing her to live rent-free in your brain."

Easier said than done.

I mull over this thought, sinking further into the couch cushion as I do. "I'm out of my element here. I don't know the first thing about relationships and what's worth the fight or not," I admit, tugging my lip into my mouth with my teeth.

"I don't think you have to be a relationship expert to know when you are treated well or not, and you can always decide if the relationship brings you joy or causes you too much suffering."

"It's all mixed up together, the joy and the pain. How am I supposed to disentangle everything I felt in the whirlwind that happened in just two weeks?"

"Well, how about reframing the question. Would you be disappointed if this relationship never happened, despite all of the heartaches?"

The memories feel like weapons as I fight my way backward through the short time I have known Hayes. There was an instant attraction and connection, which is unusual for me. He didn't have to give a silly Southern belle the time of day, yet he was kind and helped me when I needed it. He promised to worship my body when I was ready, and boy did he follow through. I've never been so in control of what I wanted than when I was with Hayes, and that thought buoys me up out of the current with a clarity I have been lacking.

"I would do it all again," I whisper, feeling the truth in my words like a golden tattoo emblazoned on my soul. "I would take every heartache and betrayal to have that connection with Hayes again."

Alex takes both of my hands in his and gives me a long look. "There's your answer. The pain was worth it to experience what you did."

Six

Paige

I pace the short distance between the two windows in Alex's living room on the morning of my third day in New York, looking for answers over the dark Manhattan skyline and hoping for some kind of clarity on how I can go back in time and salvage my marriage. This visit has been a balm to my broken heart. It's been wonderful to be carefree and to walk the streets of Brooklyn and Manhattan with Alex, without a single person recognizing me.

Carefree or not, a part of me is homesick, and it's not my childhood home or Savannah that I'm yearning for, it's the Buckhead mansion with an underhanded man and his giant demon dog that fills my mind on a loop.

A soft knock at the door freezes me mid-step, and I turn toward the entryway. It's just after six, Alex is still asleep in his room and didn't tell me to expect any visitors. Maybe it's one of his friends, or maybe a fling not expecting to meet a random girl in his apartment. I look back at Alex's closed door and wonder if I should get him up. No, it's so early, it's better to let him sleep. It's probably someone looking for another apartment, anyway.

I pad softly to the door in my socks and look through the peephole, but I can't see anything. I definitely didn't imagine the knock, so I make sure the chain is engaged and slowly open the door a crack to peek outside. My eyes travel down toward the mat where Cerberus is sitting like the regal, imposing guard dog he is, a piece of paper tied around his neck with a red ribbon. I scan the hallway looking for Hayes, but it's empty and I'm wondering at the craziness of seeing his dog here in Brooklyn. Am I dreaming? I take the chain off and open the door wider.

"Well, butter my backside and call me a biscuit. You're a sight for sore eyes, big guy," I whisper.

Cerberus's nubbin tail thumps the mat as I run my hands over his sleek fur and place a kiss on his big, blocky head. I drop to my knees in front of him, where we're the same height and I can better read the note around his neck.

Paige (my most favorite human of all time,
whom I love even more than my dad who
raised me, feeds me, and deals with my shit),
My dad messed up big time. So bad, not
even a pretty poem could fix it. Seriously, he

tried for hours. His ego is really big, and it hurt when he realized he was wrong. You were right to leave him for what he did. That's why I'm showing up late. He was sad (and really stupid) and wouldn't bring me sooner, but I wish I could have made you feel better. Trust me, I was mad at him, too. I took a Jurassic dump on the kitchen floor to get back at him when he showed up at home without you. You're welcome.

I giggle and rub Cerberus's face for having my back and staging a coup against his dad. I return my eyes to the note and continue reading, feeling my heart slowly thawing with every sentence.

You made our family whole, and we both miss you more than words can say. It's too quiet, too clean, and not nearly enough fun in Atlanta without you, and we want you back. You made Dad happier than I've ever seen him, and you're the only person I've liked more than him since I was a puppy. He wants to be a better man completely deserving of you. Teach him how.
It's not the same without you. Please forgive him for being a big jerk and not being honest with you. I know he doesn't deserve it, but

we're both hoping your big heart can extend
some grace to him.
XOXO,
C and H
PS - say "Apologize."

I sit back on my heels and raise an eyebrow at Cerberus. "Apologize?"

He raises his front paws off the floor and sits back on his haunches. He brings his paws together and howls so loud that I fall back into the apartment on my bottom. I start laughing as Cerberus continues to howl, begging in his best rendition of a completely tone-deaf request for forgiveness.

"Okay, okay. Apology accepted," I say quickly, to get him to stop and not wake the whole building.

Cerberus immediately stops howling and plants his paws back on the mat before he rushes in and covers my face in slobbery dog kisses that just make me laugh harder.

"His singing voice is better than mine, believe it or not."

I look up from petting Cerberus, who is all but trying to sit his massive one-hundred-pound body into my lap, and take in Hayes.

"I wasn't mad at him, so he didn't have to apologize."

Hayes tentatively steps toward the door and squats down to eye level, looking like a luxurious dark dream in his black peacoat, black cashmere sweater that hugs his chest, and charcoal slacks that mold to his big thighs. He runs a hand through his hair, but it's already disheveled like he's repeated the motion many times before this instance.

"I kind of hoped you might be a little more interested in talking to me if I had backup."

I sigh, giving Cerberus one last ear scratch, and untangle myself from his paws to stand. I think Hayes deserves a chance to tell his story, and I'm going to try my hardest to hear him out this time. He rises from his crouch and stands awkwardly on the welcome mat that says *Challah At Ya Boy* in pretty script next to a braided loaf of bread.

"Come in. No use standing in the hallway and letting the nosy neighbors listen in." I look around Hayes and catch a door shutting abruptly.

I step back and cross my arms as I move into the apartment and hear the bedroom door open behind me.

"What's going on?" Alex asks, sleep gravely in his voice.

I look back over my shoulder at Alex, wearing oversized pajamas, curly hair rumpled, holding the earplugs he sleeps with, then back to Hayes, not sure how to explain.

"I'm here to get my wife back," Hayes answers instead, his voice not exactly threatening, but not completely comfortable, either. It's a small difference I learned in our time together, and likely why Hayes is considered as formidable as he is—he has the male equivalent of a resting bitch face and the voice to match.

Alex's eyes open wider as he becomes fully awake, straightening up and walking into the living room to stand next to me.

"Well, shit. Do you want him here?" The fact that Alex is allowing me to tell Hayes to get lost is a wonderful reminder that he has always had my back, no matter the situation, or the imposing man who towers over both of us.

"It's okay with me if it is with you, Alex. This is your apartment and I'm just a guest."

Alex gives me a long look and I try to coax my features to imply that I am confident and ready for this, whatever it is. He nods slightly.

"Give me a minute and I'll go get bagels and coffee for the three... um, four of us," he says, taking in the giant black dog sitting at my feet giving him a level stare that says back the heck up. "Holy shit, what in the hell is that?"

I squat down and give Cerberus face scritches. "This is Cerberus, and he is the best dog ever. Cerberus," I say, addressing the dog now. "Alex is my best friend, and we love him, okay? You don't have to be so menacing."

Cerberus looks past me at Alex and after a pause, he finally settles onto the ground with a sigh. I stand back up and give Alex an apologetic smile.

"He's very sweet and loving," I offer.

"I'll take your word for it," Alex says, his eyes not leaving the dog. He retreats to his room where I hear drawers opening as he gets dressed.

I turn back to Hayes and have to fight the urge to run directly into his arms and bury my face against his chest. The urge is so strong I have to fist my hands in the sleeves of my sweater to keep myself from reaching for him. I want to hear him out before I fully open my heart to him again. It's better to keep my traitorous body out of this.

"I've missed you," Hayes says, his gravelly voice low and connecting straight to my lady bits.

Well, there goes that holdout; my body is right on board with whatever he has to say. I shake my head to clear it and keep from falling down that path.

"Hayes," I start, bracing to tell him I'm not sure I'm ready.

Alex bustles out of the bedroom, pushing his arms into a coat. "I'll be back in an hour. If you need me before that, I won't be far, just call," he tells me, with all the care of a protective best friend who also wants to give me time alone with my husband. Gosh, it's still weird to think that I have a husband, no matter how estranged we have become, and he's standing here now, patiently waiting for a chance to talk to me.

"I'll be fine, but thank you," I say, wrapping him in a hug. "I appreciate you so much."

Alex pulls away and approaches Hayes. "Don't fuck this up. This is your only second chance."

Hayes's face darkens at being scolded and told what to do, but he just nods and lets Alex pass through the door before closing it.

"I'm glad you have a friend like that," he says to me, without sounding like he means it at all.

"Alex is as good a friend as they come. We grew up together and he saved me from a whole lot of heartache in high school."

I catch a shift in Hayes's features and wonder if he is thinking about us now or what Garrison did to me in high school.

"Come in and sit down."

I curl up on one end of the sofa, pulling a throw blanket down and patting the cushion for Cerberus to join me. I'm extra indulgent with him because it feels so good to have complete acceptance and love from a big animal who didn't go out of his way to buy out my legacy.

Hayes hesitates, looking around the room before finally settling his big frame into a chair across from me. It's pretty impressive to see him out of his element and not completely in control of himself, or the situation, for once.

"Paige, I'm so sorry. I think that's the most important part of anything I have to say to you, so I want it out there first." He pauses to gauge my reaction, and when I lift my chin, he continues. "I messed up. I put my interests first and you were the collateral damage on my way to getting what I wanted."

I cringe and blink rapidly at his word choice, thinking of Liliana calling me collateral damage in Savannah. My heart shutters at the comparison and I fight the knee-jerk reaction to leave the room and close myself off to everything he has to say. But... I said I would hear him out, so that requires an open heart, not the resistant mindset I'm in. I take a deep breath and let it out, along with my resentment and hurt.

"Please continue." My voice may be shaky and full of hurt, but I'm trying.

"You're not just some business deal to me, but I did have less than honorable intentions when I first met you."

My heart sinks with his words that confirm my greatest fear. This is getting worse the longer I listen. I want to make it stop now before it hurts even more. "Hayes," I plead, but he rushes to speak and keeps me from finishing my thought.

"Those didn't last long as I got to know the strong and amazing woman you are, outside of the business I wanted for my own. I fell in love with you, not for what I thought you could give me access to, but because of who you are. It's impossible not to love you, angel. You're kind and sweet—maybe too much so for the depraved man I am—and your innocence is like a balm to what I realized was a jaded worldview."

"Your words are very lovely, but this doesn't begin to scratch the surface of my real issue. You kept something secret that absolutely affected me. You should have told me about it."

I'm proud of the strength in my voice and the fact I haven't melted into a puddle at his feet. I deserve an explanation, and I won't give in until I can see where he was coming from and why he thought he could be so duplicitous. I'll let my judgment stand until then.

"You're right." He drags a hand across his face and stares at me hard from those jungle pool depths for a beat before he drops his hand to his lap and continues. "I should have been upfront and honest with you. I could have told you a hundred times that I was planning to buy the Xenios Group, but I kept my mouth shut because I didn't want to jeopardize the deal we were putting in place. That wasn't fair to you, and I understand if it changes how you feel about me now."

I shift in my seat and worry at the hem of my sweater. "So why did you do it? I wasn't shy about how much the legacy meant to me." This is an answer I have been wanting from the moment I found out what he did. Why would he do this to me?

Hayes leans forward, his face cloudy with tension. "It was a business decision that was made before I ever met you, so there was less morality holding me back from making the offer. I kept going with it even after you came into my life because I let my business ambitions dictate my choices."

I shake my head. "You knew the hotels were my future. Now I have nothing. Well, my family has more money than we know what to do with after that monstrous deal you made with Daddy, but money doesn't give me the future at the helm of a hotel group I was expecting, or my family's ancestral home to remain in my life. It's devastating." My voice cracks on the last word and I have to gulp down a breath to keep myself from giving in to the emotion that suddenly feels thick in my throat.

"Your future with the hotels is just beginning. You don't have to be devastated about this situation."

"How can you possibly say that?" I ask, feeling my heart shred a little more in my chest. I rub at the physical ache his words cause. He is absolutely insane if that's how he really feels despite the way his actions have hurt me.

"The Xenios hotels make up a significant portion of the Olympus Hotel Group now. It will be a public entity, unlike privately held Olympus International, and you will have a controlling interest in it. You'll have a place on the board and will be helping to direct not just the Xenios properties, but the future of the largest boutique hotel chain in the country." He pauses and catches what

I am sure is a wide-eyed stare of disbelief. "But only if you want it."

I suck in a breath as what he's done hits me. "I didn't buy any stocks."

"You didn't have to. It's a wedding gift to you from Payton and Zander. I know you were expecting to run a hospitality company on the East Coast, but now you've got something a little bigger to influence and grow."

"I can't believe they would do that. They barely know me," I say, feeling the shock settling in. This is big. Huge. While being the owner and CEO of the Xenios Group was a lifelong dream because it was the family plan, being on the board and helping influence a much larger, nationwide group will carry far more weight without the day-to-day operations of the hotels to worry about. It's different knowing I won't own any hotels outright but having even partial ownership in something so big kind of eases the sting of losing my legacy, including The Mansion, the Fairchild family home that started it all. *Almost.*

"They know enough to feel confident in placing their trust in you to sit as equal with us in this endeavor. We all feel pretty shitty for how we've left you. It's the least we could do after we dismantled the very thing you wanted most." His hands hang tightly clenched between his legs as his left knee bounces.

My face softens and the ache in my chest blooms into something softer. Something full of love. "All I wanted was you."

The urge to touch him makes my hand lift off my lap and hover for a moment before I bring it back down in a clenched fist. I'm as stupid as a cat in heat when I have my hands on him, and I need to keep a level head, at least until I know what the heck I'm doing next.

He springs out of the chair and kneels in front of me, his movements remarkably smooth for how large he is. "And I want you. More than anything, I've realized." He drags his palm across his face and brings his deep green eyes up to meet mine. "Even feeling the way I do, I was desperate to make that deal work and I hurt you in the process. That's not going to fly from here on out. I learned my lesson the hard way that the things that affect you need to be made known from the beginning. If you give me a second chance, I'm not going to gamble with it."

I pet Cerberus's massive head where it's resting against my thigh. "What do you think? Is it worth trying again?"

He chuffs once and closes his eyes. I lean toward Hayes until our foreheads barely touch.

"I think I can find it in me to give you a second chance. That first one was kind of a trial run if we're being honest. Besides, even when I was mad at you, I still missed you, and I think that's where relationships are made. If you're still madly in love with your partner when they absolutely don't deserve it, maybe you care about more than the initial things that brought you together. I'm hoping we have a fighting chance at doing life together."

The brilliant smile that lights up his face is stunning, and I feel every bit of his happiness radiating from him. He reaches toward me and pulls my hips forward until I'm off the couch and straddling his lap, his hands moving to my back and holding me close as my arms wrap around his shoulders.

"We have more than a fighting chance, baby." He slants his mouth over mine and kisses me like he's never had something so sweet. I meet his ardor, twisting my tongue and tasting him back. This kiss feels like coming home. It's an unexpected breeze off the Savannah River finding you on a veranda in the middle of a hot and humid July. It's a cozy blanket and hot cocoa in front of the fire in December. It's exactly what I've been missing and everything I've needed.

I could draw this out and make him grovel. I could ask him to prove through acts of service and grand gestures that he's worthy of a second chance. I could make him jump through hoops to show he's learned his lesson, testing him over and over again to ensure he's not lying to me now. I know I have every right to demand more proof of his miraculous turnaround. I could hold this over his head and keep it as the elephant in the room as long as I wanted to.

I also know that feels wrong.

I don't want a relationship that lends itself to game-playing. We didn't take the time to have the typical feeling it out phase, instead, we went straight into believing in what we have together so ardently that we got married, even if it was for convenience, so I don't know how to judge the apology any better.

All I know is that I love him, and this feels right.

It may feel right, but it also feels absolutely insane to be this deeply in love with someone I have known for such a short period of time. But I also know we will have plenty of opportunities to grow and find our rhythm as a couple the longer our relationship progresses, and that will give us plenty of road bumps and detours to navigate that will help us develop this relationship together.

I hope.

I pull away from Hayes's mouth. "I'm really glad you found me, and that you brought the demon spawn. I missed you both so much."

Hayes reaches out and ruffles his hand along Cerberus's ears. "This shithead has been a pain in my ass all week. He was not happy when it was just me who came home. You really did break my dog." He drops his hand to my thigh. "You broke me, too, angel."

I tilt my head and purse my lips. "What are you talking about? I'm pretty sure it was my heart that was stomped on when I learned of your business betrayal." I poke him in the chest, and he captures my hand against him.

"Baby, watching you walk out and not knowing where you were for days was the most helpless I've ever felt. I kept thinking about all the things that could have happened to you, but the worst being what I did." He shuts his eyes tightly and moves his hands down to grip my hips. "The look on your face when you found out haunts me. I'm your husband. I should be making you smile. Instead, you were devastated and in pain, and I did that to you. Worse even is that I wasn't the one to tell you, you had to learn of my betrayal from your mother."

I tip his chin up and kiss him quickly before I sink into the familiar headspace he's reminding me of. I pull back, my hands on his cheeks. "Did you ever stop to think how you would have felt if someone bought out your father's company before you could take it over? How much would that have changed your own life?"

His eyes open and he studies me. "I don't think I've ever put myself in the position of the businesses I have acquired." He grows introspective and pulls back a bit. "I probably wouldn't be as successful if I did this every time, but I see what you're doing now. You're right, it would have completely changed my life."

"Yes, it does. I hate not knowing what my future looks like now that the thing I've been working toward is no longer an option. Even with a board position, it's not something I'll need to be working on daily. So what do I do with myself? I was planning to start my general manager position at The Mansion in the new year. Now I have... nothing."

He shrugs a shoulder. "You can be my beautiful wife and we'll make a life together. You're an heiress socialite and billionaire yourself. Shouldn't be too hard, right?"

I smile indulgently. "If you think I'm going to be sitting at home or shopping all day while you're off building your empire and taking over every business you can, you don't know me very well."

"You really are an enigma, woman. How can you refuse to take the easy life I offer? You're not even the slightest bit interested in being a trophy wife?" He shakes his head right along with me. "In that case, how about carving out your very own empire in the liquor business?"

My brows scrunch and I shake my head. "What do you mean?"

"I have it on good authority that Underworld Spirits has a beautiful new owner lined up. Think you'd like to make a run of it?"

"Oh, Hayes, you didn't." I sit up straighter and hold his shoulders at arm's length as he nods. "But why would you do that? I thought you loved the business."

"I couldn't think of anyone else I'd rather have running it than you. Besides, I owe you a belated wedding present. All I have is my heart and a few businesses under my belt, so I went in this direction because you already own my heart."

"How are you known for your ruthlessness yet so willing to distribute your holdings? I can't believe I'm married to a man who is so generous with his businesses." I laugh and scrunch my shoulders up, feeling completely inadequate and unprepared for this. "You really want me to run it? I don't know the first thing about the liquor business."

"But you have spent your whole life learning how to run a successful business, and that's what matters. You won't be doing it alone. There is an entire staff ready to implement your fresh ideas and work with you to take over the South, and even farther. And you automatically have an entire hotel group that will be ordering everything you have to offer." He kisses my nose. "I think your first order of business will need to be increasing production because the demand is already there."

"Can I make you a VP? I would love to have you on my team." I'm only half joking.

He laughs off the question. "I'll always be available for consulting, but I want this to be yours. You were raised to run an empire, and I'm just making sure you have what you need."

"I just need you."

His hand rises and cups my face, thumb stroking my cheek. "You have me, angel."

Seven

The Atlanta Haute List

E lusive Billionaire And His New Bride Are Shaking Up The Business World

We previously reported that Hayes Olsen and Olympus International had bought out the boutique hotel empire, Xenios Group, from right under his bride, Paige Fairchild's, nose. It appears that wasn't the only business transaction to take place for Olympus International in the last few weeks. We have an exclusive tip that Olsen is going out of his way to impress his estranged sweetie, likely to win her back after his business betrayal that earned him her scorn and subsequent separation. Olsen went so far as to transfer ownership of his Atlanta-based liquor darling, Underworld Spirits, to Fairchild. The young lady may have a business degree, but she has no experience to speak of when it comes to running a multi million-dollar enterprise. Will Fairchild have what it takes to bring this fledgling company to the forefront of alcohol sales, or will it flounder before it ever gets going? We were surprised enough with this development but call us shocked when we caught wind of another recent business acquisition Hayes has procured and just as quickly gifted.

Olsen bought Savannah-based Daniels Industries and gifted the entire enterprise to his new father-in-law, William Fairchild, in what appears to be a bid for his approval. We're not business analysts, but we can see how this may have softened the hotelier when it came to selling his hotel group to Olympus International. Whew, that was a lot of businesses that have changed hands in such a short amount of time between Olsen and the Fairchilds! So, Hayes, if you have another company just lying around, you know we would be happy to take it off your hands!

But why Daniels Industries? Our sources say it has to do with a rivalry between Olsen and Garrison Daniels, heir to Daniels Industry, who was previously linked to Hayes's new bride. There may have been some interest from Paige's mother's family business, in the Daniels Industries cotton processing plants, as well. Clearing out the competition would certainly work in his favor when wooing the Fairchilds into selling, despite how it looks now that the business deals have all come to light. Does Hayes remove all obstacles in the path of his conquests—both in business and love—this way? We're looking into it for you curious kittens.

We're not sure how the Fairchilds will use their new gifts, but we'll be watching. Click Like and Subscribe for all the Haute gossip.

Eight

Hayes

"We're not headed to the airport?" Paige asks, turning in the backseat of the black SUV to look at me as we cross the Williamsburg Bridge into Manhattan.

"I figured you came all the way to New York for a reason and may like to stay another night," I answer, taking her hand from where it strokes Cerberus's head that rests on the seatback between us from his spot in the rear of the vehicle. "Would you like to see my apartment?"

Her eyes gleam with curiosity. "Of course you have a place here, too. Penthouse somewhere on the Upper East Side?"

"With a view of the park," I add, feeling a smile curling up my lips. "But it's not just mine. The apartment belongs to Olympus and both of my brothers also use it when they are in the city for work."

"I'm really glad you found me," Paige says again, her voice soft. "I thought I made the worst mistake walking out when you didn't come after me."

I want to erase the pain I see in her face and punch the version of me that was too fucking stubborn to fight for her the night she left me. I know I should have chased her down, kept her with me, and hashed it out right then and there. I should have taken all of her ire and hatred just so she knew that I would never let her go. But I didn't, and I let her walk out without the fight she needed to see from me. It was the stupidest mistake of my life.

"Angel, I will always come for you." My phone vibrates, stopping me from going on about what else I would do for her. I pull the phone from my pocket and see Payton is calling. At Paige's nod, I answer the call. "What?" I snap.

"We've got a problem," he says over the line, and I feel the tension jacking my shoulders up already.

"Fix it," I reply, keeping my voice low so as not to scare Paige.

"We need you back in Atlanta. One of our mines collapsed and we have to do damage control whether you figured shit out with your girl or not."

"Which mine?" I bark, thinking of our Georgia metals and the newest acquisitions that have yet to be retrofitted for the operations we want them for.

"South Africa," Payton answers, sounding distracted. "How soon can you be here?"

My stomach seizes. Of fucking course it's a new platinum and palladium mine that cost a fortune to acquire. "I'm in New York. I'll head straight for the plane and be there in a few hours. Pull everyone in. We have to get this covered now before the word gets out."

"I'm already on it but this is big and there's not much we can do but be reactive. I'll see you in a few hours. I'll email over the initial reports." Payton hangs up and I'm left with a big mess at my feet.

"I'm sorry, I have to go back to Atlanta. I want to take you with me, but I understand if you prefer to stay here. I can take you to the apartment before going to the airport and you can stay as long as you'd like." I kiss Paige's knuckles and hope she will see how much I would rather stay here with her than fly into a shitstorm and have to deal with a worst-case scenario.

"What happened? You asked which mine, was there an accident?" she asks, her big green eyes worried.

"Yes, at a new acquisition, too, meaning we are going to look like the assholes not living up to safety standards and putting peoples' lives at risk for the sake of profit. No one is going to give a global conglomerate the benefit of the doubt, so we have to both fix the problem and avoid becoming the villain."

"I don't want to stay in New York by myself, not when we've just reunited." She grips my hands in hers. "I'm coming back to Atlanta with you. Having a united front for your personal life may help."

Once the plane lands, I head straight to the Olympus International Tower in downtown Atlanta. I would have loved to have Paige at my side, but I didn't want to subject her to this mess, so I had a driver take her and Cerberus straight to the house from the airport. The elevator doors open to complete chaos, people hurrying between offices, phones ringing, an air of panic permeating the air.

"What in the fuck is going on," I say, catching sight of Carina, my assistant, waiting for me.

"Mr. Olsen, can you please come with me? I have your brothers in the boardroom ready to discuss what is happening overseas," Carina says, gently guiding me by the elbow away from the elevator bank and into the office proper like I'm a shell-shocked child.

"Fucking finally, where have you been? You're even later than expected and we don't have time to deal with your shit," Zander says, chucking a ball of paper at my head with more force than necessary.

I bat the ball away from my face. "I got here as fast as I could. Now, what the fuck is going on," I repeat, this time to my brothers rather than the general air of disruption that has a hold of the office.

"The Mine we just acquired had a massive casualty. We're getting reports that twenty-four of the workers have been killed, and it's looking like safety equipment wasn't up to standards. We're trying to get ahead of this, to route the media inquiries and change the narrative so it doesn't rain a shit ton of bad press and disapproval on Olympus," Payton says, scrolling through a tablet and putting muted live news reports onto the boardroom televisions.

"Already the finger is being pointed at us for not up-dating equipment and practices fast enough. They want our heads on a stake," Zander adds, shuffling through a stack of fresh printouts his assistant just handed him.

I glare around the room as a way to give my growing frustration an outlet. "How can it be our fault? We just bought the mining outfit last month, and we haven't even had a full rollover of staff or fully vetted the information from the sale. It was fast and dirty; our team still needs to clean up the pieces."

I run a hand through my hair and take a seat at the table. Adding the overseas mining operations was phase one of our expansion plans for the end of this year, whereas the hospitality takeover was phase two. We went directly from getting the mines to taking over the hotels, with no pause in between. There hasn't been time to do what we are being called out for now.

This is bullshit. The South African mine is one of five that was acquired, we have a team for each that is integrating everything we can from those companies, but it takes time to fully investigate all of the infrastructure and current practices being used. Our teams have barely had a chance to dig into them, let alone implement the kind of changes that might have prevented this disaster.

"The press and popular opinion won't care about the timeline, only that our name is on the paperwork when it comes to who is at fault. We need to spin this, somehow," Payton says, his fingers flying over the screen of his tablet, working his media magic in some form, I'm sure.

"Can we push this onto one of the subsidiaries, out of the Olympus name but still under the umbrella?" Zander asks, his brain following the same trajectory mine had immediately taken.

"All roads lead back to Olympus and, unfortunately, this one was already under the company name. We can't change what has been filed and made available to the public," Diego Vallarta, my senior vice president of finance, says, his phone out, fingers typing out a message to our team as he talks.

My eyes track around the room, from each of my brothers to our executive team and support staff that have turned this boardroom into a war room, electronics out, voices quiet as each part of the team approaches the problem, looking for viable solutions. I pass my palm across the back of my neck and think fast because while this is brand new for us, I know it took enough time getting to us that there are plenty of people out there calling for our heads.

"We need to make a public statement, right now. We can't wait to address the accident at the mine, or even investigate the cause to get a better idea of how to spin this. The workers need our direct attention, and we need to address the press." I look at Payton. "I need your team to draft a public statement that we can put online within the hour. It has to have a personal, heartfelt tone. Zander will give the speech at the press conference we'll hold this afternoon. Call the media outlets and let them know they can attend, but we won't be taking questions at this time." I turn to Diego. "I need finance to send aid right the fuck now to the mining outfit. Compensate the families of those killed and keep them as happy as we can. Don't admit fault, just express our deep condolence and concern we have for the wellbeing of the entire work-force."

"They may see that as us trying to buy their silence," Diego hedges, but he's already nodding at his team to make it happen.

"In a way, it is, but just for now before this can be distorted into something beyond our control. Just circle the fucking wagons and prepare for the backlash anyway, because it's coming no matter what we do."

Nine

The Atlanta Haute List

S afety Issues And Shoddy Equipment The Cause Of Devastating Mine Collapse

The Olsen men of Olympus International are in the hot seat today when a mining accident at a subsidiary held by the company killed twenty-four and injured dozens more. Youngest Olsen brother and Olympus CEO, Zander, stepped out to face the crowd gathered at Olympus International Tower for a press conference that was more of a company statement, as questions weren't allowed. This blogger found the statement, printed below, to be a little lackluster given the calamity that happened, but it is admirable that one of the brothers actually made it, rather than foist it off on the PR department.

Already, cries for more action can be heard as activists lament the working conditions of the mine, the lack of sufficient safety equipment on hand, and no real training for the workers. Do our favorite billionaire brothers have blood on their hands from this blatant disregard for the safety of their lowest-paid workers? They've been profiting off lowly workers for a decade. Maybe it's time to cancel the Olsens and Olympus International. They've bought up enough of the South, and have their hands in piggy banks the world over, when will enough be enough? We'll be keeping an eye on them even more to see what changes the brothers will make, if any. As always, hit Like and Subscribe for all the Haute gossip!

Statement given by Zander Olsen, Olympus International CEO, Monday 2:32 PM EST

"It is with heavy hearts and our deepest sympathies that we are here today, addressing the collapse of a recently acquired mining outfit in South Africa. We have staff on their way to assess damages and help the local team reorganize with a focus on safety above all. While mining has always been at the heart of Olympus International and a fundamental part of our business structure, branching out into foreign markets is new and comes with many hurdles of various degrees to ensure that other outfits align with our US safety standards and practices. None of our reports from the acquisition of this mining operation led us to believe that any safety precautions had been circumvented, but it is now on us to see what went wrong, fix it, and address any issues that may be raised to ensure it never happens again. We respectfully ask that you keep the people most affected by this tragedy in your thoughts and prayers. Please know that we are taking direct action to help members of the mining force and the families of those involved in this accident because we care about all members of the Olympus International family. No questions will be taken at this time."

Ten

Hayes

"**T**his has been the day from hell," Zander says, taking a deep drink from a tumbler of Underworld Spirits bourbon brought in from my office after the press conference earlier today.

I sip from my own glass and eye my brothers across the boardroom table. "This isn't even close to over. We've been playing catch up trying to clear the rubble and figure out the best way through this disaster. We're still not ahead of it, and it won't give us the benefit of a night off to regroup."

"The media is crucifying Olympus, and us. They're saying we're not doing enough. That we were negligent and put our workers at risk for profit," Payton says with more pep to his voice than his statement warrants.

I give him a nasty look as he scrolls on his tablet and ignores me. I will never understand how he can be so optimistic and unfazed by even the worst of the world. It's like he relishes when shit hits the fan.

"We've done what we can with the media. They will run whatever they want until the next news cycle produces a bigger story. Our focus needs to be on the people. The ones who were killed, injured, or at risk since the mine is currently shut down. We have to show the integrity of our business." Silence descends in the room, papers still, and all eyes turn toward me.

Luca De Silva, SVP of operations, meets Payton's eyes and a silent conversation passes between them. Payton turns back to me.

"We have an image problem. It's been brewing for years, but this disaster finally sealed the deal. We *have* to address the media, and change the way we are viewed, both with this event, and moving forward."

"Image problem? Who cares about what anyone else thinks of us? All that matters is we get shit done and mow through whatever obstacle is set in front of us," Zander says, brushing a stack of papers out of his way so he can lean his arms on the table.

"That's exactly it," Luca says, casting a graph onto the screen from his tablet. "You won't be able to keep mowing down competition and gobbling up companies without developing a stigma in the business world that will leak into public perception."

"Olympus doesn't have stock that's publicly traded, just a few of our subsidiaries. Why does public perception need to matter right now?" I ask, trying to follow what Payton and Luca are saying, and how it relates to our next steps.

Payton stands and moves toward the screen. "We're being held to some higher standard *because* of how we have operated in the past, and the image we've created about being business first, people second, or much further down the list."

He taps the screen showing a downward trend on a graph.

"Public perception means everything when you have people researching their materials, looking for corporate accountability and sustainability. The raw materials we mine go into everything from computer chips to high-end jewelry. We have more than our direct customers to answer to moving forward."

He swipes through more photos of the end products and sales graphs and lands on one that pulls all the headlines we have attracted in the last few months.

"Our shipping and aviation departments use up incredible amounts of fossil fuels and dump tons of carbon emissions into the atmosphere. Our workers are paid fairly for their area of the world, but we have moved into industries in a lot of third-world locations, and it looks bad that they're paid so little for the often dangerous or backbreaking work."

"So, you're saying we have to reevaluate our image, along with cleaning up a mine disaster, navigating a media shitstorm, and recouping losses and operating costs in the shutdown and reconstruction of a brand new investment?" Zander asks, his voice giving away his irritation at the expectation. "It seems a little contrived to roll out a new publicity campaign to change our image right now, but we can begin by taking public actions that speak louder than any shitty promises in writing ever could."

I'm in agreement with Zander on that. Money is always the issue, and the scope of work Payton is proposing could bankrupt the mining entity.

"We're better off selling the mine and washing our hands of the issue. It'll be down too long to be profitable in the foreseeable future and will be hemorrhaging money trying to get back in operation at a pace that makes sense for why we picked it up to begin with," I say, steepling my fingers in front of my face, glaring around the table. My head always goes to money, understandably. As the CFO, it's my job to ensure Olympus operates well into the black with all of our acquisitions, especially the newer, riskier ones like these overseas operations. It's my priority to cut the losses before they sink the ship, and this is looking like a big fucking loss.

Zander plants his hands on the tabletop and pushes his chair away, standing. "Selling the lot and throwing money at a problem doesn't have the personal touch this situation needs. Making statements from the gleaming lobby of our high-rise headquarters seems cold and removed." He looks around the room. "We need to put words into action and boots on the ground. Pack your bags, boys, we're going to South Africa ourselves. We'll leave tomorrow."

I slice a hand through the air. "You will leave tomorrow. I need to stay in Atlanta and ensure our other holdings are not affected by the backlash that's happening overseas."

That and make sure my wife doesn't want to go through with that divorce she may have been considering just yesterday. I have to be a man of my word and show her with my actions that she is more important than anything Olympus has thrown at it. Hopping on a jet and traveling halfway around the world now would just show her I can't be bothered to work on our relationship when it needs it the most.

Zander scrutinizes me across the table, nodding tightly. "Fine. Payton and I will take our teams to South Africa to handle this at ground zero. Unless you have something you would rather be doing here, Payton?"

"My schedule is cleared, and we can get this handled and be back within the week," he says, finally setting down his tablet.

"Don't we have a controlling interest in some of the media outlets firing cannons at us now?" I ask Payton, who heads up the media portions of our conglomerate, along with operations.

"We do, but it doesn't look good to send a notice to the free press telling them what they can or cannot write stories about. The most we can do is lay low and let them hunt down another juicy story. That and clean up our act now to reverse the tide that is turning our way with accusations."

I fight the urge to roll my eyes. We should be able to do whatever the fuck we want when we want to. I sigh. Payton is right, though.

"Call it a wrap tonight. Go home. I've got a wife who needs some tending to," I say, rising from the table.

Zander wolf whistles. "I told you my plan would work! No wonder you don't want to leave the country with that pussy back in Atlanta where it belongs."

My lip curls into a snarl at his words, but before I can move to throttle him, Payton steps into my line of sight, effectively blocking Zander from the punishment he deserves for speaking crassly about Paige once again.

"Don't let his words get to you. Go home and take care of your marriage before we have more of those *are they or aren't they* stories to deal with. The Atlanta Haute List hasn't reported you being back together yet, since the mine collapse seems to be more appealing. Take her out, show her off, and make sure the world, or at least Georgia, knows you're all good despite everything else. A united front and all that bullshit. We need the better press, one way or another."

"That's an order, Hater," Zander says, leaning back in his chair to see me around Payton. "Make a bigger story than a mine collapsing. Knock her up, already. That should get their attention."

"Fuck off," I say, too tired to add the normal vitriol I would usually throw at him. The thought is far too appealing, however, and the practice to get to that place isn't a burden in any way.

Eleven

Paige

I hadn't been gone for long, but coming back to Hayes's house felt like I was entering a museum to what our first magical week together had been. I didn't think it would feel like home as much as it did, and that thought got me caught up in my feelings again, wondering if we could get back what we had—before he destroyed the one dream I'd had my whole life.

Stop thinking that way, Paige, I chastise internally. It won't help me get to a place with Hayes that everything to this point has hinted at. We have so much potential, and I want to give him a second chance to see what blooms from that little bud of happiness.

Hayes had me driven back to the house from the airport when he realized the mine collapse would be taking all of his attention at work, and I wasn't mad about it. But walking in by myself, seeing the home that had been my refuge from the storm Mama created, and not having him beside me to experience it, was... weird.

Now, Cerberus's ears prick up at a noise, and I follow his gaze to see headlights cutting across the front of the house. *Hayes.* I rise from the couch and pad barefoot after Cerberus to the front door, opening it as Hayes strides up the stairs.

He doesn't stop until his hands are tangled in my hair, tipping my chin up as he brings me in for a kiss that needs no prelude and has me standing on my tiptoes to meet his intensity. My fingers curl into his shirt and instantly, flames are licking through me, igniting my core, making me ache. His tongue works across mine, drawing out pitiful whimpers from my throat. When he pulls back, nipping my lip with his teeth as he sets me back on my heels, I'm hazy and almost surprised by the heat in his dark, jungle eyes, sparking up what was set to be my darkest night.

"That's what I've been wanting all day, angel. Your mouth on mine making everything better," he rasps, his lips still close enough to feel the heat of his words against mine.

A fire is roaring in my lady bits and the week apart has me desperate for him. My back arches, pushing my body against his, my arms twining around his neck as our mouths meet again. This time my tongue delves in and takes every drop of his minty sweet taste. He groans against my mouth, and I feel him, hard and thick, pressed against my belly.

Oh, I missed this. This physical connection and willingness to nearly climb into each other's skin just to be close. I draw him with me as I step back into the house, wanting to find a horizontal surface. I want to strip down and really fit together, but he stops me with a hand under my chin and a nip to my lips. His hands slide down my body, skimming my curves until he joins our hands by interlacing our fingers.

"Going somewhere?" he growls. A predatory smile breaking across his face.

"To bed, if we're lucky, but I'll settle for any flat surface," I respond, my eyes heavy-lidded and my voice coquettish. I take a few steps back, letting our clasped hands stretch between us and tug. Hayes's eyes light up at this, and he follows slowly, letting me lead him to the stairs, where he stops me.

"Do you need me to fuck you, angel?" he asks, sliding up behind me and whispering the naughty words in my ear as his hands come around my front. His body molds to mine as his hands plump my breasts and work lower to the junction of my legs where the source of this fire resides.

Okay, maybe we *can* get back what we had. I moan in response to his touch, a throaty plea for more. He spins me around and hauls me up his body, wrapping my legs around his hips and starts climbing the stairs. I let out a yelp of surprise, clinging to him like a monkey as his long, powerful strides take us higher.

The bed dips under me when he lays me down in his room, his body still covering mine and his lips making their way down my neck. My hands slide down his back, pulling his crisp white button-down out of his pants and giving me skin to explore.

He lifts off me enough to pull the shirt off, giving my hands more skin to touch. I rake my nails up his back and hook my fingers over his shoulders. Hayes groans into my neck, biting softly against my shoulder as he continues his exploration of the skin that shows around the neck of my sweater.

"You didn't answer. Do you need to be fucked properly like a good girl?"

My eyes widen in surprise, more at my physical response to his filthy mouth than the words themselves, because I just felt my body squeeze and my panties dampen with my desire. Holy moly, he's good at this.

"Yes, fuck me," I whisper, caught up enough in the moment with him to let the curse slip into my answer.

Hayes wastes no time removing my sweater and peeling the leggings from me. He kneels at the edge of the bed between my legs and his big hands push my thighs apart.

"You're wet for me, baby," he says, running his nose across my panties and making me shiver. "I want this tight pussy dripping down my face before I fuck you."

I gasp when he draws a large finger across my opening, hooking my panties and moving them to the side so his tongue can sweep through my folds. He nibbles at my skin, flicking his tongue out and catching my clit, sending sparks dancing at the edge of my awareness. "That... again," I rasp, wanting him to continue.

His chuckle rumbles against me, and I feel it zinging up my spine, bowing my back with the brush of his chin at my center.

"You liked... this," he says, flicking my clit again before he truly gets to work worshiping my body.

All I can do is hang on for the ride because he's driving. My hips buck against him, and he presses me down with one thick forearm, continuing his sweet torture as I writhe under him.

"More, please," I beg, missing the fullness of him in this hazy moment of awareness.

He obliges and gently slides a finger inside my body, stretching me as my center instantly clamps down on him. The feeling of his finger dragging through me is nearly enough, but I whimper, knowing there is still something missing. He pulls his finger back and slides a second in, and I feel impossibly full, finding exactly what I was looking for.

He caresses me inside, and his mouth continues the delicious ministrations to my clit. He makes short work of taking me over the edge, as my body shudders and I release into waves of bliss that radiate through my whole body with a wordless shout.

"That's my girl," he says, voice deep and satisfied from low down my body.

I feel my panties dragged down my legs, and Hayes leaves me for a moment to remove his pants. The next moment, he is above me, lifting my hips and pushing in as my core continues to throb with waves of pleasure.

"So tight," he groans, slowly fitting himself into my body.

I remember to relax at the tugging stretch, willing my body to take him in all the way so I can be as full of him as possible. I grip his shoulders and pull him against me and raise my hips to meet his thrusts.

"Hayes," I say, my voice breathy and hesitant. "Fuck me like you mean it."

"You're going to be the death of me, angel," he groans into my neck. He leans back, hauling me up to straddle his thighs as he settles himself back on the bed. "Ride my cock like you mean those filthy words," he commands.

A wave of power rolls through me at his words, and I start moving in earnest, grinding against him.

His hands settle on my hips, helping me find a rhythm that sends the embers of a release spinning through me again. As I start to slow and tense, he pounds into me from below, setting off the orgasm so all I can do is ride out the pleasure. He rolls me over and thrusts into me hard, my entire body jerks with the motions. I am too languid to push back, content to take each punishing thrust and enjoy the sensations that build in me on the heels of the last orgasm. I feel the sparks roiling at the base of my spine and arch as another release rolls over me. I gasp and claw at Hayes's back as he fucks me senseless. With a roar, he slams all the way in and I feel the pulse of his release along with my rhythmic waves.

He collapses forward, burying his face in my hair as we breathe through the moment, or minutes, it takes for our heartbeats to slow and our breathing to even.

"That was... whoa," I gasp out.

Hayes releases a contented sigh. "Hell of a way to welcome a man home." He gathers me in his arms and rolls us to the side, his hand sliding lazily along my side. "I missed you."

It's only been hours since I was in his company, but I missed him, too. I know what it's like to be separated from him for much longer now, without the assurance that I will see him again at the end of a workday. It was reassuring to have him come back to me in the end.

"How was work?" I ask, nuzzling into the perfect nook his shoulder and neck make for my head.

"Fire and brimstone, bad PR, and a lot of shit-talking from the media," he says, the words rumbling against my ear that's pressed to his chest. "Payton and Zander are going to South Africa tomorrow to deal with the fallout on the ground."

I pull my head away so I can look at him. "Why aren't you going with them?"

It doesn't make sense for just two of the three heads of Olympus to put in an appearance. It may seem less than contrite for one of the brothers to be missing if this is a push to show they're taking the accident seriously.

"I'm needed right here," he says, tapping my chest, just above my heart. "That, and I want to keep an eye on the rest of the holdings to ensure the negative fallout doesn't cost us even more."

My chest gets warm and gooey where he taps. He could have easily said the trip was the most important thing to focus on right now, which I would understand, but he *chose me*. I see him trying, and it means the world to me.

"Do you think the trip will accomplish what your brothers want it to?" I ask, hesitant to question what they choose to do with their giant conglomerate.

"Zander seems to think so, and it's a smart move, publicity-wise. We're getting crushed. And while we've always taken a very hands-off approach to our public image, this should show we care, or at least that's what Payton says."

"What do you think? Will it be enough?"

"I think one small showing like this isn't going to turn the tide of negative press, but I also don't think a full one-eighty where we appear to be completely socially aware will have the effect we want, either. It's a fine balance of keeping our heads down and ensuring our practices are without fault going forward."

"You can't change the past," I say, tracing a finger along Hayes's jaw and relishing the rasp of his five-o'clock shadow against my skin.

Hayes sits up, gently drawing me with him. "I had every intention of scooping you up and taking you out when I got home before I was distracted by how much I needed you. You need to eat, and I know just the place. Come on," he says, leaving the bed and leading me toward the bathroom.

I follow, loving the view I get of his naked body, so strong, masculine, and sinfully hot. My thighs are sticky with our lovemaking and a shower sounds excellent right now, even though I just washed my hair and would prefer not to have to blow it dry again. I put it up in a bun as I walk to remove the need.

Hayes pulls me into the shower, giving us both a good rinse and lathering me with body wash. He is so methodical, careful, and sweet as he washes me from neck to toe, thankfully leaving my hair out of the spray as his fingers paint designs through the bubbles along my skin. I stand patiently for him, enjoying every minuscule moment of our connection. It's little things like this that make me feel cherished and taken care of. He gives himself a much quicker wash and finally rinses us both off before grabbing towels.

When I've had a chance to put myself back together and dress—in one of the outfits I shopped for that first full day in Atlanta that feels like years ago—Hayes is ready and waiting on the edge of the bed. He looks amazing in a black cashmere sweater and gray slacks that mold to his strong legs. I look down at my tight, knee-length, cream-colored dress and heels and contemplate changing. Maybe my hem is too low to be fashionable, and I could always trade for a pair of strappy stilettos instead of these leather platform pumps, even though they are more comfortable. He makes me want to look half as good as he does if we're going out, and I suddenly feel dressed for the wrong occasion.

"Don't you dare underestimate your innate sexiness or how you're dressed," he growls, practically reading my mind.

I must get better at not letting every thought cross my face.

"Just wondering if I should change. Where are you taking me?" I ask, self-consciously tugging at the cling of my dress so it pulls away from my generous hips where it's tightest.

"Rare. It's a nice steakhouse, and you're dressed perfectly. Everyone who sees you will want to eat you up." His eyes take on a territorial gleam, and I wonder if he'll say something possessive that sounds like it's out of a romance novel. Instead, he just smiles wickedly, and I'm left wondering at the thoughts that brought it on.

"What's that smile about?" I ask when I can't stand not knowing.

"I like that other men will want you, and women will want to be you. I love how sexy you are without even realizing it. I fucking love you, Paige."

I feel my cheeks flush with the compliments and his ability to handle me being sexy without wanting to cover me up or hide me away out of possession. This feels healthy for a relationship, and I'm so thankful to have him as my husband, allowing me to explore who I am and not have Mama dictating my choices.

"I love you, too. You are way sexier than me, though, and I'm so lucky to be yours and have you choose me over and over."

"Angel, I will always choose you. No matter where you go, or what happens in this life, I will pick you every damn day. I will never stop loving you, no matter what."

My smile at that is brilliant, and I let him lead me downstairs and into the car still feeling the heady elation that he is mine.

The drive to the restaurant takes longer than I anticipated, the dark streets of Atlanta slowly clearing of rush hour traffic and the evening crowd on the roadways. Hayes drives up to a valet stand in front of Rare, in what I can only assume is a trendy area because of the foot traffic that looks to be made up of influencers snapping photos, fashionably dressed models, and people looking pleased with themselves. He opens the gullwing door of the Mercedes SLR McLaren for me, pulling me out and into his arms, where he stops to place a lingering kiss on my lips as the valet waits.

I feel my cheeks heat and look around us when he guides me toward the restaurant with his hand on the small of my back. A few people have stopped to watch us, one or two with phones out and pointed in our direction like we're some kind of attraction. I tuck myself in closer to Hayes's side and stay silent until a host directs us to a table that isn't as secluded as I imagine Hayes would want.

"Have you been here before?" I ask, wondering if, like Napoletana, he has also invested in this restaurant and is a regular. *With or without all the women he's likely had over the years,* a small, vicious part of my brain reminds me. I blink to end that self-sabotaging thought and let him scoot my chair in as I sit.

He rounds the table and settles himself before placing his elbows on the table, his hands clasped as if in supplication. He levels me with those fire-lit, emerald eyes. "Never been, but I hear from Zander it's the best, and that is what you deserve." He drops his arms to his lap and leans across the table, toward me. "Are you okay, Paige?"

Hearing him say my name when he's been calling me other endearments shakes me from my internal ramblings.

"It's just..." I begin, looking around the restaurant and, again, catching a few people looking our way and whispering. "I've been having to dodge a lot of questions from people who feel far too comfortable delving into my personal life the last week and I'm getting that same feeling here. I was never much to talk about in Savannah until you happened." I slightly angle my head toward the couple two tables over who have their phones up and are blatantly taking photos or videos of us.

Hayes narrows his eyes at the couple, and they immediately turn back to their meals, but their eyes continue to stray our way. He raises a hand and catches the attention of a server, who hurries over.

"Good evening, Mr. Olsen. How may I be of assistance?" Hayes may not come here often, but the restaurant knows who he is at the very least.

"Either get rid of the assholes with phones pointed in our direction and let us eat in peace, or we're out of here," he says.

"Yes, sir," the server says, before rushing to a back hall and disappearing for a moment.

"Can you really do that?" I ask, marveling at his assuredness. "I can deal with it if needed, it's fine."

"They're making you uncomfortable when you should be enjoying yourself at dinner. Fuck them and their unwarranted interest. They can eat at McDonald's if they want to act like that."

A moment later, a man I assume is the manager approaches the onlookers' table and has a brief conversation. The couple quickly experience a range of emotions that flash across their faces, from shocked, to upset, then resigned as they stand and leave the restaurant, casting irritated looks back at our table several times. All because Hayes commanded it. Holy moly, he's more powerful than I even imagined to have that kind of sway at a restaurant he has no vested interest in. And the very first time he's been here.

Our dining experience significantly improves once the gawkers leave, and we're well into our meals when I feel eyes on me again. I pat my lips with a napkin and cautiously look around for the source of the feeling.

There is a man staring hard at Hayes, occasionally dragging his eyes to me, then back. Our eyes meet the next time he looks my way, and a flood of cold streaks down my spine. He's familiar in that *I can't quite place it, but I know I've seen you before* way. I quickly look back to my plate, my mind spinning through possibilities to make sense of this. *Why would I know anyone in Atlanta?*

"Something bothering you?" Hayes asks, his voice low and rumbling with heat.

I look up and shake my head, plastering on a contented smile, like I've always done when Mama questioned my mood. "I'm fine," I say, adding extra cheer to my voice to sell it.

"Don't gloss over whatever it is. Your face... that was a look I don't want to see on you. What's wrong?" he asks again, reaching for my hand and running his thumb along my knuckles when I take his.

"A man was looking at us and I just… I just had a feeling I've seen him before and I can't place it. But it wasn't a good feeling, even though I have no recollection of why it would be bad," I admit. I'm struggling to make sense of the foreboding I feel, and why my flight instincts would be so torqued up I want to hop out of my seat and flee the restaurant.

Hayes looks around us, nearly turning in his chair to catch the offending gaze I mentioned, but when I look at the table the man was sitting at, it's empty. I feel so dumb. There's absolutely no reason to feel that prickly feeling along my spine here with Hayes. It's not like I know anyone, and I haven't made a habit of making people want to threaten me—not as far as I know. I can only chalk it up to the run-in with Liliana and the horrible way every accusation felt in Savannah. She knew exactly how to hurt me, targeting every insecurity and worry I have.

Thinking of my run-in with Liliana sparks a connection in my brain, putting together the frayed threads that are loosely woven through my consciousness. I think I may have seen that man in the park the same day I fled that horrid interaction. He bumped my shoulder on the path when I was walking home. A cold dread passes down my spine, and my heart rate quickens once again. I look past Hayes, but the table is still empty. I decide it isn't worth pursuing, and reach for his hand, just wanting to be closer to him as the adrenaline pumps through my system and puts a tremor into my hands.

"He's gone," I say so Hayes will turn back to the table and settle down. "Thank you for noticing the distress, even if it wasn't warranted." I bring his hand, still clasped in mine, to my lips and kiss his knuckles. I smile against his fingers when I see him visibly soften, his shoulders drawing down, away from his ears, and his posture loosening up a fraction.

"You let me know if anyone creeps you out again," he says, a note of wrath in his tone. "I'll move heaven and hell to keep you safe and protected," he promises.

I do not doubt for a second that he would do just that if his one command at a restaurant got other patrons removed and the previous altercation we experienced outside of Napoletana are anything to go on.

"If I have to hire a security detail to keep you safe when I'm not around, I will. Actually, that's not a bad idea. We have a security contract for the company; it would be easy enough to arrange."

"Kick back, killer," I say with a hint of amusement. "It was nothing, just an overreaction on my part for no reason other than I've been a little jumpy with all the attention lately."

The white lie slips easily out of my lips, wanting to appease Hayes rather than throw him into an overprotective mode for likely no reason. He tilts his head at me and the face of disapproval he makes speaks loudly enough that I continue.

"But of course, I will let you know if anything else happens that freaks me out."

"Good." He nods in approval. "Do you feel up for dessert?"

I tug my lip with my teeth and watch as his eyes zero in on the movement, intensity heating the jungle-pool depths in the low lighting. I let my lip go and smile.

"I smelled churros when we were in front of the restaurant. Do you think there is a cart nearby we can try to find?" I don't know why, but street food always appeals to me, and the buttery, cinnamon-sweet dessert sounds really freaking good right now. Comfort food is the best way to deal with possibly seeing the same stranger in two different cities, right?

Hayes laughs and shakes his head. "You have a whole dessert menu at a five-star restaurant to choose from and yet you want food from a cart," he says softly, with real warmth.

"Yes, and with caramel dipping sauce. Or maybe chocolate? I don't know, it depends on what they have," I muse, really craving the treat now.

"And now I have to find you this damn churro cart, or I'll be buying a whole bakery tomorrow to sate that desire," Hayes says, a glint of challenge in his eyes.

Twelve

The Atlanta Haute List

B ad Boy Billionaires Cleaning Up Company Image

Atlanta's favorite trio of billionaire brothers are stepping up their humanizing qualities, with two of the three making a transatlantic trip to their mining operations in South Africa mid-week. It is reported that Payton and Zander Olsen toured the facility and the open portion of the mines, helping clear rubble (shock!), and visiting the injured workers still in hospital after the devastating mine collapse that occurred a week ago. This is the first time the brothers have made a point to provide assistance in person or show up for more than a shareholder meeting or corporate takeover. They typically stay at the top of their skyscraper, far away from the huddled masses who do their bidding. Could this trip mark a turning point in the Olympus agenda?

We don't think so. Judging by a long string of past activities, the brothers are playing a game of just showing us what we want to see after receiving harsh criticism from the public as of late. They'll have to do more than one trip to a now-closed mine to change our minds.

Olympus International holdings all over the world have come under scrutiny for allegedly horrible working conditions, outdated or nonexistent safety equipment and procedures, and industry-wide low wages for the workers doing the back-breaking labor that makes the brothers rich. This may be the first industrial accident that has made headlines, but it's likely not the only one to ever occur at an Olympus-held entity. You know we will be digging through their dirt and finding what secrets they are hiding, or seeing just how deep the rot goes.

Where was big brother Hayes while Payton and Zander were on a humanitarian mission? He was spotted out on the town with his lady love, Paige Fairchild, rather than crossing oceans with his brothers. The pair were seen dining—ahem, *canoodling*—at trendy hot spot, Rare, and eating street food for dessert after. Is that a dig on the fare at Rare, or just a penchant for a good dessert? It made our cold little hearts happy to see the love birds reunited and back to their PDA-filled outings around Atlanta. Maybe the eldest Olsen is learning that your significant other should be placed before business, and that's why he didn't make the trip with his brothers. What forced the newlyweds apart for over a week prior to this randy reunion? We're still stumped on that, but happy nonetheless that our favorite It Couple is back in the arms of Atlanta again.

As always, hit Like and Subscribe for all the Haute gossip!

Thirteen

Hayes

"We're being sued. A class action suit brought by the workers of the South African mine, represented by a nasty New York firm that has a history of looking for opportunities like this," Zander informs me through the phone call playing through my car speakers.

I scowl, even though Zander can't see it. "Have legal deal with it, that's what they're paid for," I reply, my patience already too thin for this conversation.

"It's not just Olympus that is being sued. It's us. You, me, and Payton. They want to hold us accountable in addition to Olympus."

"That's bullshit! There is no way this will hold up."

"Well, like it or not, that's what the suit says, and it will be public knowledge in a short time. We're going to be crucified in the media even more so than when the mine collapsed last week. Our team is combing through the suit and finding everything they can to combat this, but it's still a real issue we have to face until we can make it go away," Zander snaps. Clearly, he's already been down this road and doesn't want to deal with it. My brothers returned from South Africa feeling hesitantly optimistic a few days ago, so this unexpected new roadblock is once again slowing down our progress at pulling Olympus out of the mud.

"Get PR to work on a statement. We need honesty, not culpability. This is a publicity nightmare, and I would guess there is more to it than just the ambulance-chasing law firm cashing in on the opportunity of a lifetime. We have enemies, and they want to see us fail at every turn. There's money and power backing this bogus claim, and we need to figure out that trail before we can know what we're really dealing with."

"Payton is already drafting statements with PR. You can join them and add your two cents when you finally deem us worthy of your presence today."

"I was working on another problem. I'm almost there; don't get your panties in a bunch wondering about my schedule," I say before I hang up.

Making sure Paige was fully satisfied before I introduced her to the team at Underworld Spirits for her first day as head of the company took priority this morning.

Now, I'm thinking she's getting the better deal finding her place at a new, and unblemished, company than I am with the string of issues mine is facing as of late.

I can feel the tension when I step out of the elevator at Olympus, eyes averting as I stride through the office space heading for the boardroom. Are we having a crisis of conscience with the staff in addition to all of the rest of the shit that is falling on us? We'll have to improve morale before they start talking and leaking sensitive information to the press, or worse, the Atlanta Haute List.

That stupid blog. It's not even a real media outlet, yet it has so much sway over what happens in Atlanta and the South at large. What they report often gets picked up by actual media sites and goes viral for some reason. I'll be checking the company NDAs today to make sure that they're iron-clad in case I catch wind of a rat in our midst that needs to be dealt with. I have no problem letting someone with loose lips go, no matter what their title may be.

"Good of you to join us, Hayes," Payton says when I push into the room and settle into my seat at the head of the table. Zander may be the CEO, but we all know I run things and get the coveted spot anytime the three of us are in the same meeting. Sometimes being the eldest has its perks.

Carina quickly places a stack of documents with sticky notes attached in front of me. She's been taking notes in my absence. She also settles a fresh mug of coffee in front of me, assuming correctly I will need the forti-fication for what's to come.

I nod my thanks and turn my attention back to Payton.

"Break it down for me. Who is really behind this, because I know it's not just some scammy law firm seizing the day and hitting us with a bullshit lawsuit."

"We're working on cracking that now. We have people in New York positioned close enough to gather the intel, but it will take more time to root it all out. Time we don't have. So, we have to be proactive and address what we can now, and be ready for more to hit us," Payton says, tapping his tablet and sending what's on it to the main screen for the rest of the room to see.

"Our main objective is addressing concerns in the suit that we were somehow aware of the issues with the mining equipment and structure yet didn't plan to fix anything. We don't want to be seen as negligent, but we also have to contend with the fact that the quickness of the sale kept us from doing our due diligence and we actually put off those inspections in favor of buying the property as-is," Diego says from my right, tapping a pink sticky note in my pile.

I lift it and see a waiver of inspection attached. Great. Now practices are being called suspect. This is how we do business, often blasting through a deal and waiving whatever we have to in order to make it happen on our timeline. It's a common enough practice but can look a bit risky from the outside.

"Second, we have to address the allegations of human rights violations in the working conditions of the mine. It's carefully worded, but there is blame being passed to us that the workers were not allowed to unionize and were punished for bringing safety and workplace concerns to management," Luca adds.

"Not to mention they have managed to corral the remaining workers to put this together so quickly. Someone is working against us on the ground in South Africa. Maybe the former staff we are in the process of replacing?" Zander muses from the other side of the table. "They were all happy enough when we showed up, checks in hand, ensuring they were paid for the year and all medical bills would be handled by us last week. I don't know what would have changed their minds so fast to want to be part of a lawsuit now."

I nod in agreement and see his eyes narrow that I'm not disagreeing or finding a way to fight with him. I point to the legal team. "I want whatever information we have about the condition of the mines, and how we may have missed that they were in danger of a collapse. Was it covered up in any documentation, or not disclosed in the sale, to begin with? This will be a definitive point for us to stand on, or fall to our death, so be thorough."

Heads nod and notes are scribbled while one of the members quickly leaves the room to get the rest of the team started.

I look to Payton and Luca and their motley mixed band of PR and operations staff. "We need an even better statement to release today. No in-person needed, just something we can distribute quickly." I snap my fingers, thinking of the main wording. "Olympus International, as well as the Olsen family, are deeply troubled by these allegations and are doing everything in our power to discover all of the details. We are known for our integrity and accountability and find no truthfulness in the suit brought against us by an opportunistic law firm representing a consortium of people we have already aided." I wave my hand in the air, looking for input after that start.

"We can work with that, but it won't fly as is," Luca muses.

"Too much blame casting. If we're addressing this, we have to keep it straight to the facts and not look shifty or like we're unable to accept when we've fucked up," Payton adds.

"Then bring up the real facts. Address the inconsistencies of the suit and the false information they are working with. When have we ever colluded to rob workers of rights? Never. We want the best value for our money, but we don't go out of our way to harm anyone, especially the workers." I wave my hand around at our own gathered assembly in emphasis. We are a Fortune 100 Best Company To Work For, and that extends to every level of our operation.

"Good labor is hard to come by and we have only ever replaced management at new properties so we could have our company values prioritized," Zander says, and the look of anger on his face likely matches mine. "That's probably where our problem lies. Look into the replaced upper management at the mine operation. See who may be kicking their feet for losing out on their job. They were likely crooked or not doing their job to begin with, but that gives them all the more reason to make a fuss and try to get their revenge now."

I nod in agreement and motion for Diego to run with it. "We cut the fat quickly, so we'll have to check with human resources and the acquisitions team to confirm who was on staff before we took over that isn't there now. We can hunt down some unhappy rats," I say, knowing there is likely a gleam in my green eyes that would scare anyone else on the receiving end of it.

I'm known as the bringer of death for a reason. At least in the business world. My actions are swift and decisive, and I never spare feelings when it's my bottom line at stake. Fuck with me in my personal life and you're likely to see the same side, though even less congenial.

"Local workers aren't powerful enough to put this together so quickly," Zander muses out loud, leaning back in his chair. "Who did we beat out of this deal?"

I stare at the ceiling, trying to remember the tiniest details of this acquisition. I was more worried about the numbers and making them work for Olympus than who we were bidding against, if anyone.

"Rex Omnia was sniffing around the operation before we jumped on it. They were the only real contender, though," Payton answers immediately. His mind is a veritable database of every detail of our business. It's scary how much he retains and has easy access to given the slightest provocation. His eidetic memory has come in handy on many occasions, and helped us take over some pretty hostile companies when he was able to produce some *compelling* reasons why they should agree to our terms.

I lower my gaze from the ceiling right along with my heart as it drops into my stomach. "Rex... as in Octavius Rex?"

Payton nods and sits back, crossing his arms and staring me down. "Looks like the ghost of Christmas past is coming back to haunt you, brother."

Fuck me.

"How was he even able to be considered a contender? I thought he lost everything a few years back," I muse, knowing full well he did. I took it all from him.

"He partnered with some big names on several projects and earned himself a nice reputation for making smart deals rather than always playing it fast and loose. He's definitely worth watching out for, now."

Rex was always one to watch out for. No amount of crumbling legacy or shattering of life as he knew it would end that notoriety. I met Octavius, or Tavi, as he went by back then, while doing my MBA at Wharton. We were both set to take over family businesses, feeling smug and cocky at twenty-two as we aced exams and saw the world as ours for the taking.

Things started to go downhill for Tavi several years after graduation when my brothers and I took our family mining business and expanded in every direction we could, gobbling up smaller corporations that expanded our holdings and inflated our own bottom line. Rex, Inc., a transportation conglomerate that had fallen on hard times, was one of our eventual purchases, though we picked it apart as we often do with acquisitions. Not only did Octavius's father get bought out, but he was also ousted from his leadership position at the company that had been in the family for generations.

What Octavius could scrape together from the company afterward became Rex Omnia, but it was a minor thing compared to the legacy he had planned on inheriting. I guess he didn't rest on his laurels if he was actually competition for us on this mine deal. It means he's expanded and is coming after Olympus size deals.

"He definitely has a motive to sink our reputation. Hell, he has every reason to want to see Olympus burn to the ground. He's based in New York, too. A million bucks says he has his hand in this lawsuit," I say to the room, and the grave faces that look back at me are reflections of what I feel on my own.

Fuck.

Fourteen

Paige

My impractical heels clack along the polished cement floor of the distillery as I follow Brandy, my aptly named guide for all things Underworld Spirits on my first day. We've covered what feels like miles of the multi-floored distillery rooms, operations offices, and the tasting room. The scale of this business is looming over me with each new floor we cover and every new machine and process we encounter. I'm feeling the intimidation of taking the helm and not having what it takes to execute my job adequately as the newness of everything surrounds me.

The day started with a meeting that brought in all department heads and the executive team where Hayes officially handed the company over to me. I had met most of the people at the launch party a few weeks back, but I had no part in the company at that point, so this felt more official. There was less trepidation in the air than I had anticipated. I was welcomed heartily, the familiarity they have with me thanks to the launch may have had something to do with that. Only a few people gave me looks of discomfort, and I don't blame them. I'll still have to work to win over the employees who showed hesitance to accept me as the new company owner, and that's best done by actions rather than words. Once the formal meeting was completed, I was shown my office, which belonged to Hayes previously, and given over to Brandy for my tour when Hayes headed over to Olympus to deal with his own business.

We've covered so much ground in the last two hours I'm starting to feel the effects in the balls of my feet. I'm wondering if we will ever finish the walking portion and get to the sitting part when Brandy abruptly spins at a door.

"This is the last part of the tour," she says, and I immediately let out a quiet sigh of relief. "This is where our newest gin stills are located, so be prepared for the pine-like aroma of the juniper berries, it's really strong right now."

I nod at her, but I'm not prepared for the wave of juniper that washes over us as she holds the door open and ushers me in.

"It smells like Christmas," I say, surprised by the evocative reaction the scent garners from me. I've only had gin a few times but typically ignore it out of spite because it's Mama's favorite drink. I don't think I noticed the intrinsic flavor when I tried it because it was mixed with other ingredients. I think I have seriously been missing out. I expected the sort of hot mash and grain smells that we experienced within the vodka and whiskey rooms, or the oaky scent in the barrel room where the bourbon is aging, but this is fresh, albeit, reminiscent of nail polish remover under it all, and I kind of love it.

"That's what Hayes said when he first toured this space, too," she says, smiling and bobbing her head so her ponytail swings.

That's when I notice her candy cane earrings. Christmas is coming up quickly, and I haven't found a present for Hayes. What could I possibly buy for a billionaire who has no real hobbies because he's a compulsive workaholic who buys whatever he wants as he sees fit?

"Y'all are so cute. I just love that he gave you a whole business for your wedding present," she pauses when she sees my look of confusion. "At least that's what I read on the Atlanta Haute List, is it not true?"

"Something like that."

Her question has my guard up and I'm once again facing the very real stigma that I haven't earned my place as the owner of this company in her eyes, and likely many others. They may believe exactly as she does, that this is the result of a besotted husband trying to impress his wife and shower her with extravagant presents rather than based on my ability. I'll have to work twice as hard to prove that I belong here as head of this company.

I also didn't realize the Atlanta Haute List was still reporting on everything Hayes and I do, including what he's doing on the business end of things, but I begrudgingly nod.

"Do you actually read that gossip site?" I'm genuinely curious about the reach it could possibly have. This is a prime example of why I don't do social media and stay off the internet as much as humanly possible. I may need to set up an alert for my name now that I am suddenly thrust into the public's interest, thanks to being married to Hayes. That way I will know what people are saying and not be blindsided by strangers with way more information than I'm comfortable sharing.

"Oh, yeah, of course I do! Practically everyone in Atlanta does. They've really taken a liking to you," she says, a note of admiration in her tone.

I highly doubt she would enjoy being in the spotlight on that blog if it was the intimate details of her life splashed across their website.

"I call it obsessive and not at all necessary. I'm really boring and there's nothing special for anyone to speculate about," I reply, my cheeks heating at her open stare and curiosity.

"Girl, you are living a fairy tale life in my opinion. I swear, it reads like a romance novel sometimes, how quickly you two fell in love—like it was fate. And the presents! They're so extravagant. How did you meet, anyway? The Haute List hasn't been able to crack that one and I am dying of curiosity." Brandy's blue eyes are intense as she leans in conspiratorially, and I take a step back from the scrutiny, masking my discomfort by peering closer at the second distillation process happening near us.

"We met at a party. See, nothing special," I say, downplaying the enchanting night I ran into Hayes in a dark garden as I fled my mother and my responsibilities at my debutante ball. I love that only Hayes and I know the details, just a little piece of our story that we can hold dear. I certainly don't feel particularly forthcoming with a virtual stranger who is far more interested in my life than she should be. It still surprises me that anyone would care about me or my relationship in the slightest. There are so many more important and interesting things to worry about.

"I've been dying to know what happened to keep you guys apart for over a week right after you were married. Did Hayes buying the hotel group from your family have something to do with it? I would have been so mad, so I don't blame you for walking away from him, but I know a lot of people probably didn't understand. But you got back together, so there must have been a reconciliation. Was that when he gave you Underworld Spirits? I would die of excitement if someone apologized by giving me a company. Is it super glamorous being married to an older billionaire? I know the billionaire part is probably a given, but it seems so sexy to have someone more mature pursue you. You stayed here in Atlanta with him, right? What's his house like?" She finally takes a breath and I take a step back from her barrage of questions and postulation.

"I'm really not comfortable talking about this." The words come out stilted and awkward, my need to stop the conversation in its tracks outweighing my desire to avoid confrontation of any sort. It's worth the cringey horror I feel to get her to stop asking intrusive questions.

"Oh, I'm sorry!" she says, finally realizing my discomfort. "I get carried away sometimes and it makes me nosy. I'll finish giving you the tour." She appears only partially contrite but it's better than the prying questions.

I really dislike that gossip site and all of the mess it's brought to my life just by throwing me into the ring for everyone's entertainment. How does one go about staying under the radar when they're married to a billionaire that has already caught the attention of everyone in the city?

I follow Brandy through the copper gin stills, stopping and admiring the top-of-the-line machinery and learning about the cutting-edge technology Underworld is using in their distillery without really knowing what the process is, or the reasons why one is used over the other. I keep adding words and phrases to a mental list and realize I have a lot of homework to do as we trace our steps back to the operations side of the building, where she deposits me in my corner office with floor-to-ceiling windows that look out over a sliver of Lake Clara Meer and Piedmont Park several miles away.

I pull my phone out and send a quick text to Hayes.

> Paige: Hey! I hope your day is going well. Underworld is more massive than I thought. There's so much I don't know. I hope things are going better for you *hearts around head emoji*

My phone vibrates on the desk a moment later.

> Hayes: It's a mess here. I envy you having to learn about a new company when mine is a shit show. Lean on the team at Underworld. They're top of their class in chemistry, marketing, and production, so the information and talent are all right there in that building.

I tap out a quick reply, knowing we both have plenty to keep us busy today and I am likely pulling his attention away from more pressing concerns just by texting when he should be focused on the work at hand.

> Paige: Sounds like you have your hands full! I will be just fine. I'm sure I'll be here late trying to make sense of the process and the why of everything, but it's fascinating. Stay

I open my laptop and make myself comfortable at the massive desk, probably ordered by Hayes when he was the company owner, and search the web for the history and the processes of distilling. The history is fascinating, and the commercial practices that have developed over the years keep me busy.

A knock at my office door has my head popping up from my overwhelming research. "Come in," I call.

The door opens and a petite brunette in clear-rimmed glasses pokes her head in. "Um, hi, I'm Sierra Tremayne, director of chemistry and development?" she says with a note of a question in her voice. "I'm here to give you a crash course on our distilling process. Your husband, uh, Mr. Olsen, called and made the request. Oh, and he made me bring you a whiskey cake from the café because you probably haven't eaten."

I wave her in and chuckle at how well Hayes knows me. It's just like him to pull strings to see to my needs and ensure I have someone close by to help even when he's dealing with his own work crisis.

"It's so nice to meet you, Sierra, I'm Paige. Thank you so much for your help, I could really use it right now. I was getting a little deep into things I don't quite understand with my research. I hope you don't mind me picking your brain."

She comes in and sits across from me, her dark eyes wide behind her frames as she pushes the plastic container of sticky sweet cake and a fork toward me. "It was kind of a shock to get a call from him directly. He's pretty intimidating."

"He can be, for sure, but he's very down-to-earth when you get to know him," I assure her, despite knowing that Hayes likely never shows his soft cinnamon roll side to anyone but me.

My husband is a secret romantic, a cuddly, affectionate, sweet man who is only ever like that with me, I realize. I'm lucky but also know it will be hard to convince anyone else of his amazing qualities when he stays so intimidating with others and incredibly ruthless in his business practices.

I take a bite of the cake and let out a sound of approval. It's amazing. I will have to thank Hayes for his intervention on behalf of my stomach when I get home.

"He mentioned that you were interested in the distilling process. Do you have time now to go over that?"

I smile and silently thank Hayes for not telling her how in over my head I am with my lack of knowledge. "Yes, this is perfect. I'm sure it's no surprise that I know nothing about any of this given my background is in hospitality. I'm eager to get to know everything possible to ensure I'm doing all I can to steer this company in the right direction."

"Okay, let's start with the basics, without getting into the nitty gritty. Only a chem nerd like me actually needs to know about carbonyls, sulfur compounds, terpenoids, volatile phenols, and heterocyclic compounds."

"Yup, I am lost already. I'm glad you have that knowledge, though, I am sure it's incredibly important. How about focusing on what sets the Underworld Spirits products apart, so we can incorporate that into our marketing and sales structure?"

"Oh, okay, yeah, I can do that."

Sierra launches into what we do that is classic to liquor distillation, then follows up on how we have changed certain aspects through micro-craft distillation to create a superior quality and finish. She explains why we have used different botanical varietals for flavor variations, and experimented with grain percentages in the various formulas to get a smoother mouth feel and taste. It's fascinating to see where the chemistry comes in, and how Underworld has broken from tradition in certain aspects while remaining true to the heritage of the liquors we produce. It gives me a ton of ideas to think about. I want to really play off the reinvention of our heritage aspect. It's fitting, given my own reinvention.

By the time Sierra has thoroughly supplied the history of distilling, laid out in a very rudimentary way the chemical processes for each of our liquors, and given me insight on the constant tweaks the team has made to get to the current formulas, the sun is setting. The sky outside my office windows is a riot of oranges and pinks, dotted with fluffy clouds that are mirrored in the lake below. I guess that means it's time to go home.

I take a quick look at my watch. It's after five, yet the darkness of night is quickly stealing any daylight left. As the calendar is nearing the winter solstice and the shortest day of the year, it makes sense, but I can't believe I have kept Sierra here so long.

"You have been such a help today. It was so kind of you to spend so much time with me making sure I understand what I'm leading now. I hope I didn't pull you away from anything too important just to catch me up."

"Oh, no, it's slow in my division right now. With the recent launch, this isn't a time we want to be making changes to the chemistry or formulations of our liquors. Also, with the holidays so close, it's really busy for sales and production, but the rest of us get a bit of a break. We're closed the week between Christmas and the New Year, usually, so they are working extra hard to get orders out in anticipation of the downtime." She pushes her glasses up her nose and gives me a quick look. "Unless you have other plans now?"

"No changes coming from me," I assure her. "I look forward to holiday downtime as much as anyone else, and y'all deserve it after the launch. I hear things are going well." I actually have a stack of the sales numbers and profit and loss sheets on my desk that support this claim. At least that side of the business is familiar and didn't give me any trouble to decipher.

"It's been very good. I know shipping and receiving is having a hard time keeping up with the constant in and out of product, which means there is a bit of a backlog that is happening."

"Sounds like I need to hire more people and ensure our workflow is regulated to adjust to the new demand." I'm just musing aloud, but Sierra nods.

"Probably a good idea. I can get you connected with people from each department who have good insights. It's not always the managers or heads of department, though."

"I would appreciate that so much." I look over at Sierra shyly, wondering if I am pushing my luck with what I want to ask her. I figure it's worth the risk and go for it. "Would you mind if I tapped you for more information and help in getting me acclimated to this role? You are incredibly knowledgeable and seem to be very in touch with the operations, and you put up with my incessant questions with a great attitude."

Sierra blinks behind her glasses and I wonder if she's about to tell me I'm annoying her in the direct way she uses that I have come to appreciate in the hours she has spent in my office. She doesn't seem much older than I am, and I think she would be super helpful, but what I am asking is out of her scope of work.

"I would love to. Your questions were thoughtful and inquisitive, which makes me think you were actually listening to me. Not everyone does when I get to the technical side of the distilling process, so it was nice to talk about my work with someone who paid attention."

I smile and feel the relief of not being turned down in corporate speak, which would have sounded like *sorry, I don't have the bandwidth to take on additional duties at this time*. And if we're working together more, maybe Sierra and I could become work friends. I'm severely lacking in the friendship department, as I have come to realize in the last few weeks.

It would be nice to develop some friends here in Atlanta to hang with outside of work and away from home where Hayes is the biggest part of my life. But for now, just having someone who knows everything about Underworld Spirits on my team and is willing to put up with my ineptitudes is a win.

"Deal. I'll listen to the chemistry even when I don't understand it if you'll help me figure out this whole thing. As for today, you have more than delivered and I won't keep you longer. It's about time I called it quits, also."

Sierra smiles and I think we're off to a good start. "I'm kind of surprised you want to be as hands-on as you are intending to be. Mr. Olsen may have owned the business and knew the bottom line, but he wasn't here much. You could probably coast along on the same level of detachment if you wanted, but I like that you're willing to be here with us and take ownership at more than face value. You're going to be great, Paige." She stands and waves as she leaves my office while I sit in complete disbelief and gratitude for her offhand comment.

I pack up and leave the office, saying quick goodbyes to a few of the employees who are still in the building as I find my way out of the labyrinthine structure. It's dark as I hit the fob to unlock the doors of the Mercedes G-wagon Hayes continues to let me drive as I don't have any of my own possessions here in Atlanta. I really need to head back to Savannah and collect a few items, or maybe find replacements to keep here to make my life feel more normal.

My mental list of things to grab is interrupted by my phone vibrating in my purse, and I fish it out, hoping it's Hayes saying he's on his way home as well. My hope is dashed when I see it's actually Mama calling me. I slide into the car, turn it on, and let my phone connect to the speakers before I answer her.

"Hello, Mama," I say, voice neutral. I haven't spoken to her directly since she called and told me Hayes had bought the Xenios Group from Daddy and I would no longer inherit the hotel legacy.

"Paige Fairchild, you have some explaining to do," she starts immediately.

I roll my eyes, knowing I'm about to get an earful of her sharpened and honed Southern guilt trip. This is why I didn't want to answer her call, despite feeling the familial obligation.

"Your father and I have been worried sick about you. Why wouldn't you call us and let us know you had left that man? You know we would have welcomed you home and helped you get rid of him for good. Then I hear from that horrid gossip site that you're flying all over the Eastern seaboard, and seen back in Atlanta with *him*," she says, treating Hayes's name like it's a dirty word she doesn't want to say.

I sigh and put the SUV in reverse to head home, knowing this will be a long conversation and I'd rather end it by coming home to Hayes than being stuck in a dark parking lot.

"Mama, I'm still working through some feelings I have over what you and Daddy did, so I had no desire to come running home to you. Besides, I'm an adult with my own apartment to go to and I will visit Alex if I feel like it without running my travel plans by you," I explain as patiently as I can muster.

"Oh, Paige, you have to get over that!" she insists, and I can just imagine her swatting the thought away like a summer fly on her verandah. "It was a good option at the time. We just want what's best for you."

"Oh, so you think a rapist was a better choice than the man I actually married? That's rich, even for you—oh, my Lord!" I say, startled by a man standing in the driveway when I pull out of my space and turn toward the exit. I hesitate, slowing as he stays rooted in place. Does he work here and is just leaving at the same time? He's staring directly at my car, his eyes squinted against my headlights, and I notice something vaguely familiar that sets my teeth on edge.

It's him. The man I saw at dinner at Rare, and in the park back in Savannah. My heart is thundering in my chest, and I've completely blocked out that Mama is on the line until I hear her repeating my name. I step on the gas and pass the man before I can think twice about it. Three times I've seen this very same man. It can't be a coincidence. *Can it?*

"Paige, what's wrong, for heaven's sake! You can't worry my nerves like this. Are you okay?"

I drive a little too fast down the road away from Underworld Spirits, signaling to get onto the highway and away from my fright. When my breathing slows and I can talk over my innate fear, I respond to Mama. But seriously, why does he freak me out so much, and more importantly, why am I seeing him again?

"It's nothing, I was just surprised by something in the road. It's fine and I'm on my way home now."

Another white lie. It's not like the man could be dangerous, right? He hasn't done anything other than show up in the same place I've been a few times. It could be a coincidence, though it seems unlikely after the third time. I'm sure it's nothing to worry about, so I won't make anyone else worry, either.

"Home," she sneers, and I bristle. "I do not know what has gotten into you. You used to be such a reasonable girl, understanding your duty and place in this world. Now, I hardly recognize who you've become. I'm worried for you, Paige."

"Mama, for the last time, I am a grown woman, so you can stop dictating every aspect of my life now. I get to decide what is best for me, even if it goes against your wishes."

That was a little harsh for Mama, but maybe it's about time we put some distance between us. I can't be her little doll to dress up and parade around forever. My hands shake and I tighten them on the steering wheel. I don't know if it's from the encounter with the strange man, or from being direct and confrontational with Mama, but the adrenaline pumping through my system has me jittery.

The line stays quiet for a long moment, and I wonder if she's hung up on me, or if our connection was lost. I check the screen on my dash. Nope, the call is still connected.

"Very well. I need to discuss a few matters with you. Is this a good time?" Her voice is glacial and so formal it makes me cringe. She is ferociously angry, yet she's moving forward with a conversation, which is a change from her usual dismissal and the hang up I would have expected any other time I sassed her.

"Of course, Mama. I wouldn't have answered the call had it been a bad time." I try to keep the crossness out of my tone, as I would like to repair our relationship eventually, and sandbagging it now won't help.

"Christmas is coming up quickly and it will be the very last time we get to celebrate at The Mansion. Will you... and that man... be attending Christmas Eve dinner?" Two steps forward, one step back.

I pause, not sure how to answer. Had she asked me a month ago, I would have predictably said yes, because of course we spend every Christmas Eve at the fancy black-tie dinner that caters to the top of the Savannah social elite. Now, I have my own family to think about, and it may not be in the cards.

"I just started a new job and don't have all of the details for it, or what Hayes's schedule will allow. I will speak with him about it and get back to you no later than tomorrow," I finally say, hoping that appeases her. I don't know what Hayes does for Christmas, so I can't make plans for us without at least consulting him on the matter.

"It's really bad form to respond so late to an invitation," Mama replies, her words cutting with a cold inflection.

"Seeing as how I didn't receive a formal invitation in the mail, and you are asking me the week before the event, it would seem you are on the wrong side of Emily

Post when it comes to etiquette, not me," I retort, not wanting to feel bad when it's her faux pas.

She sputters and I swear she may have dropped the phone at my disrespect to call out her manners. "Fine. Please reply at your earliest convenience," she drawls, her voice syrupy sweet yet crackling with her anger before the line clicks off.

Well, that's one way to really irritate Mama.

I'm flooded with relief when I reach the gates of the Buckhead mansion I'm calling home with Hayes. I press an automatic opener and drive through, winding through loblolly pines, towering oaks, leafless hickories, and a few spreading magnolias on the way to the house itself.

Hayes's Mercedes sports car is in the garage as I pull into an empty bay of the large and packed space. I scan the cars, noting a few exotics I can't begin to name, and a few that are more familiar, but likely rare models that very few would actually be able to attain. Hayes really has a thing for cars, expensive ones at that. Should I try to find a rare or vintage car for him as a Christmas present? It's the kind of thing he would do for me without batting an eye, but I don't know what kinds of cars he hasn't already bought himself that he could still want.

"It's about time you got home."

I look up with a smile as I step out of the car and gratefully slide into the open and welcoming arms Hayes holds out to me.

"You're a sight for sore eyes," I tell him, my voice muffled where I've pressed my face into his chest.

"Tough day at work?" he asks, taking my bag from me and turning us both for the door to the house, his arm slung around my shoulders.

I kiss his hand where it rests on my shoulder and hum a noncommittal noise. "Not so bad, just a lot all at once. I realized how truly little I know about the liquor industry—how anything is made, any best practices, procedures, or even how to market the stuff. I spent hours with Sierra learning about how the liquors are distilled and the chemistry that goes into the process. Thank you, by the way, for calling her in to help me. She was incredible and the company is absolutely fascinating."

Hayes chuckles. "Oh course, angel. Sierra knows her stuff, but it sounds like you took to it like a fish to water. You'll have the lay of the land soon enough. Don't think you need to be the foremost expert in anything the company does. Your role is to lead. Let them bring the information to you. You'll know what to do with it." He kisses my hair and leads me into the kitchen, where Cerberus is waiting patiently on the floor mat he knows as his place when commanded.

"Well, hey, big guy," I say, kicking off my heels in the doorway and bending down to give him plenty of pets and kisses. He shimmies in intense excitement until I release him from his perfect obedience with my attention.

"Let's get you some treats for being such a good boy," I say, feeling particularly indulgent.

Hayes is so stingy with the treats, and I'm happy to be the favorite human for giving the dog every last morsel.

Cerberus follows me into the pantry as Hayes laughs and pulls a few things out of the refrigerator. I poke my head out of the large pantry, wondering at his ruckus.

"What are you doing?" I throw a treat to Cerberus and pad barefoot back into the kitchen to lean against the island where Hayes has deposited a few containers. I pick up a bell pepper and eye the onion wondering how I will keep the tears away once it's cut. He's laid out corn tortillas and containers of rice and beans, so it's Mexican food he has planned. But... is he actually... going to cook?

"Cooking for you," he says. "Why, were you under the impression that I didn't know how?" He raises an eyebrow at me, his mock stern look is enough to bring me to giggles.

"Actually, yes, I was quite sure you never cooked."

It didn't help that I had a run in with his former-flame-turned-nutritionist who shopped and cooked for him up until I came into his life. That wasn't fun.

I know, theoretically, that Hayes is a man of the world, and as he once said to me, he does what he wants, whenever he wants, including women, but being face-to-face with one of those women made me feel every bit of my innocence and inability to please him. Now, well, I know differently and the jealousy is gone. *Mostly.*

"Never doesn't mean I can't," Hayes says, dumping a container of red meat into a skillet he's heated and oiled. "I'm perfectly capable of finding my way around a kitchen so I can feed my wife. Fajitas okay with you?"

"Of course," I say, washing my hands so I can help prepare the vegetables he's placed on the island. I roll my shoulders and begin to hype myself up to ask about Christmas at The Mansion when he interrupts my preparations.

"How would you feel about spending some time in Savannah next week? Olympus will be shutting down for the end of the year and I'm pretty sure Underworld Spirits will likely have a lot of downtime over the holidays, so it's a perfect time to get back down there."

I let the knife clatter to the island as I turn and wrap my arms around his middle from behind, so relieved I don't have to force him to leave Atlanta at such a busy time of year.

"I'd really like that." I take a deep breath and launch directly into my request without letting him go. "You know, my family has hosted a black-tie Christmas Eve dinner at The Mansion for generations. As this is likely the last time it will happen, I would like to attend, even if I'm not the biggest fan of my parents at the moment. Will you come with me?" I squeeze my eyes shut as I feel his back stiffen under my cheek. He turns in my arms and presses me at arm's length so he can look down into my face.

"I will go anywhere with you, angel. Even if it sounds a little like hell." His smile tells me he's kidding, mostly, and I return it.

"Thank you. I think you will make it a million times better, just by being with me. Besides, I want to show you the parts of The Mansion I grew up loving. They're not usually part of the tour." I release him so he can continue cooking the steak and go back to my peppers and onions. "What are your holiday traditions?" I ask, wiping at my eyes to stop the inevitable onion tears. I'm genuinely curious what his family did when he was younger and how he celebrates now.

"No formal Christmas Eve dinners with the who's who of society, that's for sure," he says, a smile in his voice. "We would actually go to a homeless shelter and serve dinner on Christmas Eve. I hated it when I was a kid because I thought it would be better to do parties and presents like my friends, but my parents were insistent, and eventually I understood why we did it. They wanted us to understand our privilege, which isn't easy when you're a white, upper-class man with generational wealth and plenty of connections." He pauses to take the peppers and onions from me and places a kiss on my forehead.

"That's so lovely," I murmur as he turns back to the stove. I wash my hands again, hoping to rid them of the smell of onions.

"We didn't do big Christmas Days, either. We would open up a few presents that were more practical than frivolous. No Xboxes or fancy phones in the Olsen household. We got practical gifts like good socks, leather journals, and one item off a wish list that couldn't be an electronic or big enough to need two people to carry it. My mother came from an extremely poor area, as redneck as it gets, and didn't approve of extravagant Christmas presents for us just because we had the money to do it."

"That is not at all what I would have imagined for you," I admit, cleaning up the vegetable scraps and tossing them in the trash. "What do you do now?" I want to fit myself into Hayes's traditions so bad it's a yearning.

"Work, usually."

I gasp and whirl to look at him in disbelief. "No, that is not at all acceptable. You have to take time off and relax, do something special, or mark the occasion, somehow."

"What would you like to do?" he asks, pulling a container of rice from the microwave. I mull that thought over as he places heated tortillas on our plates with scoops of Spanish rice and black beans.

"First of all, you need a big tree for your entryway and all the decorations we can fit in this house. It would be so beautiful and cozy, all lit up with lights and garlands."

"Done. We'll get a tree tomorrow and can decorate together," he says, like we're working through a business agreement. Now that I see just how easy it is to get him to embrace the season, I think a little harder on what I would like our traditions to be, as a couple.

"I like what your parents started. I would rather be philanthropic and give back, than do big gifts, if that's okay with you?" Extravagant gifts are lovely, but how do you top that year after year? It would eventually seem trivial, instead of special, and I don't want that.

He grunts and frowns at me. "But I like showering you with lavish gifts. What if I already had something picked out and wanted to surprise you with it?"

My eyes widen. Okay, so he has a gift. A big one. And I still haven't figured out what I want to get him. Oh Lordy, this is trouble. "How about it's not a Christmas present, then? Just a *because I was thinking you would like it* gift, rather than an *I had to go looking especially for this because of the time of year* gift."

"Mmmm," he says. "Very well. I have a *just because* present for you and I'll give it to you when we get to Savannah."

I nod eagerly, already feeling the giddiness of what his surprise could be.

"What would you rather we do for Christmas?"

I press my fingers to my lips as I think of what would feel most genuine and mean the most to me. "Can we bring presents to kids in the hospital? I can't imagine what a terrible time of year it is to be sick or not at home with family at Christmas."

"That's perfect." Hayes takes my face in his hands and looks down at me. "Just like you. I'll get someone on the logistics tonight. We'll go this week after work."

"You know what else would be wonderful?" I ask, warming to the idea and letting my imagination stretch. "Starting a program here in Atlanta that we could do all year long, so it's not just a holiday thing." I smile, really liking that idea. I want something of my own to give back in a bigger way.

His hands drop to the island behind me, bracing and leaning over me. "Your beautiful brain working out details really is so fucking sexy, especially when you're looking for ways to help others. What do you want to do?"

My breathing hitches as his body molds to mine, trapping me in his space. I fight to keep my train of thought as he places a few butterfly-soft kisses along my jaw, because it's wanting to skitter off into the recesses of dirty things we like to do together. In the dark. Like when I met him, in the Elysium garden on the rooftop of the Abyss in Savannah. The thoughts click together, and I know what I want to do. I straighten up and he pulls back slightly to take in the smile that I can feel all over my face.

"I have worked with enough foundations back in Savannah that I could reach out to for guidance, but what if we started a garden project? Something that would feed the community and give people steady work while developing business skills that they can translate into everyday life?" I'm thinking out loud, but I like the direction this is going. Our own foundation could do so much good right here in Atlanta. Something that would mean a lot to us both.

"Have you been holding back your desires from me? I didn't know you were interested in any of that. You know you can tell me all of this, anytime, right?"

I tilt my head at him. "It just occurred to me when we started talking about traditions. I'd like to create our own together. As for the garden and charity ideas, I've had to do my share of volunteering through the years as well. I always liked the projects that benefited people in underserved communities the most. It just makes sense to do a garden because of how we met, so why not make it a practical kitchen garden that extends to people who don't always have access to fresh produce? It could be our little Elysium, no matter where we are, and would help others."

"Elysium," he murmurs, his mouth dropping to my neck, breath tickling my skin. "You are full of surprises, wife."

Our conversation takes a pause, and our food grows cold, as Hayes shows me just how much he enjoys being surprised by my brain and ideas.

Fifteen

The Atlanta Haute List

illionaire And The Belle In The Giving Spirit

We may have had our initial doubts about the fast-moving relationship of billionaire Hayes Olsen and his Southern belle bride, Paige Fairchild, but we are just as head over heels for the couple now as they seem to be with each other. Our cold little Grinch hearts are growing three sizes just in time for Christmas as we watch them turn what could have been a honeymoon for the ages into a season of giving.

It was announced today that the couple has established a foundation benefiting youth in Atlanta. Think the Big Brother, Big Sister program meets your favorite Community Supported Agriculture group, but on billionaire-funded steroids, and you get the picture of what the Elysium Garden Project will be doing. Fairchild was quoted as saying, "We met in a garden, so it was only natural that we would turn to that for inspiration in creating the Elysium Garden Project. We want to provide mentorship and support while teaching valuable business skills and filling a need in the community. The Elysium Garden Project will create urban garden spaces for these communities to grow food, create jobs, feed hungry bellies, and establish local produce stands to teach basic business skills. We're excited to start the program in Atlanta and can't wait to expand throughout Georgia."

We're not crying, you're crying. And finally, a hint at how the couple met! In what garden did Hayes find this Georgia peach, exactly, and how do we start hanging out there looking for our own billionaire to pick us?

Not to be outdone by, well, themselves it seems, Hayes and Paige have also been visiting local hospitals and distributing toys to children who have to stay for the holidays. Sources say even brothers Payton and Zander have joined them on more than one occasion, so we think Paige is having a positive effect on the entire Olsen family.

This most certainly may appear to be a turn from our recent coverage of Atlanta's favorite billionaire brothers and their dastardly deeds in the business world. You must know we *are* capable of compassion as well as scathing opinions, and this is just the developing story we can get behind, and wanted to share to get all you Grinches into the Christmas Spirit, also.

As always, click Like and Subscribe for all of the Haute gossip.

Sixteen

Hayes

"No peeking." I clasp my hands over Paige's eyes when her own fingers become far too spread apart for my surprise.

"You're a madman, Hayes. You should have just blindfolded me completely if you wanted to keep me from peeking."

I growl against her neck. "A blindfold sounds like an excellent plan. Let's add that to the bedroom and see what you think."

She shivers in my arms and the motion sets off my own response, my pants tightening with each step. *Not the right time, buddy.*

"Where are we going?"

"You have asked five times already and haven't gotten an answer. What makes you think the sixth will be any different?" I kiss her head and pull her to a stop.

"I figured my persistence would eventually be rewarded. Are we there yet? Is this my present or just where I will find it?"

"Keep your eyes closed." I pull my hands away from her face and move to stand in front of her. "Okay, now you can open."

Paige blinks her eyes open and the first thing she focuses on is me, a smile spreading across her face. Her eyes dart around me and she steps back to take it all in.

"Oh, my God." She covers her mouth with her fingers and spins, taking in the park behind us. "I know this place. We're in the south historic district across from Forsyth Park, and that's my favorite house. Why are we here?"

"This is our new home in Savannah." The apartment at The Abyss was decent for a bachelor, but there aren't nearly enough spaces on which to get her naked. "Think you'll mind splitting time in Atlanta if we get to come back here?"

She smiles at me and throws herself into my arms, giving me the big squeeze around the middle hug that I like to think is reserved especially for me.

"Yes, I absolutely love it. How could you possibly know to pick this one?"

"That's all part of the magic, my love. I pay very close attention to everything that has to do with you." I take her hand and lead her through the wrought iron gate and up the ivy and royal palm-bordered steps toward the double-decker veranda. The house is a gorgeous three-story Victorian, painted white with shutters so dark green they look black setting off the plethora of windows. The landscaping is lush and gives the property the same feel Elysium has, though all of the plants thrive in the Savannah climate without the need for a greenhouse. I pull a keychain out of my pocket and turn her hand over to place it in her palm.

"Do the honors, Mrs. Olsen?"

She looks down at the key in her hand and laughs, the sound clear and tinkling. She holds up the jeweled pomegranate attached to the silver house key. "You don't forget a thing, do you?"

"You should see the keychain I got for the Maybach, it's the Batmobile." My humor is rewarded by her pressing up onto her tiptoes to kiss me, leaving behind a red lip print, if I'm lucky.

"I think I'm bringing out the fun in you after all." She turns away and fits the key into the door and pushes it open.

I grab her wrist, holding her in place as she starts to walk in.

"You know better, angel," I reprimand, my lips against her neck. She hums a pleased sound as I scoop her up into my arms and walk through the doorway with her before setting her on the other side in the foyer. "We're still newlyweds, my love."

"You and your cherry-picked traditions." She spins and takes off through the nearly empty home.

I asked the previous owners to leave a few pieces I thought suited the place, and they were more than happy to oblige when I added to the already inflated purchase price to compensate for their loss. A happy squeal has me moving to the kitchen, a beautiful space I know Paige will dirty in a second, as every surface is white, save for the gray veining in the marble counters and the dark wood floors.

Paige is leaning on the butcher block island, pulling a card out of an envelope from a vase full of stunning red roses next to a box with the Chanel logo on it. I found her a bag I thought my brothers would find fitting, so she can *carry my balls around in it*, to quote Payton.

"Oh, Hayes." She looks up, her eyes glittering with tears. "This is beautiful."

The note took me a while to craft. I'm not much of a poet other than being able to put together some rhyming couplets when provoked, so unfortunately, it won't go down in the annals of great poetry. I'm just glad she likes it. I worked it out like this:

> *I found a home most suited for the one I hold dear,*
> *Its beauty classic, full of grace, of my bride's own it's a mirror.*
> *History in the bones and love marked on the*

walls,
To hold the sound of little ones echoing
through the halls.
A place to raise our children and together
grow old,
To leave behind a legacy of love so strong it
will be forever told.
Make this house a home with me, as hus-
band and wife,
Fill it with love and noise, the epic story of
our life.

"You're beautiful." I tip her chin up with a finger and kiss her red lips until they open, and then I devour her sweet honey mouth.

Her hands move from my shoulders down my chest to my pants and she makes quick work of the button and zipper, her hands slipping inside to take hold of me. I groan against her mouth as she squeezes and strokes me.

"I want to start a new tradition." Her breathy whisper traces along my neck as she leaves my mouth. "I want you to make love to me in every room of this house, or any we have after. Even a haunted attic or scary cellar if it has them. I want any spirits that inhabit the place to know we're filling the house with only sexy moaning, so they don't get any ideas about sticking around."

My chest vibrates as I laugh. "You think this place is haunted? It has such good energy."

"Anything over a hundred years old is liable to be haunted. I used to lead history tours, in a big ball gown and parasol, no less, and there are plenty of stories about haunted houses around Savannah I could tell you."

"So, you're saying that instead of burning sage to cleanse the space, we're going to fuck the spirits out of every room?"

She purses her lips as her eyes heat. "I said make love, but I think we could do that in a few of the rooms."

"Say it, you filthy girl. I know you have it in you," I growl, my dick throbbing in her hand.

Her eyes smolder as she licks her lips and drops to her knees. She looks down at my cock in her hand, then rolls her eyes back up to me and I groan.

"We can fuck in every room."

She parts her red lips and licks up my shaft before taking me into her mouth. The exquisite combination of her speaking dirty words and blowing me in her enthusiastic, novice way nearly buckles my knees. I place one hand in her hair and slow her movements, placing my other hand around hers where it grips the base of my cock. I show her the speed I want her moving against me, stroking me as I guide her head to take more. She follows beautifully, gradually taking over and making a sound of approval as my cock throbs, the vibration drawing my balls up tight to my body. She looks up at me as my dick pops free from her lips.

"I'm ready to start right now."

I pull her off her knees, slide my hands under her dress and peel her soaked satin panties down her legs, lifting her up and setting her on the edge of the island, bared to me. I shove my pants down further and grip my dick, notching against her opening and plunging into her hot depths with a groan. She holds on tight as I roughly pump into her over and over, her nails digging into my shoulders and her legs wrapping around my hips as her head tips back in ecstasy. I grip her hip with one hand, my thumb moving to circle and press her clit, pushing her into a freefall of feeling that draws deep, satisfied moans from her throat. Her pussy clamps down and I fight to keep my rhythm until it becomes too much, and I come with a roar of possession.

Mine. This perfect angel is mine.

Seventeen

Paige

"It's Christmas Eve. There is no way someone as sweet as you can keep a vendetta against your parents today, even if I surely can."

I meet Hayes's gaze through the mirror at the vanity in the ensuite bathroom Hayes and I share in the gorgeous Savannah home that is sitting nearly empty thanks to the fact that we only started inhabiting it the day before. Thankfully, we have a bed, which was all it took to get me to stay our first night here.

I survey him as he straightens his cuffs, the movement flexing his big, muscly arms and chest that looks barely contained in the starched white shirt. I sigh a little as his masculine beauty hits me, even more powerful as he slips on a black jacket with satin lapels for the formal dinner. It's bittersweet knowing this will be the last time my family hosts the legendary—among Savannah circles, at least—Fairchild Christmas Eve dinner. Hayes has assured me that the tradition will live on even after the Olympus Hotel Group takes over, but it is bound to change, and that makes it important to attend tonight.

"I don't have a vendetta against them. It's just a little bitterness I've held onto maybe long enough."

I take a deep breath as I pass a brush through my hair one last time to soften the curls. My makeup is done in glittering golds on my eyes with the signature red on my lips Hayes likes so much, both meant to compliment the emerald velvet, off-the-shoulder dress I picked out from Haute Belle in Atlanta before we left for Savannah. I stand and take my clutch from the bathroom counter as Cerberus stretches from his spot on the rug nearby.

"Shall we do this?" I ask.

Hayes drags his teeth over his lip and appraises me. "I think one of my shirts would look great right over all that lusciousness." He thumbs toward the closet like he's actually ready to cover me up.

"You said I could wear whatever I want, and I like how this color matches your eyes."

His chest expands and he smiles, small lines framing his eyes and drawing my gaze. "I guess I can share your beauty with the world, then." He leads me down the stairs and out to the car.

"I've found a few gardeners who are interested in helping us run the community gardens," I say, breaking the comfortable silence on our drive to The Mansion. "If we can secure the land for the plots and get through the necessary space planning requirements, we can start planting as soon as the weather allows."

Hayes was so receptive to my ideas when I brought up wanting to start the Elysium Garden Project, he had to act on it immediately, so the next morning we filed the documents for the foundation and created the business plan. We got the ball rolling to make this little dream into a reality, and hopefully, the new year will bring lots of good things where that is concerned.

"That's great! The more help, the better. I have a few people who helped plan the rooftop garden at The Abyss we can work with, also."

He pulls the sleek Maybach, which reminds me so much of the Batmobile, to a stop in the parking area near the valet stand at The Mansion, pocketing the keys instead of turning them over to the young valet who rushes up to the car, only to turn away with a look of disappointment on his face. Hayes refuses to let anyone else drive his death mobile and it makes me grin. Something about it being a one-off vehicle that Jay-Z used in the Lost One music video, most likely. I've learned Hayes is a lover of 90's hip hop, and Jay-Z is one of his favorite artists, whereas I mostly just know him as the guy Beyoncé is married to.

My smile fades a bit as I take in the grand exterior of The Mansion, my family's ancestral home since the 1700s. It is a bit sad knowing this beautiful property will no longer be passed to me one day.

"I love this place." The wistful note is strong in my voice as Hayes helps me from the car. I pull on his hand and make him stand in the courtyard near the marble fountain. As a child, I threw in countless pennies wishing for friends. As a teen, I wished for patience with Mama. As an adult, I wished for someone to love me. What would I wish for now, having that very last wish finally granted?

Hayes looks down at me as I stare at the beautiful Antebellum mansion fully decorated for the holidays in white twinkle lights, wreathed windows blazing with warm light spilling out onto the front porch. "It truly is a remarkable sight."

"Just take it in, all lit up like this. Every good memory from my childhood has its roots right here." Skinned knees from chasing frogs and fireflies in the garden, family dinners in the Fairchild dining room, licking frosting from a spoon in the kitchen with Mathilde, the French pastry chef who taught me everything I know about baking. It's all right here.

"It will always be here. We won't change anything about this property. Your family legacy lives on, no matter who holds the title in their hands. Besides, your controlling interest in the Hotel Group means you can always ensure the history and beauty of The Mansion is preserved."

"Thank you." I rest my head on his shoulder and take a few more moments to revel in The Mansion, a building

I have been in love with all my life. I pull away and look at the man I love just as much. I nod to let him know I'm ready.

"Mr. and Mrs. Olsen, welcome to The Mansion," my favorite bellman says with a wink at me. "Merry Christmas, Paige."

"Merry Christmas, Stefan. Send my love to Marguerite and the grandkids. I'm sure Luke is huge now, and Isabella has to be the prettiest pageant princess ever to grace the stage."

"That they are. Izzy is so thankful for the ventriloquist dummy you sent her way. She's getting quite good at it and can't wait to show you. If I'm being honest, it kind of scares me."

I laugh. "It scared me, too. I'm sure she's far better than I ever was with it, and I would love to see one of her pageants. Just send me the information."

He nods at me with a smile and turns to open the door for us.

"Ventriloquist dummy? This I have to see."

I turn to Hayes, my cheeks heating with a blush of embarrassment. "I'm sure if you asked Mama nicely enough, she would dig out the photos and home videos for you. It was terrible. Speak of the devil," I finish softly, catching sight of Mama.

"That's my role, honey, don't give it to anyone else. She can be the harpy."

I cover my mouth with my hand as I nearly choke on my laughter. "You are so bad. I really hate that I have the visual of Mama as a harpy now and I can't unsee it."

"Paige," Mama calls as she winds her way to me and Hayes, sounding just as sharp as I would imagine a harpy does. "It's about time you got here. The Declans have been asking about you and I am tired of making your excuses."

"Good to see you too, Mama. Merry Christmas." I kiss her cheek and force her to hug me even though she's flustered.

"Caroline, you look beautiful. Thank you for having us tonight. There is nowhere we'd rather spend Christmas Eve than with family."

Mama snaps her beautifully coiffed blonde head toward Hayes and narrows her eyes as if speculating on the validity of his statement.

"As Paige is our only child, I'm sure you can imagine how important spending time with her is. I'm actually quite surprised you didn't whisk her off somewhere in an attempt to keep her away from us out of spite."

"Mama, there is really no need to be rude. Hayes and I are happy to be here tonight, and we won't settle for you borrowing trouble where there isn't any. Where's Daddy?" I divert her attention from sniping at Hayes and she looks over her shoulder with agitation at the crowd gathering in the lobby.

"Oh, Mayor Declan got his claws in early and is buttering your daddy up for reelection campaign funds. Come on then, we'll go together." Mama turns and leads us into the Christmas Eve fray.

Hayes and I greet Daddy and rescue him from Mayor Declan, who attempts to solicit Hayes for his support without any subtlety, before we can extricate ourselves from any social obligations and introductions for a moment.

I am more than relieved to not see hide nor hair of the Daniels family. I don't think I could have taken another run in with Garrison, walking free and untouched from his past deeds. They're probably afraid of the dirt Hayes has on them, and rightly so. That may have been part of the reason the Daniels didn't fight to keep their company when Hayes bought it and gifted it to Daddy and Mama.

The loss of a business isn't as bad as the possible scandal of their coverups for their rapist son coming into the light of day. It would be especially bad since the same son just passed the bar and is supposed to be a law-abiding citizen and lawyer, not a rapist whose parents paid off his victims to keep them quiet.

I shudder even thinking about it now.

The only saving grace is that Hayes knows the truth of him, with plenty of proof to keep them on the right side of the law. Hopefully that will be enough to keep Garrison from doing it again.

I do, however, see Liliana Bailey and her family, and that is nearly as bad as seeing Garrison.

When she spots me, her lip curls and she gives me a quick head-to-toe once over as she starts our way in a fluttering peach dress. *Peach? In December?* I turn back to Hayes to avoid the continued appraisal. I'm fine, there is nothing to worry about, I repeat in my head.

"Paige, you *must* introduce me to your new husband and tell me all about your whirlwind romance."

I cringe hearing Liliana's voice behind me and know I did not get lucky enough to avoid her, after all. Hayes feels me tense and protectively tucks me into his side before turning us both toward her, leaving his arm around my shoulders. I desperately look around for someone to demand our attention, but Liliana has us cornered and even Mama is busy elsewhere.

"Liliana Bailey," I say, my voice cracking as I try to make the proper introductions. "This is Hayes Olsen, my husband."

"It is a pleasure," Liliana says, coming in close and grasping onto Hayes's arm, which he hasn't extended to her. "I have heard so much about you. Paige and I go way back," she gushes to Hayes, and all I can think of is how she made me cry the last time I ran into her.

My eyes prick with the same feeling now, and I force myself to breathe deeply and stave off the waterworks of frustration and shame.

"Paige has never mentioned you. I guess you weren't that big a part of her life," Hayes says, cutting, yet not cruel enough to really sink through her thick skin.

Liliana releases Hayes's arm like it burned her, then covers the move by smoothing her auburn hair behind her ear like that was her intention all along. "Well, we will have to fix that. It's been too long since Paige and I have had a chance to catch up. If you two are free tomorrow, you can stop by the Christmas celebration at my parents' home. Paige, you remember where they live?"

I nod, but Hayes speaks before I can make our excuses.

"We will be far too busy to make it," he says in answer, but his eyes are on me, drinking in my face, and traveling lower with a look of deep appreciation. "Paige keeps me very busy these days, and well, there's not much else that I would rather do than make sure she is incredibly satisfied... with every aspect of our life together." He strokes a thumb along my jaw and turns my chin up so he can place a slow kiss on my lips. It is chaste enough not to be criticized by the crowd, but is full of enough heat and longing to make his point to Liliana.

My cheeks are burning when he finishes, but I'm not embarrassed, I'm triumphant. Hayes is my champion, but he is all deference to my sexiness and his desire for me, and that gives me a boost of confidence and power that Liliana normally crushes out of me just by existing.

Liliana's face is a mask of rage when I finally turn her way again.

"Sorry," I sing-song, not at all apologetic.

"Get a fucking room. You guys are disgusting," she huffs, dismissing us and turning away to scan the room for her next mark.

"Not as disgusting as your behavior," I mutter, hoping it won't carry.

Liliana whips around and glares at me. "What was that, slut?" she says, her eyes narrowing and her words sharpening.

This feels like high school all over again, and I can't help retreating into myself, trying to become a smaller target. I swallow the lump in my throat, wondering why I had to goad her when I could have let it be. She was done with us, and I got her attention again.

I glance at Hayes and his eyes are sharp, appraising the situation. He's letting me take the lead, but I can feel him ready to jump on this and end it for me if needed. I shake my head, warning him off, because I dug this hole myself and I might as well straighten my spine and tell Liliana what I have thought of her for so many years now that I've opened the door.

"You are a disgusting bully who puts others down so you can feel bigger. I don't know why you can't leave behind the judgment you thought was yours to cast in high school," I say, my voice high, and a little shaky.

It's not easy for me to be confrontational, and Liliana has been a tormentor for so long that I've made her into this giant in my head that I could never conquer. It's about time I tried to slay the dragon, even if it takes every ounce of strength I can muster just to take the first charge at her.

"That's rich, coming from the most disgusting girl at Prep. You really haven't changed, still a whore, opening your legs to get what you want," she says, rolling her eyes and crossing her arms over the frilly bodice of her peach organza dress. It really is the worst choice for a winter dinner, but I'm not here to critique her fashion sense.

Hayes stiffens at my side, hearing now what my posture and tension have alluded to, putting him on the defense of me.

I think the only reason I can answer her vile accusations is because he knows the truth about me, and I would rather lean into that than hate how she makes me feel. I'm done letting her get to me, done letting her make me feel defenseless.

"You made up every nasty rumor there was about me at Savannah Prep, so I guess your imagination was what was disgusting. You should work on that if you have a problem with me," I say, before softening my tone. "We're not in high school anymore, Liliana. Maybe you should grow up and find something worthwhile to pursue, rather than trying to make my life hell."

"God, Paige, you're so sensitive, you can't even take a joke. Work on your sense of humor already."

Liliana's resort to gaslighting makes me question my ability to read the situation, and it's so reminiscent of how Mama makes me feel regularly that I almost believe it. But there is a part of me, however small, that knows she's wrong and is just trying to save face now that she's been called out. Once I grasp that small flicker of truth, my heart softens and I'm able to cut the noose Liliana has had around me all these years.

It's not about me at all, it's about her, I realize. Every rumor she started with me in the spotlight was about behavior she herself exhibited. I knew it instinctually when it was happening, but it's only now that it really hits me.

She created her own double standards and forced me to be her proxy to make herself feel better. Gosh, how much she must hate herself. She doesn't need me to hate her at all when she's doing that job well enough on her own.

I actually pity her.

"You know what? I don't think you want to change, and it's not my job to make you. Enjoy your life, Liliana. I think we're done here. Hayes, we have more important people I would like to introduce you to. Come on." I turn us away and don't think twice about whatever Liliana may want to say.

"Your big heart will never cease to amaze me, angel. You showed far more restraint and grace than I would have for that nasty piece of work. Damn, I love you so fucking much," Hayes says, tucking me into his side and pressing a hard kiss to my head.

"I love you, too, and I liked you as my menacing back up. That was exactly what I needed, to have the devil himself looking over my shoulder to make sure Liliana wasn't too horrible and letting me handle it, even if I wasn't great at it."

"Oh, don't worry. I have my own plans to make sure she gets exactly what she deserves. Her last name is Bailey, right? I'm going to bury that family of hers and ruin every bit of business they do in Savannah, and I'm not even going to offer to buy their company." Hayes's voice is far too chipper for the oath of obliteration he just gave me, and I give him a side-eye.

"Is that happy tone totally necessary?" I say with a laugh that dies as I see the serious set to his face.

Hayes pulls us to a stop and faces me. "You may be able to find forgiveness for the terrible things she said to you, but I don't have to. I want her to hurt as badly as that look on your face hurt my soul."

Hayes brings my hands up to his lips, kissing my fingers in turn and looking at me from under his lashes. His green eyes gleam malevolently, and I shiver. This is the ruthless king of the corporate underworld that the world knows and fears. I've been lucky to see the softer side of Hayes, but this is who he is to everyone else. He is fearsome, and I'm more than a little turned on by his territorial aggression and promise to strike down my enemies, necessary or not.

I shake the dirty thoughts from my mind and try to wrap my head around the situation at hand. "Why? It's clear she hates herself enough for the both of us."

Hayes takes my face in his hands and stares deep into my eyes, looking to sear my soul. His words are cold as he continues. "She needs to feel as small and powerless as she makes others feel. I will make hell rain down on her for what she said tonight, and even worse for what she has put you through over the years."

"You don't have to do that, though. We can let this go now and she will still be a miserable person without our interference."

"Sweet angel, you are too pure for this world," Hayes says.

He takes a seat on a settee along the hall outside of the dining room and pulls me down to perch on his lap turning me to face him.

"It's my deepest desire to ensure that anyone who even looks at you wrong is fucking crushed." His words ring true, like a sword unsheathed and ready for battle. "Women who say nasty shit like that to one of the sweetest people I've met are nothing but bullies who need a taste of their own medicine. As it so happens, I'm quite good at dishing out vengeance."

The gleam in Hayes's eyes is possessive and, if I'm honest, it makes me happy to hear someone say those things in defense of me for once, but... in a twisted way? He's the wolf at the door I was told to be wary of, and now he's mine forever.

I shiver and lick my lips under his continued stare. Before I can overthink it more, Mama catches my attention and waves us over to resume our rounds of introductions. I rise from Hayes's lap and draw him up with me to go to her. His hand is firm and heavy on my low back as we cross the room and I thrill to his touch.

"I saw that look, angel," Hayes whispers into my ear before we reach Mama. "Be a good girl and I'll fuck your tight pussy while telling you exactly what kind of vengeance I can exact for what she did to you."

I feel my mouth make an *O* of surprise as my lady bits tighten along with Hayes's grip on my hip. I have to compose myself quickly as Mama takes my arm and steers us to a group of people waiting near the dining room doors.

"Judge Whitaker, this is my new son-in-law, Hayes Olsen," Mama says when we run into Alex's parents. She seems to take great pleasure in introducing Hayes as her son-in-law to guests, which surprises me. She must not mind the pairing as much as she says she does. I think she will eventually have to get over the fact I made a choice for my life that she didn't have control over, and it didn't turn out the mess she expected without her guidance.

It's about time we learned to be less codependent of each other, even if she would prefer we always stay attached at the hip. I'm ready to be my own woman, free from her dictatorial ways whether or not she is.

"I have heard so much about you, young man."

Hayes reaches out, offering his hand. "All terrible, very bad things, I'm sure," Hayes responds with a clever smile.

The Judge chuckles and turns to me. "Hello, Paige darling. I heard you visited Alex in New York recently. How is sh—*he* doing?" he asks as he hugs me, tripping up on the pronoun swap Alex has made. He's trying, though, and has been working on it for Alex's sake. I'm sure it's difficult for the Judge and Mimi, Alex's mother, to embrace this change after almost two decades with their child assigned a different gender than the one that felt the best for Alex. They're very open and at least trying, which I appreciate on Alex's behalf.

"Alex is living his best life, and New York suits him," I say, happy to provide the update. "I'm sorry he couldn't come home for Hanukkah. Work seems like it's keeping him busy these days."

"You know how it is for young people," the Judge says, conspiratorially, as if I am not a young person myself. "They get busy and their families have to let them go on adventures, really get to know themselves without their parents being the wiser."

I sure hope Mama is listening and sees other parents let their kids live their own lives.

We are called into dinner at that moment, and the crowd begins to meander toward the Fairchild dining room, where Nanny Fairchild sits at the head of the long table, as regal as a queen in her black lace dress and pearls. I pull Hayes along the table, heedless of the place cards telling us where we will be sitting, because I know where my place is—at the end of the table nearest to Nanny to keep her company.

Nanny prefers not to mingle before dinner, and always gets seated first to avoid the headache of schmoozing.

Ahh, there it is. I spot our names as I get closer and see Mama has still managed to keep my last name as Fairchild on my card. I haven't made a move to legally change my name yet, and I'm not sure if I will. Hayes hasn't mentioned the change, but he does call me Mrs. Olsen fairly regularly, so I will have to feel him out to see what his thoughts are on the matter. Keeping the Fairchild name going in some way is important to me. I may have lost the legacy, but I won't lose my name as well.

"Hello, Nanny!" I bend and hug the septuagenarian around the shoulders, feeling her pat my arm in response. "I would like to introduce you to someone very special."

"Hello, honey, it's nice to see you. Is this the new husband I've heard so much about? Hayes, I've heard is your name. My, you're a tall one, and handsome as the dickens. Oh, Paige dear, you did well."

Hayes smiles warmly. "Mrs. Fairchild, it's a pleasure."

"Paige has never brought home a boy, let alone a husband. You must be something special. Now, would you like to hear about Paige as a little girl? She was quite the awkward child, probably why her mother put her in all those cotillion and finishing classes, to school out the gangly limbs and penchant for slouching." She pokes my ribs with her cane, and I yelp, jumping away with a laugh.

We settle in and Nanny regales Hayes with stories of my childhood, trying to embarrass me every which way with some of the things she comes up with in the hours-long dinner. My cheeks are sore from smiling by dessert.

As after dinner cocktails wrap up and guests begin to make their exits, I squeeze Hayes's hand under the table and lean my head onto his shoulder. Nanny is no longer here to entertain us, having been whisked off by her caretaker around ten when she began to fade from the exertion.

"Getting tired, honey?" Hayes asks, placing a kiss on my head.

It is nearly midnight, and that's kind of my limit when it comes to social events.

"A little. I want to show you something before we leave, but we have to slip away without Mama and Daddy being the wiser. Let's say our goodbyes and then make a quick exit."

"That sounds promising. Lead the way."

We say our goodbyes to the Whitakers and make our way to Mama and Daddy, who are saying goodbye to guests.

"Mama, Daddy, thank you again for making this dinner such a special part of my life. We'll see you for Christmas brunch tomorrow, right?" Hayes and I asked to have brunch with my parents at our new house. We will spend all of Christmas in Savannah, and head back to Atlanta for New Year's to possibly meet Hayes's parents, effectively splitting our holidays. There's a lot to being a couple I had never considered before Hayes swept into my life and made me part of a pair.

"Of course, Sweet Pea, we can't wait to see your new house," Daddy says, kissing my cheek and straightening to extend his hand to Hayes. "Son, take care of my baby. Merry Christmas."

I feel a fierce, crashing love roll through me at him calling Hayes son. That is a huge step forward and an indication of his respect and approval. I hadn't thought it possible, given Hayes's recent procurement of our business and me running off with him and getting married without their blessing.

"Are you sure you don't want me to bring some of the food Mathilde is preparing for tomorrow? You don't have to make everything yourself."

I indulge Mama's worry.

"How about you bring your delicious biscuits and sausage gravy? It's not Christmas without them, and I think that would make the perfect addition to what I have planned."

Mama stands straighter in her deep merlot-colored dress with a look of superiority on her face. "I thought you might have forgotten about our Christmas morning tradition with your new life keeping you so busy. It's like I never see you anymore."

She's seen me plenty and should be able to handle a few weeks away, but she's prone to dramatics and is hyper-focused on my life. "I could never forget anything about you, Mama. We'll see you at nine tomorrow morning." I kiss her cheek and hug Daddy.

I tug on Hayes's hand and head toward the front lobby, glancing over my shoulder to make sure Mama and Daddy are preoccupied before I cut through to the side hallway and pull Hayes up the service stairs to the upper floors. When we stop at the topmost landing, I pause to pull out the all-access keycard I've been privileged to have all of my life, thanks to my friendships with the staff and my constant need to explore. I let us into the room I've been wanting to show Hayes all night, giddy with the anticipation.

"Where are we, exactly?" he asks, looking around at the storage area in the attic, the sloped ceiling giving away our location before I can tell him.

"The antiques are stored up here for seasonal rotation, but it's what's beyond the furniture that you have to see. I used to play up here as a little girl. I made up stories and imagined I was Rapunzel stuck in my tower." I wind a familiar path through the dust-cloth-covered furniture to the big round window that rarely gets its chance to shine. "Look at this. It's the best view anyone can have of Savannah, maybe even the most beautiful thing I've ever seen."

"Nothing comes close to your beauty, angel." Hayes wraps his arms around my middle and pulls my back into his chest as he looks out the window with me. "But this is pretty close."

I smile and lean my head into his. "You know what the best part of pretending to be a princess locked in a tower is, right?" I feel Hayes shake his head. "Knowing there's a prince out there ready to battle witches and slay dragons in order to free her. That's you to a T. Now you get to kiss the princess." I turn in his arms and cup his cheeks with my hands to bring his face down to mine.

"Fuck being a prince. You know I'm the devil, and you better know I'm not going to stop at just kissing you," he growls against my lips.

My cheeks heat at his words. "I'm not wearing panties and that just made me *really* wet."

Hayes pushes me back until I'm resting against the plush arm of one of the sofas and crouches in front of me, a predatory gleam in his eyes. He drags the hem of my long dress up my legs, taking in the sheer black stockings I'm wearing. He bites his lip when he reveals the black garters that are keeping the stockings up attached to a satin belt at my waist. He drapes my dress over my hips and his hands spread my thighs apart, a shudder working through him.

"Jesus, baby," he groans.

"I always knew there was a man out there who was perfect for me. It didn't have to be a prince, just my match, and I'm glad I found you."

Hayes doesn't respond. He just grabs my bottom and presses me against his mouth as he begins to devour me. I hold on to the couch for dear life, one of my legs lifting to hook over his shoulder as the pleasure fizzes through me in popping bubbles of anticipation and feeling.

I gasp as his fingers plunge into my center, the pressure and beckoning motion he uses combining with the feel of his mouth on me. It doesn't take long for my gasps to become moans, and his name to spill from my lips as the orgasm washes over me.

"Oh, Hayes. Hayes. Hayes!" My head thrashes with each exhalation of his name.

He works me through the release before he's standing and turning me. His deft, strong fingers unzip my dress, letting the green velvet pool at my feet. The pressure of his hand bends me over the arm of the couch in my garter belt, stockings, and heels before the waves have even stopped. His hands drag down my spine making me shiver as I anticipate his next move. I don't wait long to feel his cock press against my opening, nudging in slowly as my body clamps down on him.

"You're so fucking tight. So wet. All mine."

I shiver at his words, spoken in a harsh whisper into the curve of my neck and sounding dark and sinfully perfect.

"And you're all mine." I thrust my hips back against his body and ignite the primal side of him that promises every worldly pleasure I could ever hope for, and more.

Hayes is my dark prince, the king of the underworld, and he's claimed me body, heart, and soul.

Eighteen

Hayes

"**O**h, good, you haven't left yet."

I freeze at the voice, but keep my focus on steadying Paige, who giggles as she hops on one foot while struggling to put her shoe back on as we leave the service staircase into the lobby. Once she is back in both stiletto heels, I look over at the face of the speaker, already knowing full well who it is, despite thinking I would never run into him again.

"What are you doing here, Rex?" I tuck Paige against my side, not wanting her to capture his interest.

"Just seeing what kind of property would make you renounce being single after all these years," Octavius Rex says, straightening his suit lapels. "You have a little..." he says, wiping the corner of his own mouth with his thumb, indicating I must have some of Paige's lipstick on my mouth.

"I didn't get married to buy a property and that can't actually be why you're here on Christmas Eve. What do you want?" I wipe at my mouth absently as I take him in.

He's polished marble, perfect in every way despite the lateness of the evening, even now with the crescent-shaped scar he sports on his left temple—a souvenir of a brawl we once tackled together after a late night studying for finals at Wharton. Rex aced his finals despite the concussion he sustained. He's too smart for this, and I'm on guard knowing it.

"You're right. I heard about your recent marriage and decided I had to meet your bride for myself. There's not nearly enough about her online to learn secondhand." Rex puts his hands in his pockets, pulling a practiced, slouching stance only a fuckboy brick house at six-three can pull off and still be crack for women. He is doing it to try to disarm Paige.

I clench my jaw and feel my shoulders rise, boxing out my frame and sending back my own practiced stance that should be loud and clear. Rex gives us his signature roguish, dimpled grin, brown eyes flashing with mirth, and I want to deck the smug look right off his fucking face. He knows exactly how to get under my skin, and I need to get my shit together. I feel all of twenty-five again, instead of thirty-five, and I don't want to be the hotheaded dick I was back then. I take a deep breath and reach for the boardroom fortitude that usually sustains me.

"Don't even try, Rex. I know every last one of your fuckboy tricks," I growl, still working on the control I seem to have misplaced since running into my rival. Not just my rival, the fucking mastermind I know is behind the lawsuits surrounding the South African mine collapse.

"Oh, come on, Hayes. How about giving me a break from this macho bullshit. It is Christmas Eve, after all—" The grandfather clock in the lobby cuts him off as it bongs out the time and Rex tilts his head in acknowledgment. "I guess it's Christmas, now. So, how about we put aside our differences and get into the holiday spirit? If I'm able to put aside my feelings about what you did, then you should, too."

Paige grips my arm, and I look down at her face, growing alarmed when I notice she is more distressed than she should be running into someone only I would know.

"That's the guy I saw at Rare," she whispers. "He was also at Underworld Spirits on my first day, and here in Savannah before that."

I'm instantly on guard. "Are you following my wife?" I snap, my attention fully on Rex now. My instinct to protect Paige is riding an adrenaline rush I can feel thrumming through my veins, hot and bitter. Red creeps into the edges of my vision and I don't care where we are or who is around, I will end him if he's done anything to make her feel unsafe.

"I told you, there wasn't enough about her online, so I had to see for myself. She really is beautiful. And so... innocent," he says, his eyes growing dark as his attention slides to Paige.

I feel her stiffen beside me and there is a part of me that wants to roar and smash Rex's head against the marble column beside him. I force myself to stay rooted in place to not act on the instinct for violence.

"Eyes off, Rex." The threat is thinly veiled, and I don't have to tell him what will happen if he looks at Paige too long.

"You and I have something in common, Paige," he says, heedless of my warning. "Hayes took a family legacy from me, as well. You see, he has quite the habit of coveting other people's businesses and doesn't care if he fucks over his best friend, or his wife, to acquire them."

I feel, more than hear, Paige's intake of breath from where I have her pressed to my side, and I want to scream that's not what happened. To shut down every word he says that puts Paige on her heels about me—about us. But that wouldn't be entirely true, because no matter what my intentions were, I did what Rex said. It doesn't matter how much I fucking hate him for weaponizing it now.

"We're done here." I turn away from Rex, my arm around Paige to bring her with me and get her away from this situation. It feels like it could go one of two ways—Rex will say something that makes Paige look at me differently, or I will.

"Not exactly, Olsen. We have a lot to talk about, you and I. Paige, too, if she wants to know the kind of man she married."

This mother fucker doesn't know when to stop.

Paige pauses and places a hand on my arm to get me to stop. She looks up at my face and gives me a smile that just about breaks my heart before turning slightly to include Rex.

"I know exactly who my husband is. The good and the bad. I'm sorry for what happened to you, and the part Hayes played in it. I know how devastating that can be, but I don't think this is the proper time or place to be having this conversation. Good night, and Merry Christmas to you."

She takes my hand in hers and leads us out of The Mansion to the Maybach without another incident.

"I suppose you want an explanation," I grumble, starting the car once I have settled her into the passenger seat and taken my own.

"Do you owe me one?" Her voice is deadly quiet, and I have to strain to hear.

Fuck. I don't know how to answer that without admitting guilt or having to stumble over some shortened version of the events in question.

Paige tends to retreat into herself when she's attacked, and she's had two run-ins tonight that should be turning her inside out. She doesn't deserve this.

I rub a palm across my face, leaving it over my mouth for a moment before starting the drive away from The Mansion.

"That was Octavius Rex—he was called Tavi back when I met him. We were friends once, probably the closest I've had to a best friend," I say with a begrudging sigh, knowing I do in fact owe her an explanation.

"It seems like something went very wrong in your friendship, given the interaction we just had."

That's an understatement. She strokes my arm where it rests on the center console, and I'm so grateful she's even touching me right now. She could have withdrawn completely after what she just heard.

"When my brothers and I took over my father's company, it wasn't much. I mean, it was doing great with the mining side of things, but it wasn't diversified. One of the things we started doing pretty quickly was acquiring businesses to complement our mining operations and grow where we needed to. It just so happened that acquiring the Rex family company would get us into transportation. He didn't love that."

"Why did you pick his company when you could have found another and kept your friendship intact?"

"I did him a favor by taking on that business because it wasn't a healthy company. Tavi was too close to the situation to be objective. He couldn't see that his father had wrung out every dollar he could from the company and was doing a shit job of running things effectively. I thought I was doing him a solid by paying way more than the business was worth, which got his family out of debt. I helped him while helping myself."

"And he couldn't see it your way, right?"

I risk a glance at Paige and see her eyes focused on her lap, her hand motionless on my arm. I'm fucking this up, no matter how truthful I am and I'm at risk of pushing her away if I keep this up. Still, I'll tell her what she wants to know because she deserves that much from me. No matter how badly it will make me look.

"No... he called me an opportunistic asshole and told me he'd make me pay someday." I just hope my past mistakes aren't about to take Paige down with me if that retribution is coming for me now. "I haven't seen him since. Now it looks like he's after Olympus. We think he's behind the lawsuit over the mines, and now he's fixated on you and I'm not letting that happen."

Paige blinks her bright eyes up at me and I quickly take in her solemn face as I wind through the dark and silent streets of Savannah to our house.

"I don't think he's actually fixated on me, it's you he wants to get to and I'm just a soft spot. As for coming after Olympus, can you blame him, if you put yourself in his position for a moment?"

Fucking hell, I don't like when she forces empathy on me. It makes me... uncomfortable. I've been fine making business decisions without emotion. If it makes sense for our bottom line, I don't even consider the casualties. That's how business should be done, without all the feelings and mushy bullshit that complicate matters when you think of the people involved.

But... now I'm actually thinking of Rex and what he must have felt. Betrayed, likely. He was my closest friend and I saw the opportunity to take something from him that would benefit me, so I put that over our friendship. Just like I put acquiring the Xenios Group over my relationship with Paige. *Hoping she would see it my way.* I really am an asshole. Fuck.

"What would you do, now, in my place?" I ask because I don't have a fucking clue. It's easier to ask for her to give me the right answer she wants to hear me say than it is to be the man she actually wants me to be. I can't live up to that and I'll just disappoint her.

She interlaces her fingers with mine on the console and bites her lip in concentration. "You do the right thing, even if it's hard."

My fingers flex in hers with impatience. That's easier said than done, obviously. It's not practical. I pull into the drive of the gorgeous Victorian I bought for Paige knowing she would love it. Knowing it was the right thing to do to make sure she could be close to family and her roots here in Savannah. I am capable of doing the right thing, when it suits me, but the right thing by Rex? What does that even look like? Giving him back the parts of Rex Inc. we absorbed? Making him a business partner? Not fighting the lawsuit and letting it cripple the overseas mining division of Olympus? Nothing is easy when the situation is so convoluted that I can't even predict what the right thing is.

I stay silent as I park and exit the car, drawing in deep gulps of the cool night air, tinged with an underlying brine from the coastal inlets that feed Savannah. Our house is lush with greenery even in the midst of December, and it beckons as a solitary retreat for me but I have Paige to answer to and can't fall into the melancholy that comes on the heels of the holidays. I round the car and help Paige out, pulling her to her feet and into my arms, crushing her to my chest, and hoping I can steal some of her fortitude and emotional intelligence. What if she thinks differently of me now, seeing the results of the evil ways that are so ingrained in me? Will she pull away, close the chapter on us because I can't live up to the image she has of me as a man with integrity?

Her arms snake around my waist and she hugs me back without hesitance. I breathe a sigh of relief and know I'm a lucky bastard to have a wife who will love me despite my inherent darkness and desire to take what I want. If only I could be the man she sees me as instead.

"Let's go to bed. It's late and there's no use beating this to death right now," I say into her hair instead of letting my thoughts take us down a path that will end in a fight, or worse.

Nineteen

Paige

Christmas brunch is less awkward than it could have been due to our appearance at the Fairchild Christmas Eve Dinner buttering up Mama, but I didn't sleep well and I'm feeling the effects of the emotional strain of the last few weeks. Meeting an old friend of Hayes's, and realizing we suffered the same fate at Hayes's hands, was troubling. It reminded me that my husband is a ruthless man willing to go to any lengths to get what he wants, regardless of the casualties. It kept me up, tossing and turning, so now my brain is foggy, and I'm distracted, which is bad news when Mama is intent on making things more difficult any chance she gets.

"Paige, there's a matter your father and I would like to discuss with you," she says, between delicate bites of her biscuit, like that's not the most ominous phrase to utter to your daughter.

I blink gritty eyes at her and swallow my own bite of French toast that now feels like a lump of coal going down slowly and settling heavily in my stomach.

"William, would you like to tell her?" she prods.

"Darling Caroline, this is all your doing. Please, if you will, tell her yourself," Daddy drawls, cup of coffee in hand.

My eyes grow wide and my movements still. This is as good as telling Mama to eff off, as he has always steadfastly backed her up when she got on a wild hair. Whatever she has to say doesn't bode well for me if Daddy is openly disagreeing with her, even in as genteel of a manner as he has.

Mama glares at Daddy momentarily before composing herself with a tight smile and returning her gaze to me. "We must start planning your wedding, dearest."

I stare between them before flicking a glance at Hayes who sits quiet and motionless beside me. I don't think either of us had this on our Christmas bingo cards.

"But... we're already married," I say.

"You did it all wrong and we must make things right for people to think this will last," she says forcefully, and finally her true feelings are on display.

"Mama, I don't care what *people* think. Hayes and I are perfectly fine with how we did things, there is no reason for us to get married *again*."

I was thrilled at the idea of escaping the big to-do Mama would have made of a wedding by eloping. This conversation now makes me feel like I didn't escape a thing and I'm about to be under her thumb once again. A beautiful butterfly she's pinned to a mat to put on display for all to see. Hayes places a hand on mine where I've gripped my fork so hard my knuckles are white.

"Why would you want to host a wedding now?" he asks, his question startling Mama and forcing her to look his way.

She visibly bristles. She may enjoy introducing him to her high society circles, but she still doesn't like him very much.

"Paige is our daughter; we want what's best for her and don't want her to regret her decisions down the road." Mama, ever the practiced control freak, is in fine shape. "Not having a formal wedding is a travesty. I can't let her forego this tradition just because you coerced her to elope."

"I wasn't coerced, I chose to marry Hayes exactly how I wanted to," I say, my voice wobbly with the effort not to devolve into the whining of a contrary child arguing a tired point yet again.

It was wishful thinking to imagine I could get away with an elopement and rob Mama of this opportunity to have the final say in my life once again. She would never willingly relinquish her control over something so sacred as a social event, and a wedding is the biggest of its kind. Maybe I was too hasty in my attempt to repair our relationship and allow her back into my life. She's just as calculating and twice as ornery now that I've started to push back. If I'm not careful, she will be picking out my wedding dress and telling me what to wear to the rehearsal, just like so many other functions in my life.

Mama scoffs. "Paige, you know that isn't true. You chose the easy way out to avoid your obligations. Now, we must do our duty for society." She holds out a hand to stop my pending protest. "Whether or not you understand it now, a wedding is exactly what you need. As horrible as it is, that nasty gossip site has focused its attention on you and *his* business," she says, indicating Hayes with a flick of her wrist. "Give them something else to focus on, or the scrutiny will eat you alive and leak into every aspect of your lives."

"You want to give them a distraction by hosting a wedding?" Hayes asks slowly.

"I want to throw the wedding of the century, you deceitful man. They won't be able to contain themselves." Mama actually smiles like she relishes the idea. "And we need to do it next weekend. A New Year's Eve wedding."

"Mama, I say this with respect, but have you lost your mind? There is no way to plan the kind of event you are talking about in a week. It's impossible."

"When money is no object, anything is possible, and we have more money than we know what to do with," she replies, and I gape at her unlikely disregard for what would otherwise be a taboo subject. Fairchilds do not discuss money, no matter how much we have.

"The Mansion is still ours through the end of the year. We can make it happen. We will call in whatever backup we need, we have the staff, and I have a planner already on retainer. This will happen, and it will be next weekend." Her voice is firm. There is simply no arguing with this hurricane of event planning schemes.

"Daddy, please tell me we aren't doing this." I look to my normal ally against Mama's most absurd machinations, but he just shrugs a shoulder at me and looks defeated. Daddy is simply no match for Caroline Thackery Fairchild when her heart is set, and her plans laid.

"Your mother is insistent, sweet pea. There is no stopping her, unfortunately. I tried. Now we just hold on for the inevitable storm to roll through."

"Hayes, please tell her this isn't necessary and will just put us in the spotlight even more," I say appealing to his natural inclination to keep a low profile in a last-ditch effort to stop the situation from completely getting away from me.

"I wish I could say she's wrong on this, but she has a point." Even he has turned on me. "We can have a wedding to make your mama happy and to draw some more positive attention toward Olympus. What do you say, angel, would you marry me all over again, even if it's in front of all and sundry?"

The fight goes out of me when I see the unsure look on his face. Here he is, doubting my feelings for him and maybe even wondering if we can survive everything that has been thrown our way in the short time we've been together. He's probably thinking a big wedding could be the bandage our relationship, and his business needs.

Mama's voice draws my attention away from Hayes. "I'm willing to strike a bargain with you. Be a willing participant in this wedding—the way I want—and I will relinquish control of the trust. It'll be yours to do with as you wish, as will your inheritance, *without* my interference."

Shock of a different variety settles over me, and I feel my mouth gaping. Mama would *never* willingly relinquish control over the tightly held Thackery trust that she has wielded like a weapon against me on so many occasions to get me to fall in line. For her to tell me my participation would grant me access to the inheritance that has always been held over my head to make me behave, is a shot at freedom I never expected. It's not even about the money—marrying Hayes made me a billionaire in my own right—it's about the chance to remove one last shackle that would effectively sever the control Mama has always held over me, forcing me to be compliant and codependent. She knows the exact way to get me to concede, once again. The gleam in her eye shows me she knows she's won before I can even respond.

"Fine," I sigh in defeat. "But I'm picking my own dress and Alex will be my man of honor without any additional bridesmaids."

Mama claps her hands. "Good. I'm glad you could see things my way. We have a tasting appointment with the caterer and baker tomorrow at noon, followed by an appointment with the florist at three. We can squeeze in a dress appointment before the tasting or after the florist, but you'll have to hold back at the tasting so you're not bloated if you choose that option."

Mama quickly appraises my oversized green Christmas sweater as if looking for my current shape and being dissatisfied at not being able to tell if I have gained any more weight since my debutante ball.

"I've already had Cecile at the bridal shop pull every dress on the rack in your size, but it may still be slim pickings."

I bring my hands to my forehead, pressing the heels of my palms into my eyes as my head spins. Good lord, Mama had the audacity to set events in motion before she even approached me about the subject. Her confidence in her ability to wear me down and get me to capitulate to her demands is a disturbing insight into our dysfunctional relationship. I'm about to recant my acquiescence just by sheer overwhelm alone, the trust be damned. And I haven't begun to imagine all of the possible ways Mama will be leading the charge this week. This is a mistake, and it will be awful.

"Mama, I—" I start, but she cuts me off.

"I have a photographer from New York booked already. She has an impressive portfolio and a great eye. She will shoot your bridals two days before the wedding, so I booked a hair and makeup artist for both days, also."

I drop my hands to the table and push my chair out with a scrape, earning me a squawking protest from Mama. I turn and run out of the dining room and up the stairs as she calls after me. I'm fleeing my mother, who has overstepped once again, but it's not a new response from me. I have a bad habit of running from my problems, but right now, it feels like the only option when the alternative is to sit at the table and have her grind my independence into dust under her Jimmy Choo heel.

I feel the hot tears of frustration gathering and I am about to lose it. I would have said a few unkind things to her had I stayed at that table and continued to listen to everything she has planned for me. I fling myself onto the giant four-poster bed in the bedroom as the first fat tears leak out of my eyes. They slide in hot tracks down my face and into my hair while I stare at the ceiling, decorated in plaster trim work above me. The bed dips as Cerberus hops up, slowly making his way over to me and dropping his massive head across my middle with a sigh.

"I can't take it, big guy. Mama has no boundaries at all." I run my hand along his silky head and pet his stubby ears as the tears subside. He chuffs in response and nuzzles my ribs.

I don't know how to separate the entwined relationship my mother and I have into a semblance of something healthy. She is a thorny vine wrapping around my trunk and choking out the life from any budding flowers of independence that may have bloomed if given half a chance. Instead, I'm a stunted version of myself, unable to make even the smallest decisions without being told I've done it wrong and she will save me by making me do it over until she approves.

If I could have planned my ideal wedding it would have been very close to the elopement Hayes and I had in Las Vegas. Just us and Cerberus, somewhere beautiful, like the Elysium Garden on the rooftop of The Abyss. I would wear a dress of floral lace taken from Nanny Fairchild's own wedding gown, put flowers in my hair, and walk through the greenery of the garden to Hayes, waiting at the waterfall in front of the Titan Arum, to a string quartet playing Taylor Swift's Wildest Dreams. Hayes would wear a classic black-on-black tux and would look incredible with his eyes matching the verdant greenery around us.

So, I may have thought this out a little, even if I told Mama I was happy we eloped. I've found myself daydreaming about this very thing a few times over the last few weeks, and there may have been a brief moment in time—like within the firing of a synapse in my brain brief—where I thought I could have this very dream when faced with the possibility, now, of having a big wedding. It was quickly snuffed out by Mama's manipulations.

I know for a fact that the wedding I dream about wouldn't be anything close to the monstrosity Mama is conspiring to throw, and it makes my heart heavy. Do I let her take over once again, giving up the hard-won independence and distance I've put into our relationship so recently so she can have the event of the century, as she called it? Is unfettered access to my trust worth it?

There is so much I could do with that trust. It is exactly what I could use to ensure the Elysium Garden Project takes off and becomes the philanthropic delight it should be. I could use it to pay for the salaries of permanent gardeners and staff, ensure we could provide a living wage to those in the community who would work the produce stands and need the urban oases the most, and feed the neighborhoods they serve without worrying about where the money to do so would come from. I may not need the trust myself, but others sure do, and there's no reason only Hayes's money should be going into a foundation we are creating together. I need to secure that trust so I can make bigger things happen with this new dream of mine. And that means I have to bend to Mama's will once again. My heart sinks with this realization just as quickly as it rose at the prospect of all the good it could do to have access to the trust.

"Glad to see Cerberus is being of assistance," Hayes says, sitting on the edge of the bed and ending my loop of questions. "I can send him down to the dining room to remove the unwanted interlopers if you want."

I smile, though it still feels sad. "I'd like to see Cerberus try to defeat Mama. He may have met his match in her."

"That's actually a good point."

I turn my head to see Hayes eyeing the dog speculatively.

"My money's still on him, but it wouldn't be an outright win, that's for sure. Your mother... is something to contend with."

"That's an understatement," I mumble, rolling to my side and displacing Cerberus's head. He shifts to the end of the bed, and Hayes takes the spot, facing me with his head propped on his hand.

"We don't have to do any of this, you know. We are married, and no matter what your mother insists should happen for people to think better of us, all that matters to me is your happiness." He strokes a tendril of hair away from my eyes and out of my face. His fingers glide around the shell of my ear and down my neck, stopping when his palm is over my heart. "What do you want, in here, angel?"

I shiver under his touch and the burning green stare that is deep enough to drown in. "I want to make everyone happy." The words are whispered, but they come from a part of me that shies away from the light of day.

I recognize I may just be the world's biggest people pleaser as I admit that. I don't want to disappoint anyone, especially my mother, and it's always been my own happiness that's lost out when there has been a choice. It's been easier that way when the alternative was to deal with Mama's legendary wrath. The tiny seed of choosing myself that was planted could wither away, again, should I fall back into the habit of doing what others want, and I stubbornly want to give myself a chance, for once.

"What would make you happy? Do you want to run off to Turks and Caicos for New Year's instead of sticking around here? You mentioned that once before. I can make it happen, just say the word."

I smile, remembering the moment of brutal honesty when he asked me what I wanted and I said I wanted to be with him, then took it back out of mortification and said I'd rather go to Turks and Caicos.

He remembers, too, it seems. That was the moment I started to fall for this man because he held me to my original statement and ran off with me, away from Mama and her crazy arranged marriage schemes. He let me choose and continues to nurture that power in me.

"If we get married again, I still want it to be about us, not just some production Mama is planning for other people. Do you have any input about what would feel like us?"

His eyes smolder, burning bright as he contemplates my question. "I really like you in white," he says, his voice deep as he traces a finger along the length of my neck. "That night you walked into my garden, you were luminous in the moonlight coming through the greenhouse glass. I was enchanted. I'd want to do that moment over again."

I feel my cheeks heat with his words. "That's what I was thinking of, too. A small ceremony in the garden. And..." I pause, wondering if I should tell him the extent of the daydream and the thought I've put into it now that Mama is intent on steering the ship.

"And...? What's going through that beautiful brain of yours?"

"If we made the ceremony what we want, I think I can compromise and let Mama throw a blowout reception that would make her happy."

"I think that's a good way to split the difference with Hurricane Caroline."

I chuckle at the new moniker. "She really is something, isn't she? I wish I had half of her insistent confidence and brazen disregard for anyone else."

"Your mother would be lucky to have half your empathy and kindness. How she managed to raise a daughter like you, her opposite in every way, I may never know."

"So, we should go through with this?" I sit up, and Hayes follows. He takes my hands in his.

"Only if it will make you happy, angel. Fuck what other people think. We don't have to defend our relationship by bending to the perceptions of others. I love you, and I'm willing to do whatever is necessary to make sure you know that without a doubt, and not just know but feel it. Even if it takes letting your mama plan our wedding to make her happy and keep your relationship intact."

I take a deep breath and let it out slowly as I make my final decision. I may regret it a million times before the week is over, but Mama was right to bargain with unfettered access to my trust when I have a new project that could benefit from it. She played her trump card and we both know it. I can't turn it down.

"Are you ready to bring your bargaining skills to the table with a hurricane when it's my happiness on the line? Mama won't like it one bit, and I'm going to need you on my side to ensure I can ask for what I really want."

"I am always on your side, and I will fight any battle for you. I'll handle this if you want."

I nod, feeling my confidence at being able to ask for what I want from Mama sliding away. Hayes won't have the same problem. "Please."

He grabs my hand and hauls me off the bed so we can head back downstairs. Cerberus trots at my heels down the staircase, and Hayes lets him lie at my feet when we settle ourselves back at the table.

"Are you through with your hissy fit, young lady? It was very rude of you to leave like that."

I feel my shoulders hiking up at Mama's words, and Hayes senses the tension in me. He smooths his hand down my spine and leaves a warm, reassuring warmth on my hip where it comes to rest.

"I'm feeling very overwhelmed by your preemptive planning, Mama. It's okay to need to take a break from someone who likes to make all the plans for you, and in this case, I needed a moment to compose myself and figure out what I want in this situation."

"Oh, Paige, you can't mean that. I just want what's best for you, and I'm taking on the brunt of this planning to help you."

"Ah, but that's just it, Caroline. You're not helping Paige, you're planning out every aspect of what should be her day. Instead of listening to your daughter, you're taking away her agency and forcing what you want on her, as usual. Why not ask Paige what she wants for once and find a way to incorporate that into what you're insisting on despite her never wanting this in the first place? The least you can do is compromise since she's allowed you this concession of putting on a big wedding in the first place." Hayes is all patience and calm, whereas I am, once again, a rattled and intimidated daughter working through my mother's latest gaslighting attempts.

"You have no idea the lengths I have gone to for my daughter," Mama says, clutching the strand of pearls at her neck. "I am ensuring the future she deserves, despite having picked you to marry."

"Like the lengths you went to so you could hand her over on a platter to the rapist son of complicit business associates to gain access to their technology? She could definitely have picked worse, and you know it. How's the integration going down at Thackery Agriculture now that you have all of Daniels Industries at your disposal, anyway?"

Mama turns a shade of red that borders on purple, and it takes her a moment to calm herself enough to speak. "We will not talk about that unfortunate matter. It is behind us."

Daddy chuckles darkly over the rim of his coffee cup, forever the quiet observer of Mama's constant action, though he's been cooler toward her this morning. "He got you there, Caroline. That Daniels boy was a creep, and you knew it all along. We could spend hours just unpacking that little *gem* of information you kept from me for so many years, but I fear now is simply not the time. Later, my darling wife," he says in a harsh tone that is devoid of the genial warmth he usually carries when dealing with Mama.

My eyes widen at the unusual interaction between them. Judging by his comment and tone, he is very unhappy with her choice to keep certain things from him, and he's not hiding it anymore. At least not in front of us. He was civil and in host mode at the Christmas Eve Dinner, and nothing in their interactions made me think they were disagreeing at all. It makes me wonder what is happening out of the public eye, and if their marriage can withstand it. Knowing all that they have weathered together over the years, and still managed to keep a united front, I am mostly confident that they will get past this also, though it may irrevocably change their relationship.

Mama's cheeks remain rosy and her lips are flattened into a harsh line that tells me more than she will herself. This is an ongoing argument, then, and they are at a stalemate on how to proceed past it.

Daddy sets his cup down and turns to Hayes. "We're renaming the company, as you suggested, and working on the integration plan now. We will likely be rolling out the processes starting in another week or two. It was a splendid gift and has given me something to do now that my job at the Xenios Group will become arbitrary in the new year."

"I want to have our ceremony in the Elysium Garden, with a small group of family and friends, only. You can plan the reception and make it whatever you'd like," I blurt into the lull of conversation, looking to take the topic away from Garrison Daniels and what I narrowly escaped by taking my fate into my own hands.

"There's not enough room in the garden, Paige! We have three hundred people on the guestlist without Hayes's side to consider, and at least half will expect to be at the ceremony," Mama cries, almost rising from her seat at the injustice of having her carefully crafted plans upended by my simple request.

"My wife has spoken. If you want to have this lovely wedding at all, the ceremony will be at the Abyss, and

Paige and I will be in charge of the guestlist and plan for what she wants to see happen. If you want four hundred people at the most absurd reception you can muster, by all means, make it happen." Hayes's tone is firm, leaving no room for discussion otherwise.

"Who wants more biscuits?" I ask to the stunned silence that descends on the table.

Twenty

Hayes

It was torture leaving Paige alone to deal with her mother's insane schedule and planning while I went to The Abyss to work from my office here in Savannah. Despite most of the company having the week between Christmas and New Year's off, I still have plenty of catching up to do. Diego emailed me a new update on the South African mines, the lawsuit, and what they have dug up on Octavius Rex and his possible connection to the New York law firm that brought the suit against Olympus and my brothers. It's not a clear connection, and that bothers me. I thought for sure it had to be backed by Rex, as he's the one with the most to gain from our downfall. I spend the majority of my morning piecing together a plan to get through this situation but there is another matter that needs to be addressed. One I had better get on sooner, rather than later.

I pick up my phone and dial a number that doesn't get used much.

"Well, look who it is, calling the day *after* Christmas," the deep voice on the line says by way of greeting.

I smile. "You're lucky I called you at all, old man," I reply.

"Let me get your mother, she'll want to give you the dressing down you deserve," Thatcher Olsen says with a chuckle. I listen to the sounds of my father moving through their house overlooking the Chattahoochee River that flows through their small town of Helen, Georgia.

"Hayes, you old hound dog! How dare you not tell us you got married. I deserve a chance to meet any girl you bring into the family *before* she's in the family way, so when do I get to see you and this lovely new wife of yours?" Rula Mae Olsen is not one for subtleties, and she's ready to get down to the matter at the first opportunity.

"Hi Mother, it's nice to talk to you, too," I reply with all the patience expected of me.

"Tell him we've been hearing all about his romance with the heiress girl thanks to Virginia Coombes and Lotte Smithson." I hear through the line from my father, who must be sitting next to Mom.

"You remember Lotte and Virginia—"

"I heard him, Mom, you don't have to repeat everything. Just put the phone on speaker and you can both talk." My parents are not even sixty-five, but you would think they were geriatric with how they despise using modern technology and all of its conveniences. Speakerphone should be a breeze since they take calls together all the time.

"Is this how you do it," I hear Mom say faintly before I can hear Dad clearly.

"Just that button there, that should work," he says.

"So, when do we get to meet this hotel heiress girl?" Mom asks again.

"Her name is Paige and she's not a girl, she's twenty-one," I explain, knowing it will do little good.

"She's an infant if anything. You are too old for that girl, but what good is it for me to tell you now that you've gone and gotten yourself hitched to her," Mom complains. "She's real pretty, Hayes. Virginia showed me the photos of her that the gossip site posted a while back. Y'all look really good together. I can't wait to meet her in person."

"Well, that's why I'm calling. We're having a wedding ceremony and reception in Savannah next weekend. Will you be able to attend? It's New Year's Eve and I know the town does some pretty exciting parties that night," I drawl, knowing full well Helen is busiest in the summer when tourists descend on the Bavarian-themed town to tube the river and bask in the outdoor attractions. Why my parents retired there is still a mystery to me, as they don't like tubing or being outdoors more than necessary. We were raised in Atlanta, so the tiny mountain town is a far cry from the hustle and bustle of the city, but that's likely why Mom loves it.

"Of course, we will be there. We wouldn't miss it," Mom proclaims loudly, and I hold the phone away from my ear. "Savannah is a cute little place; it'll be nice to get down there again."

I hear my dad grumble and wonder what he could be up to that would be more important than the wedding of his eldest son.

"You have something to say, old man?"

"Everyone's going to be on the roads traveling because of the holidays. It's going to take us hours to drive to Savannah."

"You have a jet, Dad, use it."

"Too much trouble," he mutters.

"Dammit, Thatcher, I deserve to be treated to a jet ride every now and again, don't I? Why'd I marry you all them years ago, raise three of your sons, and be a widow to your work for so long if not to have the chance to be treated like a rich bitch when I want it?"

"If that's what you want, then we'll do it," he agrees hurriedly, pacifying Mom's legendary temper.

I laugh. "That's the way to get what you're after, Mom."

"Well, I'm tickled pink to be meeting your sweetheart after all. Where is this shindig happening, exactly?"

"We will have a small ceremony for family and close friends at the Elysium Garden on top of my nightclub.

The reception will be at Paige's family's ancestral home called The Mansion. It's a hotel and I can get you rooms there if you want. They have a ballroom I think the Fairchilds will be using, since it's large enough for what they're planning."

"Look at you, fancy pants! You have a nightclub with a garden on it? How come you never told us about that?" Mom asks.

"I don't have it connected to Olympus at all, it's a pet project for me. Would you like to know about the pizzeria I invested in, or the drift racing team I'm working on sponsoring next year, also? That's another pet project. Or, hmm, I did just give a liquor company to Paige as a wedding present, but it was also a project of mine," I say, listing off some of my ventures.

"Oh, stop it, you smart ass, you've made your point," Dad grumbles. "I like how you've diversified, that's good at the very least."

"I learned from the best," I say, giving him the compliment he deserves.

"Back to this Paige girl, tell us about her!" Mom demands.

I run a hand through my hair and pull, thinking of how best to describe the whirlwind that is Paige. She's so much more than I even imagined when she first walked into my life. She's disarming, sweet, and her softness is something I would die to protect to keep her from growing hard with the world.

"Paige is… She's as warm as summer sunshine and as comforting as a coastal breeze. She's kindness personified. She has the biggest heart, and it even extends to people who are undeserving of her grace," I say, thinking of her willingness to forgive her parents and make amends with them when I would have written off closer people for less. "She's making me think of others, instead of just myself, and she makes me want to be a better man. Someone deserving of her." I'm rambling, but when I thought of how to explain Paige to my parents, there was no shortage of things to say.

"He sounds pussy-whipped," Mom says to Dad, like I can't hear their side of the conversation.

"That is one way to put it," I agree, letting them know I'm still here. I'll take the slight, because it's not wrong. I worship Paige's pussy.

"Please tell me you got a prenup before you jetted off to Vegas to make it official," Dad says, ever the businessman.

Ah, there it is. "Paige is independently wealthy, Dad. She's set to inherit quite a lot from her own family. She's not after my money."

"That's a no, then," he says. "You can still get a document drawn up to set some things in place. Thank God, Georgia isn't a community property state, at the very least. It's not just about protecting your assets, maybe she needs protecting from you, if she has her own money."

"We'll be fine without one. If she decides to leave me one day, she might as well take half, because I'll have fucked it up myself and sent her running. She'll more than deserve it."

"Oh, our boy's lovestruck for sure," Mom says, but the tone isn't as playful as the words sound. Rula Mae Olsen is a conservative, practical woman through and through. "Just think about it a bit, Hayes. We don't want to see some messy thing between you two in the future."

"How about we talk about this wedding that is coming up, instead?" I ask, moving the topic back where it belongs.

"If you provide the details, we'll show up."

"With bells on!" Mom adds.

"Fine. I'll send you an itinerary with your lodging information. Just be here by Friday and you won't miss a thing."

"Your brothers will be your groomsmen, right?" Mom asks. "Which one did you ask to be your best man?"

I hadn't thought that far, actually. Despite working closely with them, I wouldn't call either of my brothers my best friends. Zander drives me crazy, and Payton stirs the pot, egging us both on. I don't know if either is trustworthy enough to put in that position, but it makes sense I would. "I haven't decided yet."

"If you're having a wedding next week, you better get on that soon, son."

"I guess that's my next call."

"Love you, Hayes. Tell your brothers they need to call us every once in a while, too. None of y'all had the good grace to actually be with us or even call on Christmas of all things. But thank you for the nice orchids. They look so nice on my sun porch. Your daddy liked the wagyu beef you had shipped in from Japan. That made our Christmas dinner plans so fancy. I still put A1 sauce all over my filet mignon."

I shudder at the blasphemy she committed against the fine beef I sent them, but know it's Mom's way and there is no changing her. "Love you, too, Mom. I'll see y'all on Friday."

I shake my head when I end the call. They were in good moods today and extra chatty. Normally, it would be a quick call of them asking about work, since it's all I can fill them in on. They seem to like having Paige to talk about. I think they will love her. How could they not?

I sigh and stare at the phone again. I dial and wait for the phone to connect. Music and loud voices greet me before my brother does.

"Merry Christmas, Hater. You and our perfect little Paige having a good time in Savannah?" Zander says when he answers.

I grit my teeth and try to remember he's family and I can't disown him. "Zander. Where are you right now? It's ten in the morning and you're partying?"

"I'm in Aspen with some friends. We wanted a white Christmas and the snow bunnies provided."

I roll my eyes. Of course, Zander is off fucking some models or actresses in the snow. "I hope you don't have plans for New Year's Eve."

"Actually, I do. I was going to hit up Abu Dhabi and meet up with a Sheikh friend who throws the best New Year's parties."

"I guess you'll have to miss the wedding of the century," I say, almost glad he'll be out of the country. "Paige's family insisted on an actual wedding and we're throwing it in Savannah. I'll save you a piece of cake if I can."

"Fuck me," Zander says, with genuine sadness. "I'll cancel my plans if you let me throw you the best bachelor party ever. I know exactly what you need. No strippers and blow, I know that's not your thing, but we can do this up good. We gotta do Vegas."

"I'm already married, Zand. There is no need to go to Vegas and do some bullshit bachelor party, especially not if you're throwing it. I will end up arrested and on every gossip site in the country before the night is over. That's exactly what we need with Olympus already dealing with all this bullshit." I scrub my hand down my face, smoothing out the furrow between my brows. Zander gives me a headache. Not everything has to be an adrenaline rush and dopamine dump.

"Fuck no, man! I'm talking racing supercars at the Las Vegas raceway and penthouse suites, clubbing 'til three, and the hottest girls around falling all over themselves to sit on your lap. That kind of thing."

"I own a one-of-a-kind multimillion-dollar Maybach plus a garage full of supercars, and I can stay in any penthouse at any hotel in the world. Why would I choose Vegas and a night or more away from Paige?"

"Goddamn, you are a goner." Zander's voice carries legitimate shock like he can't imagine a world in which what he offered would be a temptation anyone could pass up. It's not even a consideration, honestly. "So, no bachelor party, at all?"

"I don't need one and there's really no time."

I pause and wonder if I actually want some sort of last hurrah to my single life. I have fucked my share of willing and interested women who got my cock to jump and scoured the world for the next car, property, or business that would satisfy my urge to conquer and have something coveted. As soon as Paige stepped into my life, my desire for any other woman, any activity that would keep me away from her, just... dematerialized. What Zander offers doesn't even give me a tiny flicker of interest.

"You can have your own party at The Abyss after the rehearsal dinner if you want. I'll give you the manager's number and you can go crazy. Just show up on time for the wedding, because you're a groomsman and can't be shit-faced at my wedding."

"You're such a downer, Hater. I knew you were no fun, but this is epically bad. You need to have something, even a small bachelor party. Don't worry, I'll take care of it. There has to be something fun to do in Slow-vannah. It can't all be historic homes and themed restaurants, right?"

"Whatever, Zand. Just be there by Friday morning and bring a tux or I'll make you rent one."

"Gross," he says with what sounds like a shudder at the thought. "Later, Hater." The call disconnects before I can say goodbye.

That's two calls down.

The third takes a while to connect, ringing a few times before Payton answers. "Speak of the devil," he says instead of hello. Why can't my family just answer a call normally?

"Talking about me, again?"

"Oh, just checking out the Atlanta Haute List this morning and seeing you and Paige front and center, once again. There may or may not be a mob of fangirls outside that pretty new house you recently inhabited. The Haute List just about printed your address for the South. Who knew doxing would make it to gossip sites that usually preserve just a tiny bit of privacy for their main stories?"

Shit. "How is that stupid site able to get this much access to us? Who do I have to fire next to make the damn leaks stop?"

"Don't underestimate the willingness of those around you to share every detail when given the chance.

Your realtor probably shared the details before the ink was dry on the papers."

He sounds almost bored, and I wonder at the amount of information in his head after all these years of searching out every last article, blog, and story about us to ensure our public image and mystique is maintained.

"Anyway, why are you calling? Shouldn't you be snorting Christmas cookies off Paige's ass or something?"

I let out a surprised laugh. "Now, that's a picture I won't be able to get out of my head anytime soon. I may have some new dinner plans."

It's Payton's turn to laugh. "Glad I could be of service."

I try to stop thinking about Paige's ass, and the delectable things I could do to it, and return to the reason for my call. "We're getting married, for real. New Year's Eve in Savannah. I want you to be my best man, so cancel whatever plans you may have had and get your ass down here by Friday."

"So, you're doing this right, after all?"

"Paige's parents—her mom, really—are insistent. She seems to think a big-ass wedding will solve our problems, both for me and Paige personally as well as helping with Olympus's rep right now."

"She's not wrong," he says, repeating my exact thoughts when it was brought to the table. "A wedding, especially a big one, with lots of media coverage, could be good for everyone. The mine stuff is working its way out of the headlines and the holidays have given media outlets more to talk about than just what we are or aren't doing for our workers overseas. I have a contact at Blush Magazine who would pay big bucks for an exclusive after the wedding."

I bristle. "There is no way I am going to sell myself, or our story, to a magazine."

"Not like that. What I'm talking about would cement your status as America's sexiest couple, and the *It Couple*'s wedding would mean your story would be in the hands of housewives and horny fans all over the country who would be talking about it with husbands, business partners, and more. Where popular opinion goes, so does the news coverage. It's good press, and exactly what we need."

"I'll take your word for it, but I don't like it. Paige is incredibly private. She won't be interested in a magazine feature, even if I sell it the way you just did."

"And thank God for that. Can you imagine if Paige was live streaming your entire relationship for the world to see? Every interaction would be even more dissected than it already is. If she was posting cutesy photos and videos of everything nice you did, or vague posting about every fight, how much more fire would that feed?"

I shake my head, wondering at the social media-averse woman I fell in love with and how it could have been so different. I'm a lucky sonofabitch.

"So, you'll be my best man?" I ask, not liking where my brain goes when it imagines the other possibilities for my life, and how easily I could fuck up the best thing I've ever had if I'm not careful.

"Of course I will. Did you tell Zand already or does he think he's planning some God-awful last-minute bachelor party for you?"

I chuckle. "I told him he was a groomsman and could have a party after the rehearsal dinner if he wanted, but it wouldn't be a bachelor party for me. I don't want one."

"Of course you don't," Payton says with finality. "There's nothing that could compare to spending another night with Paige, even if her mama is gonna do everything in her power to keep you separated the night before the wedding and you'll have nothing better to do."

An icy chill goes down my spine. Would Caroline insist on just that, despite us being legally married already? Yes, she absolutely would. "Fuck."

"So we'll do something small and classy, just a few guys from Olympus. You're inviting at least senior leadership, right?"

"I will now. Caroline has been pretty closed fist on all things wedding planning. I had to put my foot down to get her to loosen up her chokehold so Paige could ask for the one thing she actually wanted out of a big wedding, and that wasn't a pretty fight. We could use someone like Caroline Thackery Fairchild on our negotiating team. No one would stand a chance against that titan."

"She sounds fierce. I can see where Paige gets it from."

A smile turns up the corner of my mouth. "Paige is something else entirely. She doesn't have to be fierce to be a great leader. She has everyone under her spell without having to crack a whip."

"Okay, that's enough swooning for now, save it for the Blush feature. I'll get you connected with Jenyssa, my contact and she will reach out for an interview and photos once the wedding is over. Text me the itinerary and what to wear. I'll see you later."

With that call ended, I'm finally able to go back to work. It doesn't take long to be so engrossed in everything that the door opening to the office startles me.

"Hayes? It's after six." I look up and catch Paige's worried face. Despite that, she looks incredible, wearing a soft-looking camel-colored sweater dress and knee-high boots that make her legs look so goddamn good. She turns to shut the door and her ass is a sight in the tight dress. Payton's quip about Christmas cookies comes back to me, and I'm growing uncomfortably hard at an alarming rate.

"I'm sorry, angel, I didn't mean to stay so long." I hold out my arms and she comes over, draping her soft body into my lap with relief. "How was your day?"

She wiggles her ass into my crotch as she adjusts, and I throb against her. Either she doesn't notice, or it was that bad of a day to not get a response from her.

"Mama is insane, but that's not news. What she's planning and has in mind is way over the top. I would never in a million years want half of what she's insisting on. There are going to be aerial performers, Hayes. She's ordered eighty-thousand dollars' worth of flowers, in December, when everything is out of season. She's even rigging the ballroom to look like a forest and has giant trees she's going to put silks in so she can make aerialists dangle all over the room the entire night. It's going to be a spectacle."

I smooth Paige's hair and press her head into my shoulder, soothing her as best I can to bring down the tone of hysteria a notch.

The way Paige defers to her mother in all matters is troubling. She reduces herself to a meek and obedient child when faced with confrontation.

It's one thing to compromise, but Caroline is a steamroller and I hate how easily she squashes Paige in all things. I want to build up Paige's confidence and ability to ask for what she wants, but it's two decades of learned behavior to change. For Paige, it might not be worth it.

If I had my way, I would punish Caroline for every instance she has belittled Paige or made her feel less than perfect. But that's not my place and I continue to bite my tongue and let Paige lead the interactions with her mother.

The moment she wants that to change, there will be a world of hurt on her mother's doorstep. I'm good with exacting revenge. Right now, though, I realize Paige needs my support more than anything.

"We're still going to do things our way, honey. You get to have the ceremony of your dreams, while your mama plans a reception of our nightmares."

"She is inviting half of Savannah, and the food will all be things that look pretty but taste terrible. I finally got her to agree to allow mac and cheese bites as a passed hors d'oeuvre in exchange for the fairy garden she has planned for the lobby."

"At least we'll have something to eat if all else goes wrong," I say kissing her head. "What about the cake and the dress shopping?"

"The cake will be a five-tiered monstrosity with buttercream, gold dust, fresh flowers, and five different cake flavors and fillings. I couldn't decide what I liked best, the chocolate with fudge filling or the chocolate with raspberry. So Mama picked everything but those options and it may be a mystery up until we cut the cake as to what we are getting. Probably some bloody-looking red velvet, which is just gross."

My jaw pops as I clench my teeth at the injustice. She looks so miserable. Weddings are supposed to be the happiest time of a woman's life, and here she is not even able to decide what kind of cake we get at the wedding due to her mama's overbearing ways.

"Is wedding cake even good, though? Maybe we won't be missing out on anything."

She pulls her head off my shoulder to look me in the eyes. "I take cake very seriously, Hayes. It is an essential food group."

I kiss her nose and smile. "I'll call the baker tomorrow and insist you get your favorite flavor choices on at least two layers. If they try to argue I'll just buy the whole damn operation and they won't be able to say no to me."

"You can't just buy out everything that displeases you."

"I can and I will if it means you are happy."

"Well, the cake was easy-peasy compared to dress shopping with Mama." Paige shudders. "Everything was wrong, and Mama wanted to see me in the most hideous gowns. Nothing felt like me at all. I couldn't find a single dress I loved, but Mama has three on hold in case I change my mind."

"Why don't we go see your friend at Haute Belle in Atlanta tomorrow and see what she can do? She's been spot on the two times you've gone to her, and I bet she has wedding dresses too, right?"

Paige brightens and kisses me on the nose this time. "You perfect man, that is just what I need. Angela will make me feel like an actual bride instead of a stuffed cupcake."

"Stuffed cupcake, huh?" I ask, rolling my hips into her ass. "I can make that happen."

Paige's lips twist into a sneaky smile. "I'm not wearing panties."

It takes no effort at all to turn her to face the desk and press her into the mahogany top from behind. "Don't tempt me. I'm already hungry for you."

"Please," she begs, her hands clutching at the edge of the desk as she arches her ass back for me. "Make today better."

"As you wish, my love. Stay just like that," I command, pushing the soft skirt of her dress up her thighs with an agonizing slowness that draws out the lust for both of us. When her ass is exposed, I shudder in relief. "This perfect peach belongs to me." I roll the globes of her ass in my hands, getting a purr of contentment from Paige.

"That feels so good," she says, her face still pressed to the wooden desktop, eyes closed and a smile turning up her cheeks.

I use my thumb to spread her open, dipping into her wet center and finding her hot and slick for me already. I could get lost in this moment, with the feel of her against my fingers, but I want to make her come for me and beg to have me filling her before I have my own rewards. I bring my thumb along her seam to her ass, circling delicately and pressing just the tiniest bit to see her reaction. Her hips still their rhythmic movements, and she turns her head to look at me with an unspoken question furrowing her brow.

"Would you let me have your ass, angel?" My voice is guttural with the question, a need building in me to claim another untouched part of Paige.

Crimson blooms across her cheeks and she blinks big green eyes up at me. I want to see that color all over her body, flushed and needing more.

"I don't know how to answer that," she says softly, and I watch the thoughts cross her face one after another, her cheeks growing redder with each one. "I've never... Well, I've never even imagined that. I don't know if I would like it or not... but I trust you."

The beautiful gift of her trust opens a new part of my soul I didn't think existed, and I am even more in love with her than I was before. There's still a very feral part of me that is wickedly delighted by the prospect of having another part of her that will be all mine. I want to destroy her, make her beg for me to fill her ass again and again and love every punishing moment. I rein in the depraved thoughts and remind myself this sweet woman is just that—sweet and innocent. I can't fuck her ass right now and have her like the experience any more than the idea I just presented to her. Her hesitant trust is not a free-for-all pass to do the very unhinged things that are currently circling the gutter of my filthy mind, only that she is willing to explore the ideas, and I can do that.

"We'll go slow. I don't have to fuck your ass to see if you'll like it, there's plenty more we can try first."

She slowly nods and I'm proud of my sweet girl for being open to a new experience. I won't take that trust lightly.

I push my chair back and kneel behind her, pressing my mouth to her center, using my tongue exactly how she likes it, and feel her hesitance release with the familiar motion. When her hips are pushing back against my face, I slip in first one finger, then two, and feel her butterfly soft squeeze already starting. I slide my tongue away from her opening and along her ass cheek while I beckon inside her. I give her the barest touch of my tongue along her rim and feel her tense. Not quite ready for that, but she trusts me, and I'll get her there, eventually.

When she is dripping down my hand and her body shaking, right on the edge, I stand, removing my fingers from her depths and unbuckling my pants to shove them down my thighs. I can't wait to be inside her, so I pull her hips away from the desk and slide into her pussy like it was made for me. Her gasps and moans are soft as she tries to relax around me and take in my full length. She's more open to me from behind, and I'm deeper than she's used to, so I give her a few soft thrusts to help. I wrap one arm around her hip and find her clit, stroking while I start a slow pace for us, my other hand on her hip, keeping her in place.

Looking down at her ass and seeing my cock sliding in and out of her tight pussy is glorious and I could come just from the sight alone. Instead, I focus on prolonging this pleasure, forcing myself off the ledge so I can get Paige there first. She's starting to tighten around me as I work in and out of her tight hold. Again, I place my finger against her ass, but this time, she is so close to climax she doesn't tense against me, and I slide in a digit right as she comes apart around me.

"Fuck!" Paige swears, her hands white-knuckled at the top of the desk as she writhes through the waves of pleasure that drag me right over the edge. Hearing her use filthy words when she's coming is my new favorite depraved delight.

I slam home once, twice, and a third time before I'm coming with her name on my lips. "Goddamn, Paige, you're too good."

Twenty-One

Paige

"You can't leave, we have too much scheduled! It's imperative that you are present for all of these appointments, this is your wedding, after all. We're on a tight timeline and there's no time for deviations to appease your desire to try on dresses hours away."

Mama is apoplectic, nearly blowing a fuse when I broach the subject. You would think I had told her I was headed out of the country, not going to Atlanta overnight to dress shop.

"I'll be back tomorrow, I'm sure there will be plenty of time to make me review table linens or what cardstock to use for the place cards," I cajole, my voice wavering with the effort to argue in the face of her anger, but I'm managing to stick to the decision I've made rather than let her dissuade me.

Slowly, I'm winning more of the battles I pick than losing. It gives me the confidence to keep insisting on my own happiness, but it's not easy. Resetting my default is no joke, and walking the razor-thin line of being the willing participant in this wedding despite hating every second of it so she'll relinquish the trust is exhausting. I'm constantly weighing the risks of pushing back too hard or on too many details, and it adds an extra level of anxiety to my already fraught state.

"You have to take this seriously, Paige. Your future depends on it. You. Cannot. Leave." She punctuates those last words by clapping her hands like I'm a simpleton in need of short sentences. It rouses a fire in me that I wasn't sure I had when faced with her displeasure, and I'm mad now, too.

"You can pick out whatever you think is best if it can't wait a day," I insist, knowing that's what would happen, anyway. It doesn't matter if I want a different option, Mama will end up going with her choice regardless. I'm a redundancy that makes her feel like she's letting me be a part of the selection process when I'm just an observer.

"Paige Fairchild, you will stay here even if I have to lock you in myself," Mama threatens, moving toward me like she's going to physically restrain me to keep me from leaving her house.

I take a quick step back and find the wall at my back. I'm not exactly worried Mama will resort to violence, but I also can't put it past her.

Hayes steps between us, done with being the silent observer as I wage war with my mother. He is radiating anger and his eyes flash darkly. "That's enough," he rumbles, his voice carrying the terror-inducing and destructive force of an earthquake. "You will not threaten my wife like that ever again. You should remember to address her as Paige Olsen going forward as she is no longer just your daughter, but a powerful woman in her own right who deserves your respect."

Mama stops her advance toward me with a look of surprise crossing her face. Maybe she realized how out of line she was being, or maybe she's just stunned someone stepped in to defend me for once against her tirade.

My mouth drops open at his tone and the words he just spoke. I look up at him, grateful for his interference, but this is a boundary I have to defend myself when it comes to the relationship I have with Mama. I'm also glad I'm not on the receiving end of that look and don't envy Mama for it, even if she can launch her own scary looks right back. I reach for Hayes's arm and keep him from unleashing his fury on Mama, who rightly deserves it.

"I've made my choice of where I would like to look for a wedding dress, on my own, and I'm going whether you want me to or not." My voice is steady, thanks to the reminder from Hayes that I am powerful and I do deserve her respect, which is a win on its own. "I requested that I would pick out my own dress when I agreed to this whole thing. If I want to go to a store that I know carries dresses I like and I'm comfortable in, it's worth a lost day of planning with you."

"Mothers are supposed to be there when their daughters try on wedding dresses. It is my right to be a part of this process," Mama argues, clutching at her chest like she's been personally affronted by my assertion.

Hayes makes a noise of frustration next to me and I know he's a second away from letting her have it. I gently run my hand up and down his back and turn to Mama again.

"You're the one that insisted on this tight timeline. If we had more time, we could have all of the normal wedding planning mother-and-daughter moments. As it is, you had your chance yesterday, and I wasn't satisfied with the experience. We're doing this our way or not at all. You can get on board and still have the event you want so bad, or you can let this all be for nothing." I cross my arms over my chest to keep my hands from visibly shaking. I'm doing a decent job of standing up for myself, but it comes at a price. The guilt, anxiety, and frustration coalesce in my belly and turn into a vile thing that has me unsure if I just made the worst decision ever, or the best.

Mama stares me down, her expression is fierce and her own arms crossed. Slowly, the anger recedes, and she looks away first, conceding the battle so she can win her war.

"Fine. Go to that godforsaken place and leave your mother out of the process. I guess I'll never have that moment with you when you find the dress of your dreams." Elation fills me that I have won this fight, small as it may be.

"Mama, it doesn't matter if you see me in the dress the moment I find it. We were able to have the bridal shop experience together and that will be enough. You'll be the one buttoning me into the dress on the wedding day, and we can have that special moment together then," I say as a peace offering, despite still thrilling from the moment of victory.

"You wound me, Paige. That's hardly a consolation."

"That's what you're getting, Mama. Count yourself lucky to get that much with this debacle you call a wedding."

We flew into Atlanta this morning after leaving Mama's and I'm making the most of my freedom by spending a good portion of the day dress-shopping with Angela at Haute Belle while Hayes runs his own errands. I called ahead and Angela closed the shop so she could give me the one-on-one attention that was required, and I couldn't be more grateful. I picked out the wedding dress of my dreams and I didn't even feel bad about doing it on my own without Mama present. I also found something for the reception and even picked a dress to wear to the rehearsal.

I didn't have to force myself into ballgowns that didn't fit or fight for the style I wanted like I had to yesterday with Mama.

Angela worked her magic to make sure the dresses were exactly what I wanted, adding a few special touches to make them custom as a personal request. She's a magician with how quickly she can perfectly alter a gown off the rack to fit like a couture piece.

"I take it this was a successful few hours?" Hayes asks, entering the shop. He doesn't bat an eye at the stack of garment bags, shoe boxes, and jewelry cases stacked on a blush pink settee at the front of the shop where Angela and I have been chatting. He merely pulls out his wallet and hands his black AMEX to Angela, who dutifully rings up my purchases.

"Honey, you're going to die when you see what she has planned," Angela says, handing Hayes a receipt with his card and helping us carry my items to the black Mercedes-AMG G63 SUV parked in front of Haute Belle.

"Looks like you were busy, also." I nudge a few bags over to make room for my shoes.

"I can't wear just any old tux in the closet to get married to you again."

"And all the other stuff?"

"Some are presents for you, others you'll see eventually."

"Girl, you better take this man home and open up your presents. I know I would." Angela pulls me into a warm hug, which I return.

"Thank you for everything. You made this so easy, and I have exactly what I imagined."

"I'm the one who should be thanking you for everything. Since you've been shopping here, business has been booming." Her demure pink lips spread wide in a smile, and I know she is thrilled with this turn of events. It's the least I could hope for given how kind she's been to me.

I smile back. "I'm glad people are recognizing the talent and artistry you put into every dress. I guess that's the one good thing being on the Haute List has brought." I shake my head thinking about that site.

"Have fun this week and don't let your mama get you down. Do what feels right and fight for your happiness," Angela says, waving from the shop door. Not only did Angela work literal magic on the dresses, but she also was a wonderful sounding board for the mess Mama has made and gave me plenty of advice along with listening to my woeful tales.

"Are you hungry?" Hayes asks when I settle into the passenger seat.

"Starving. I could eat an entire pizza right now."

"How about I order ahead at Napoletana and we can take it home for a quiet evening?"

"You read my mind, that sounds absolutely delicious."

Hayes taps the dash and dials, placing our pizza order and asking for the chocolate cake for dessert on top of it.

I smile and curl my legs under me as I turn a bit in my seat to stare at his dignified profile. He got a haircut, I realize.

"Your hair is shorter!" I reach over and run my hand along the velvety smooth buzz on the back of his head and scratch my nails against his scalp. Thankfully, the top is still long enough to push back and even flop rakishly over his eyes when he's above me if I'm lucky.

"Fuck, that feels good," he rumbles, pressing his head into my hand.

"And you shaved!" I run the backs of my fingers against his cheeks, feeling the soft suppleness of his skin without a hint of stubble. "You had a spa day without me? How dare you," I joke, taking his chin in my hand when the car comes to a complete stop at an intersection. I pull his face toward me as I lean over the center console so I can rub my face against his and nuzzle my nose along his jaw. He feels so good. I want to rub my entire body along his. I gravitate toward his mouth like a magnet finding its match and kiss him slowly.

A horn honks and I jump away, startled, as Hayes chuckles and continues our drive to Napoletana.

"I'm really glad we ordered to go. If you're going to pet and kiss me like that, I would prefer to be home with you where I can really do something about it."

"Don't tempt me with a good time."

"You don't know what you're asking for, angel. I'm feeling extra depraved right now." His words are silk over gravel, and I feel my whole body flush in response. Knowing he wants these depraved things with *me* makes up for not knowing exactly what that means.

"Why not enlighten me, then?" I reach over and slide my hand up his thigh, feeling him warm and solid. He's not kidding, he is majorly turned on.

"Do you really want me to elaborate, or would you rather find out when I get you home?"

I pull my lip in with my teeth and think that through. "I definitely want to hear you say it out loud, first." I squeeze him then and get a hiss that is far from pain and all excitement.

"When I get you home, I'm sending you up to the bedroom, alone," he begins, rolling his hips under my hand.

"Why alone?"

"I want you to strip down to your panties and wait on the bed for me."

"That makes me nervous."

"You should be. I have plans for you, my love."

I feel a thrill hearing him call me that in his sexy growl and suddenly the nerves are all eager anticipation. "What will you be doing?"

"Putting Cerberus in his kennel so if either of us screams he's not interrupting."

Holy sugar honey iced tea. I am in for something tonight. A shiver runs down my spine and goosebumps dot my arms in excitement. Me, excited over some sexy shenanigans? Whoa Nelly, I must be really getting into this.

"When I find you, on your knees, I'm going to make you watch patiently while I undress."

I swallow hard and look at him. His eyes are that deep jungle green that promises unending pleasure and a promise to take me past my self-imposed limits without much effort.

"I love watching you. You're so graceful."

"Graceful?" he asks, sparing me a quick look with furrowed brows.

"Yes, you're graceful, even if that doesn't seem like the best word for it." I shake my head, trying to pin down my exact thoughts. "Your body is ridiculous, like something that should be in a museum. You're a Greek god made of marble, all perfect planes and sculpted contours. There is grace to every movement, and brutality, too."

"That's more like it. I'm definitely more brute than grace."

I laugh. "Back to what you have in store for me, please."

The smile that curls his lips is slow and sinful. Predatory and pleased. His eyes are growing heavy-lidded even now. "Are you wet already, baby?"

I shift and feel the full body flush rush across my skin again. "Soaked," I admit in a ragged whisper.

Hayes lays his hand over mine, making us both grip his big, incredibly hard cock. Oooh. Just thinking the word does things to me. I shiver again as Hayes slowly shifts my hand, stroking him over his pants.

"Good." The low tremor and finality of the word stokes a fire in my belly. He's not messing around. He really does have something in store for me.

"Will I get to touch you once you're undressed?"

"You will get to do anything you please. It's about time you learned how to take control and demand what you want."

I swallow audibly. This is a life lesson, not just a sex lesson he has planned. I find it intriguing. "How... How will I do that?"

"I'll guide you until you're comfortable, and then you'll try whatever comes into that beautiful brain of yours and I will be your test subject. You're going to be very good at dirty talk and role-play before long, and I can't. Fucking. Wait."

My throat goes dry, and I don't think there's enough water in the world to relieve this parched feeling. Dirty talk and role-playing? Me? The virgin up until a few weeks ago, who never even flirted with a man, will be good at that?

Hayes squeezes my hand and in turn I squeeze him causing him to groan. "And angel?"

"Yes?"

"We're going to be very, very tired before the night is over."

Twenty-Two

The Atlanta Haute List

Billionaire And Bride Making Savannah Home

It looks like our favorite billionaire is continuing to heap lavish presents on his Southern Belle Bride, securing a *gorgeous* new home just in time for Christmas! Our Haute tip inbox was buzzing with news of the pair's newest purchase, a stately Victorian built in the 1870s with over 7,000 square feet and plenty of rooms to fill with the pitter-patter of little feet (we have some major wishful thinking over here, basically writing our own Hayes and Paige fanfic, if you'll allow). The three-story home overlooks famed Forsyth Park in the hometown of our favorite belle, which leads us to think maybe they are planning to start that family sometime soon. We stan a real-life love story, and these two are goals from what we can tell.

Not only are they scooping up real estate like a real-life game of Monopoly, but we're also hearing rumors of a large event in the works to celebrate their quickie Vegas wedding a few weeks back. Could Hayes Olsen and Paige Fairchild be doing things up as we would expect from proper billionaires? It certainly looks that way. Our sources are whispering of tastings, dress fittings, and plans that look just right for a wedding. We hope we are invited to what is sure to be a blowout celebration.

The adorable pair were spotted in Atlanta today, visiting Fairchild's favorite dress store, Haute Belle, and we can only imagine the stunning creation she left with. We've perused the beautiful dresses in the store ourselves and know there are plenty of bridal options that would be perfect for a ceremony or reception, or both! The stack of garment bags Olsen carried out after leaving his bride in the store for a few hours has us even more curious.

Who is taking bets on the date? We think it'll be sooner, rather than later, and of course, we will be reporting on all things to do with this elusive couple. Remember to hit Like and Subscribe for all the Haute gossip!

Twenty-Three

Hayes

Despite stopping to pick up dinner, when we get home, Paige immediately goes up the stairs instead of into the kitchen. She doesn't even stop to cuddle Cerberus, merely giving him a quick scratch on the head as she walks.

I chuckle at her eagerness. I was hoping we could continue what we started in the car, but I thought she would at least eat first. Oh well, we can fuel up after we fuck and maybe get a round two, or three, in later.

"Not that way, big guy," I tell the massive dog, who wants to follow his favorite person.

He pauses and gives me a dissatisfied look that is comical coming from a hulking black demon dog, as Paige would say. I point toward the den, and he turns and slowly walks in that direction with his head lowered, knowing he's getting kenneled. I'll be lucky if he even looks at me tomorrow after this. Separation from Paige is almost as bad for him as it is for me.

"This is for all of our own good," I tell him as I give him a few treats and toys and close the door. I make a stop in the kitchen to put the pizza in the oven to stay warm and grab a bottle of Underworld Spirits bourbon and a glass to bring upstairs with the bag of presents I picked up for her.

When I make it to the bedroom, Paige is waiting just as I asked, on her knees in the middle of the bed, naked except for a scrap of pink lace she calls panties. Her arms are held close to her body, and she shivers a bit, her rosebud nipples tight and her smooth skin glowing like a beacon in the low-lit room.

The single bedside light plays along her curves casting some in shadow and adding more appeal than I thought possible. How did I get this fucking lucky? I couldn't have dreamt up a better, more beautiful, and more perfect person to take as my wife. This is something only the fates could have arranged, and I will gladly be paying for this boon for the rest of my life.

I set the bag on the bed next to her and step back, taking off my shoes.

"Open your presents."

I set down my tumbler, fill the bottom with amber liquid, and take a sip, savoring the burn of the bourbon instead of getting caught up in the view of my wife, nearly naked, perfectly pink, and so incredibly fuckable.

Paige looks to the bag, and back to me, torn between where she would rather have her attention. She pulls a box from the bag and starts to unwrap it while I peel off my socks and stand barefoot on the rug in front of the bed. I'm still fully clothed, so she takes a moment to focus on the box and realizes what she's holding.

"An anal plug?" she asks, opening the box and pulling out the small teal silicone butt plug. "Is this… because you want to… have my ass?" She whispers the dirty words and I swallow in anticipation. God, yes. I take another sip of the bourbon to slow myself down, then set the tumbler on the nightstand.

"You remember how it took a bit to get used to my fingers filling your pussy before you were ready to have sex? Your ass needs a little help, also. You can wear that and get used to the stretch until you're ready for my cock. Or I can fuck your pussy while you wear that, and you can experience a whole different sensation when you come."

She bites her lip and slowly puts the plug on the bed and looks back in the bag. "Lube I can understand," she says, pulling out the bottle and placing it next to the plug. "Is this bag full of sex toys?"

"Keep going." I slowly pull my Henley over my head and toss it to the side.

Paige looks back at me quickly, her hand coming out of the bag holding a set of soft restraints. "Are you… going to tie me up?"

"Maybe someday," I respond, unbuckling my belt.

"So we're not using these today?" she asks, sounding almost relieved.

"Oh, we will definitely use those tonight, but you can put them on me."

Her eyes grow round, and her mouth follows.

I want to shove my cock into those plush pink lips of hers and watch her whale eye up at me from her knees. The scene is so perfectly imprinted in my head, I have to take a deep breath to get past it and push my jeans down to my feet where I step out of them. I'm down to my boxer briefs, my cock impossibly hard and straining the material, and she can't take her eyes off my body. I remember her words, calling me graceful and brutal. She will see both very soon, all while she gets to call the shots.

She manages to pull her eyes away from me when I nod at the bag, encouraging her to find the last present. She pulls out another box and turns it over in her hands, studying it.

"Is this for you, or for me?"

"It's for both of us. It's a cock ring that vibrates. You put it on me, and it vibrates your clit while making me last longer. I'm looking forward to using that with you."

She looks up at me shyly and smiles. "I like the way this one sounds." She opens the box and pulls out the sleek, dark purple ring with the small vibrator built into the top. She presses the button on the vibrator a few times, feeling the changes in speed and her eyes light up.

"I thought you might. That leaves my hands free to do other things, or if you want them out of the way."

"I think I need some of that bourbon."

I pick up the glass and hold it out to her, just out of reach. She has to shift onto her hands and knees to reach it, and the sight is something to behold. Her tits hang full and heavy and the arch of her back that tilts her ass invitingly vies for my attention nearly as much. I let her take the glass and have a sip before she hands it back to me, wiping her lips with the back of her hand delicately.

"Now what?" she asks, settling back on her heels.

"That's for you to decide, angel. You're calling the shots tonight. I'll do anything you ask. Anything." My tone deepens on the last word, and I see the effect it has on her.

Her eyes brighten at the same time her lips compress. She is so torn, waging an internal battle to ask for what she wants despite being accustomed to meekly following in the wake of the dominant personality in any room.

I want so badly for her confidence to become second nature, for her to demand her own satisfaction, in every aspect of life. If it takes playing a more compliant or submissive role for her in the bedroom so she can test it out, I will do it.

"Please take those off," she says, gesturing at my boxer briefs.

"As you wish," I say with a smile.

"You've said that twice now. Have I heard it some-where before?"

I pause with my fingers in the waistband of my shorts. "You've seen *The Princess Bride*, right?"

She shakes her head and I let the waistband snap against my abs. "Seriously? It's such a good movie, you'd love it."

"Isn't it really old? I think it was made way before I was born. I haven't really watched anything from before the nineties. Did you watch it as a kid?"

I press my hand to my chest and lean over, catching myself on my knee, feeling every one of my thirty-five years. "You wound me, I'm not *that* old. I wasn't alive when it came out, either. I just know good movies and watched it when I was older."

Paige's cheeks grow crimson, and she sits up straighter, her tits bouncing with the movement and reviving my quickly deflating hard-on thanks to being reminded that I am almost fifteen years her senior and *really old* by her estimate.

"We can watch it later if you want to continue your goal to educate me about good movies after you educate me in anal plugs and how to use restraints."

I straighten up and walk toward the bed where she sits. "Promise?" She nods. "Just call it a butt plug, anal sounds so formal."

"Fine, how do I use the butt plug?"

I suck in a breath and feel the desire roaring back to life in me, old or not. I'll show her how much she will really like old things tonight. I pick up the bottle of lube. "Turn around."

Paige swallows and turns over onto her hands and knees. "Like this?" Her hair swings down as she turns her head back toward me.

"Exactly like that."

I hook a finger into her lace panties and draw them over the globes of her ass and down her thighs to her knees. She lifts one knee, then the other so I can remove the lace. I groan at the sight of her bared to me and selfishly want to take what I want so badly. It requires more restraint than I think I possess, but I manage to hold back and just bite her ass cheek, getting a surprised giggle from her.

"Lube is your friend. Use it liberally with ass play." I pop the cap of the bottle, drizzle it down her ass crack, and squeeze out enough to coat the butt plug. I drag the little teal plug through her center, parting her and spreading lube all around. She's too tense to stick it in her ass and have that go well, so I fuck her pussy with it for a moment, using my free hand to guide my cock under for her to rub her clit against it.

"Oh, that's not bad," she says, spreading her knees wider and rolling her hips to press harder on my cock. She's right, it feels damn good to have her center stroking my shaft and her clit rubbing against the head of my cock.

I slowly pull the butt plug out and trace it up to her ass, using my finger to spread more lube at the puckered ring and getting her used to the sensation in that area. "I want you to keep moving just like that and relax when you feel it."

She keeps up the intoxicating rhythm, her breath coming in soft pants as the sensation takes over. I gently press the end of the toy into her ass and, besides a slight hitch in her movements that quickly resumes, she seems to barely register the intrusion. I let her motion guide the toy in until it's fully seated.

"That's it, you're a very good girl," I say, tapping the end of the butt plug as she starts to moan.

I guide my cock into her center, pushing in slowly and feeling her tightness on another level with the addition of the plug in her ass. I reach around her hip and strum her clit as I move deep and slow inside of her.

There is something so delicious about watching my cock moving in and out of her from this vantage point with the addition of the teal plug in her tight little asshole. I continue to pull all the way out and fully seat myself again in her pussy, watching as she takes me greedily each time.

Paige's legs shake against my thighs, her hands fisted in the duvet as she comes hard around my cock with a gasp. God, does she feel incredible.

I still my motion and let her muscles clench and throb around me, thinking of everything but how good this feels so I can last through it. I have way more I want to do with her, and this is just the beginning.

"It's in? All of it? That's actually better than I thought it would be," she pants, her head falling to the bed and giving me an incredible new angle to work with.

"You took it without a problem. You're such a good girl. Did you like how it felt to come while so full?"

"Yes," she says without hesitation, and I smile, the motion feeling wicked. "There was so much more… sensation. I felt like I wasn't just coming apart, but shattering, and it was like two heartbeats instead of one. I'm not sure how to describe it, but it felt really good."

"You're making me incredibly happy hearing you say that."

Paige smiles and rocks her hips back against me as she stretches her arms out on the bed. Her ass and hips make a perfect heart narrowing at her waist and I'm glad I'm still buried deep inside her to get this view. I slide my hand around her hip and up her back, encouraging the stretch.

"Will you put the ring on next?"

"You're asking, but I want you to tell me. There's a subtle difference."

Paige stretches flat on her belly, my cock slowly sliding out of her pussy to bob in front of me, and she flips to her back and leans on her elbows, looking up at me. "Put the ring on your cock and lie on the bed, please."

I smile at the nicety following a very naughty sentence. "With pleasure." I pick up the purple ring from the bed and direct my still-hard cock into it, settling it at the base and feeling the pressure it puts on me. I follow her directions and lie on my back on the bed next to her. "Like this?"

"Should I restrain you, too, or is that too much to use everything all at once?" she asks picking up the cuffs and turning them in her hands.

"That's for you to decide." I would prefer to have my hands free to roam, turn, and touch her body, but this is an exercise designed just for Paige to claim her power, and I keep my thoughts to myself.

She tosses them back onto the bed and crawls toward me, straddling my hips and hovering over my body when her lips are above mine.

"I think this is plenty for now." Her pretty pink tongue slips out and she licks along my jaw, and I groan. "I feel both vulnerable and powerful, so I think your point was made," she says into my ear before biting on my earlobe and tugging gently. "Besides, I like when you touch me."

With that admission I finally allow my arms to move, capturing her body against mine and taking her lips with a punishing kiss that she willingly opens to. My hands wander just as we both want and I squeeze her ass, my fingers going to the plug and giving it a gentle tug to see how she reacts.

She bites my lip and moans in response.

I slide the plug in and out the tiniest fraction and she grinds down against my cock, inching up enough for her pussy to take in the head. I let her lead, and she slowly slides her body back to take my cock all the way in. She's lying on me, our chests and hips pressed together, legs entwined, and I can't get enough. I turn on the vibration function of the cock ring with a quick touch and Paige lets out a happily surprised noise.

She interlaces her fingers with mine and pushes up to sit, using the stability of my hands to start moving above me, hips rocking, my cock sliding deep in her tight pussy. She's provided her own form of restraints without needing to tie me up at all, and I love that she figured it out on her own.

Watching Paige ride me, her motions confident, and her body lithe, unlocks a possessive undercurrent that I've only skimmed the surface of before now. I would do anything for this woman. I would go to war for her, mow down her enemies, wreck everything just to make her happy.

She's mine, and I defend what's mine with a vengeance.

"It's... too much." Paige's strained whisper draws my attention and I catch her face as it tenses up, her mouth opening on an *O* and her eyes screwing up tightly as she tips over the edge into her release.

I grip her hip with one hand, keeping her seated as she starts to pull away from the intensity, and guide my other hand up her chest to her tits and roll my thumb over her nipple. Her entire body jerks hard as one wave after another rolls through her. The relief that floods her features and curls her lips into a smile is enough to have me rolling her to the bed, turning her onto her stomach, and pulling the plug from her glorious ass in a quick movement as her tremors continue.

"Tell me you want me to fuck your ass." My hands coast up her hips, my thumbs massaging the dimples at her lower back as I speak.

"I want you to... fuck my... ass," she says haltingly, but her hips rise up toward me, beckoning me to take her now.

"Tell me you can't wait to have me filling you up as I come deep inside of you."

"Oh, Hayes, I can't say that." She pushes her face into the bed. Her head tossing for a moment. I may have found her line when it comes to dirty talk.

I reach under her and softly stroke her clit. "Tell me what you want."

"I want to feel you deep inside of my ass. I want to come apart around you again."

I palm my cock, slipping off the ring and notching up against her ass. "You want me here?" I push in a fraction and feel her inhale sharply. I retreat and push in further. Retreat again and plunge in deeper. "Do you want me to play with you, or fuck you, baby? You gotta tell me what you want."

"Fuck me, please," she whimpers, pressing back against me and forcing me in deeper.

"Good girl," I growl, dragging one hand slowly up her back to wrap her long hair around my fist so I can tilt her face up. "Now what do you want?"

"Touch me, too, please," she moans as I slowly work in and out of her and keep my hand in her hair. "I need more of you, everywhere." I oblige, slipping my other arm around her hip so my fingers can circle her clit as I fuck her delectable ass, which feels just as amazing as I imagined it would.

Her head pulls against my fist as she takes in every inch of me, her knees widening as she starts to rock harder back into my hips, my balls slapping her pussy with each thrust. She gathers handfuls of the duvet in her fists, finding an anchor that allows her to press back against my deep thrusts.

"Oh God, Hayes, that's too... amazing... holy—" She doesn't finish her sentence. Her voice becomes a cry of relief and a moan at once, her body tightening and coming apart around me, a flurry of sensation putting a squeeze on my cock unlike anything I've felt before.

I try to hold out, enjoying the feel of her too much to want to be done with her now. I really try, but her ass is quaking with each tremor of her core, and I only manage to hold out a few strokes longer. My release comes on a hard thrust and I surge into the deepest parts of her with a feral groan that matches Paige's own cries below me.

I unravel my hand from her hair and stroke her back, her shoulders, anywhere I can touch her reverently. "You are everything I have ever wanted. You are more perfect than anything I could have dreamt up." My mouth won't fucking close as I come down off this climax. I'm not a talker, but I can't stop. "God, I fucking love you."

I drag my fingers down her back as her breaths slow, palming her glorious round ass cheeks in my hands as I slowly pull out of her. She stretches out languidly below me, boneless and shivering with aftershocks. I gather her in my arms and press her back to my chest, holding her tightly and whispering in her ear as I nuzzle. There's an anxious feeling gnawing at me now that I've had this part of her. It would kill me if I lost her after this.

"You're amazing, angel. You took all of me, every hard thrust like you were made for this. I'm never fucking letting you go."

"You can't shake me, Hayes, so don't even think about letting me go. There is no one else for me but you." Hearing her soft words as she curls into my arms calms my mind and puts the lid back on my mouth, keeping me from uttering every manic thought flying through my mind.

"Let's get cleaned up. We've been dirty enough for one evening, and I have pizza and a movie to introduce you to, next."

Paige giggles as I scoop her up and walk into the bathroom. "Dirty enough? Inconceivable."

I stop and look down at her. "You have seen the Princess Bride, haven't you?"

"I looked up some memorable quotes when you were grabbing the pizza. That was just too easy."

"I fucking love you." I bite her shoulder and think maybe she's right. There's no such thing as dirty enough with her. Despite our attempts to get clean, we end up on round two under the spray of the shower heads with Paige pressed against the shower wall as I take her from behind again.

Twenty-Four

Paige

"**I** finally understand all of the quotes and references I've heard over the years that I just thought were vaguely funny. It was actually pretty good for an eighties movie."

We've just landed back in Savannah and I'm still thinking about last night. Not only did Hayes introduce me to *The Princess Bride*, but he also broadened my sexual interests.

I thought for sure I would hate anything that had to do with my behind. It scared the living daylights out of me when he asked about having me *there*, which is not a question I ever anticipated receiving. Now? Well, now I think I wouldn't mind that again, and that is a revelation. Just because something sounds scary, doesn't mean it will be. Besides, when it comes to Hayes, I don't know if I will have any boundaries I wouldn't let him cross. He's taken me so far, in such a short time, and I haven't been disappointed once.

Hayes kisses my head and hands me my seatbelt. "I told you that you'd like it."

I watch him round the front of the sleek Maybach and get into the driver's seat. It was so nice to have a night to ourselves without having to think about this wedding stuff, or how crazy my mama is.

"I'm dreading today. I'm sure Mama's gone off the deep end because I asked for one day without her and one piece of the planning she couldn't have her hands on."

"Do you want me to make some changes to my schedule so I can be there with you?"

I turn to face him, tucking my legs under me and curling my entire frame into the seat like it can protect me from Mama's fury. I don't want him to have to cancel anything just so I have a defender. I should be able to stick up for myself and not let Mama push me around every other moment.

"No, I can handle her. Mostly it's just going with what she wants, anyway. That's not too hard when I don't care."

"What about when you do care? Are you willing to keep fighting for the little things that matter to you in this whole production?"

"I think the only part I really care about is the ceremony and my moments with you, and we've managed to get what we want in those instances. There's nothing left to fight with her about." Admitting this brings new levity to the situation where there was just trepidation before. If I can tolerate Mama's craziness a few more days, and play along at the planning sessions, this thing will be over before I know it and I'll finally have unguarded access to my trust. Whether I can stand being with Mama every waking moment for the next few days, is a different story.

"You don't want to take a stand on something insignificant just to make her work for it? That's what I would do."

I shudder. "I hate fighting with Mama. The last thing I want to do is start picking fights about stuff I couldn't care less about. Let her have her way and make this event something she wants so she's happy and it'll be over in a few days."

"I promise I will never let your mother plan another event for us. If there's something that needs planning, I'll hire the whole thing out and tell them not to bother us."

I put my hand over my heart and give him my best appreciative princess face. "My hero."

"I thought I hated public events and being in the spotlight more than anyone, but I think I found my match in you."

I salute him and grin. "Your equal in hating being in the spotlight, reporting for duty, Sir."

"Mmm, say that again." I catch the change from mirth to desire as it occurs in his face and swallow.

"Which part?"

"Call me Sir again. I like hearing that from your sweet lips."

Oooh. He's jumping from our humor to wanting more dirty talk from the naughty version of me he's created. "What will we be doing later, Sir?"

"If you're a good girl, I'll give you anything you want."

This is a bit weird for me. I'm okay using some of the naughty words while in the moment, but this has me outside of that headspace. I laugh nervously. "I think I'll have to practice that a bit more to feel comfortable doing it on command."

"It was worth a shot, and practice is always good." There is a twinkle in his eye even as he acknowledges my discomfort, so I know I didn't turn off the mood completely.

"Would you please drop me off at Mama's? Hopeful-ly, I can be finished with all of this mess if I start early enough. There has to be an end to her preparations at some point, and I'd rather get it over with as soon as I can."

Hayes pouts, hilariously pushing out his bottom lip so I laugh. "I was hoping you would stay with me longer, but you're right. I can drop you at her house and head straight to the office."

When I walk in the door at Mama and Daddy's, all hell has broken loose. There are multiple strangers at every table and seat in the parlor. Some have fabric samples, others have laptops out typing furiously, some are painstakingly creating a seating chart with beautifully handwritten calligraphy, and there are a few orbiting Mama like little moons as she moves from one room to another, dictating her wishes to each group. I hang my garment bags in the hall closet and make my way toward Mama, fighting through the throng that surrounds her.

"What's going on?" I ask, as soon as I can make it close enough to hopefully grab her attention.

"Oh, Paige, you're here. Finally."

"I told you I would be gone overnight, and now I'm back. What's on the schedule for today?" I work to keep any frustration out of my tone. I don't want to upset her first thing after taking away a day of her precious time by doing my own thing.

"We are finalizing all of the reception details. I brought in extra help from the Savannah College of Art and Design to make it go faster, so I'm overseeing each team and ensuring they're doing it correctly." She looks over the shoulder of a girl who can't be older than me, holding out fabric samples with locations written on cardstock pinned to them. "Not like that, you buffoon. We are not using blush pink in the swags from the ceiling, it's ivory only, with green on the walls. The pink is just for the tablescapes."

The girl scurries away, clutching fabric samples in her hands when Mama is done dressing her down. My eyes widen in horror at her tone and the way she spoke to the girl. I know the feeling all too well of being on that side of Mama's cutting remarks.

"Was that necessary?"

"They need to know their place and how not to mess up. I let them learn the hard way and the lessons stick better. Now, did you manage to find a worthwhile dress in that godforsaken city, or do we need to return to the bridal boutique to try on the dresses I have on hold again?"

I beam at her, despite her disbelief that I could have achieved my goal without her. "I found all of the dresses I will need. I put them in the hall closet."

She raises an eyebrow at me. "How many dresses do you expect to wear to one event?"

"I have a ceremony dress, a reception dress that's a bit easier to move in, and something less formal for the rehearsal dinner."

"Hmm. I want to inspect these dresses. Your bridal shoot is tomorrow, and we can't have something completely wrong on hand. Maybe we should head to the bridal shop now while we have time," she muses.

I take a deep breath and pray for patience. I knew she would second guess all of my choices, not trusting me to pick out anything worthy of the image she has for the party she is planning, but it hurts anyway.

"The dresses are perfect. They are altered and fit my body exactly as they should, and I feel so beautiful in them."

Mama purses her lips and looks me over, taking in my slate blue silk blouse and cream skirt like they offend her and any dress I could have picked will be just as terrible.

"Very well. Show me what you bought. You there," she says to a passing young man with artfully messy hair and a septum piercing. "Take the garment bags in the hall closet upstairs to my bedroom and hang them on the wardrobe."

"Yes, ma'am," the unidentified man says, hurrying out to the foyer.

"I'm perfectly capable of carrying the bags myself," I remind her.

"We have the extra hands, might as well make use of them." She waves off my concern and turns to the three people still trailing her. "You three start on the place settings. I want to see all of the options we have when I return."

They scuttle off toward the dining room and I feel sympathy for them welling up in me. Who knows what she has subjected this army of assistants to in the last twenty-four hours? And where did they all come from? SCAD should still be on holiday break. If she went dredging up all of the wayward souls left in the city during the break, she really must have been desperate for help.

My thoughts of the assistants are cut off as Mama places her hand on my back and marches me into the foyer and up the stairs to her room. I try to shake off her hand, but she just moves it to my upper arm instead and I roll my eyes, submitting to being dragged along with her.

The garment bags are hanging on her wardrobe when we enter her room and I smile at the white bags knowing what's inside will have to pass Mama's inspection. There is no way she can complain, though she will try.

I go to the heaviest bag and unzip it, folding the edges around the hanger and pulling the bottom of the dress out of the bag so the train can be displayed. "This is the ceremony dress."

Mama walks up to the dress, her eyes squinted as she takes in each piece that makes up this fabulous creation. While she runs her hands over the lace, pulling it away from the lining, I open the second bag.

"This is the reception dress. It doesn't have a train like the ceremony dress does. If I have to dance, this is a good option."

"Hmmm," she says, leaving the ceremony dress and giving her attention to the long gown that will swirl around my feet without tripping me up. "I don't like it as much as the ceremony dress. It's too plain."

Despite the backhanded compliment, and not saying so much outright, I now know she actually likes the dress I picked out for the ceremony. The reception dress *is* plain, and I liked that about it. It is a fitted sheath of ivory silk with a straight neckline just below my collar bones in the front and dips to a V at my mid-back, with long sleeves. I felt incredibly elegant in that dress when I tried it on and thought it would be an excellent option for the dinner and dancing portion of the night Mama has planned.

I sigh quietly and reach for the third garment bag, unzipping it and pulling out the knee-length fitted dress that hugs my hips and makes me feel so very feminine. It has a squared neckline that shows just a hint of cleavage, and long sleeves made of lace very similar to the one used on my ceremony dress. I loved that it was less formal, and very sexy in the way it hugs my curves, while still being demure enough for the occasion.

"This is not at all what I would have picked for you," Mama finally says, taking a step back from the wardrobe and looking at all three dresses in turn once more.

That's an understatement. The dresses she has on hold are all ballgowns with full skirts and flounces. Mine are all simple and stunning.

"But they aren't the worst options. They're just not the vision I have for you and this wedding. They're all form-fitting. You looked so beautiful in a ballgown, like a princess."

That is a huge compliment from Mama. She hasn't outright forbidden me to wear any of them, which means she approves even if she would prefer her own choices.

"The ballgowns didn't feel like me. I loved all three of these dresses because they made me feel beautiful and sophisticated."

"But did you feel like a bride?" Mama's face shows true concern for once, and my defenses lower.

"Yes, Mama, I did. Especially the ceremony dress."

I feel a smile taking over my face as I look at the dress. It really is stunning. I reach out and run my hand over the lace tiers of the mermaid-style skirt, remembering the moment I tried it on and knew it was the one. I was giddy in that moment, my own breath short as I took in my reflection.

"The lace pattern is very similar to Nanny Fairchild's wedding dress. The fit works really well for my body type, and the lace on the straps, being flowers and leaves, is such a sweet detail. It gave me secret garden vibes that would be right at home in Elysium. I felt like a fairy princess as well as a bride, honestly." I look over at Mama and the smile slips off my face. "What's wrong?"

Mama is *weeping*. Big tears slide down her cheeks as she covers her mouth with her hands. I take a step toward her and wrap my arms around her shoulders as they begin to shake with silent sobs. I make comforting noises as I hold her, not sure what happened just now, but wanting to make sure she's okay. Mama does not cry. She may shed a furious tear or two from time to time, but this is unabashed emotion, unlike anything I've seen from her.

Mama takes a few deep gulping breaths and her sobs slow, then stops. She pulls away from my embrace and pats at her cheeks delicately, which does nothing to stem the flood of tears that has ruined her makeup.

"I wish I could have been there with you when you tried it on. I missed out on something special and will never get that experience again."

"You didn't miss a thing. We had our shopping trip to try on dresses and remember, you will be the one helping me get ready. You will see the dress on before anyone else does. Even before Hayes sees it."

Seeing my mother break down like this alters a part of my brain that considers her the most stubborn and unaffected person I know. She really cares, despite all of her controlling instincts. Or maybe it's because she cares so much that she wants to control all parts of my life? Either way, I know she cares, and I also know a little distance in our relationship would do us both wonders.

"Very well. Let me freshen up in the bathroom."

The unexpected emotion makes me want to dig deeper into her psyche and find out who this new, weeping woman is. "Mama, can I ask you a question?"

"You just did, you silly thing, but go ahead." It's never a simple response, always a critique.

I falter, wanting to dive into the whys of her actions and the difficulty she brings to my life but not wanting to put her on guard and turn this into a fight. "Do you think I am capable of living my own life, without constant input and direction from you or Daddy?" I ask, phrasing it as delicately as possible.

She walks into the ensuite bathroom, and I follow hesitantly, keeping my face placid and open so as not to rile her up. It really is a tricky situation, though I feel like we may be able to get to a place of trust and openness. Someday. I hope this is the start.

"I care about you so very much," she starts, grabbing a tissue from her vanity and patting her eyes. "It can be… difficult… to allow you to have free rein of your life with everything that could hurt you. I've seen how the world wants to eat up sweet things like you, and I want to protect you from that. I have failed over and over again to keep you from being hurt, so my instinct is to build a wall around you and make sure you stay within my defenses." The fierceness of her protective instincts forces its way into her features, pulling down the corners of her mouth and furrowing her eyebrows.

"Isn't growing up about making mistakes so you can learn from them?" I hedge quietly.

"Why should you have to make any mistakes if I can keep you from getting hurt and teach you the lesson you would have learned anyway?" she retorts.

"Sometimes it takes learning it for yourself for the lesson to stick, right?"

She flattens her lips and looks like she's about to argue, so I continue.

"What I really mean is, I don't want to make mistakes, exactly, I just want to be free to choose for myself what happens in my life, rather than always being told what to do or how to do it."

Mama sits on the bench at her vanity and drops her face into her hands, looking wearier than I think I've ever seen her. She sighs deeply and drops her hands, one arm staying on the vanity and fingering a strand of pearls lying on a silver tray with her perfume bottles.

"There are many parts of this world I wish I could shield you from. There is so much evil that would tear you apart. I've spent your entire life worried about what could happen and doing everything in my power to protect you from the worst of it."

"You've done a great job of that," I say, settling onto the bench next to her and nudging my shoulder into hers.

"No, I haven't." Her voice breaks on the word and my heart goes with it. "Despite my best intentions, you were still assaulted in high school during the one party I let you attend, and now you've gone off and married someone much too old and just all wrong for you. I couldn't stop the worst from happening to you despite my best efforts, and it breaks my heart anytime I think of my failures." A tear tracks down her cheeks and she makes no move to brush it away.

I wrap my arms around my middle and fight through my own rising anxiety at the mention of the trauma. "What happened with Garrison in high school was awful. It ruined a part of my life and took an innocence from me that I'll never get back. But it also taught me to be wary of other people's intentions. It kept me out of trouble for the rest of high school and college because I knew better than to hang with that crowd or even try to date. As hard as it was to go through that, maybe it saved me more trouble down the road, which is valuable in itself. I'm squeaky clean for this generation, and you don't see that much."

She huffs out a bitter laugh. I can feel the tension radiating off of her through the closeness of our shoulders on the bench. I want this to be the end of the conversation, but I know there is more that must be discussed before we can ever move past her betrayal. I inhale deeply and fight the tremors from coursing through me.

"Still... You made a mistake wanting to arrange a marriage for me with Garrison for your own benefit. You completely disregarded my safety and peace of mind so you could get what you wanted in the end. That wasn't done out of love, Mama, and you have to accept that it changed our relationship irrevocably."

Mama's chin drops, tears falling down her cheeks again. "Maybe I was too lost to my own ambitions to see it clearly at the moment. Your father and I have had many discussions over the last few weeks about what I kept from him and how I could have thought it was beneficial to set you back in Garrison's path," she says with unusual trepidation. "I may have been... wrong... to think that Garrison would have changed or not to have fought for you when it happened all those years ago. You're right, I made a mistake, but more than that, I wasn't protecting you at all. Even when I'm trying to protect you, I just end up hurting you. I'm a failure." Mama's voice is weak and stammering when she usually oozes confidence. Admitting fault does not come easily to her, and to have messed up so epically and having to own it now is the antithesis of her typical cool confidence and bravado.

"As for marrying Hayes—I hope you can see that I am head over heels in love with the man, despite any objections you have. Being with him has taught me to value my opinions and desires, to know my worth, and to ask for what I want. He's incredibly caring, loving, and protective as well, and he makes me feel cherished beyond anything else."

"This isn't the way I imagined you would meet your husband or fall in love. He's just... not at all what I wanted for you."

I drop my hands into my lap and spin the gold and diamond rings on my left hand. Instead of arguing the point or telling her every part of my relationship and how it came to be, I will appeal to her protective side.

"If you wanted me to be with a man who loved me unconditionally, was willing to protect and fight for me, and could give me the life you think I need, I certainly found him. I hope someday you will grow to love him nearly as much as I do, because he is everything I could ever want in a husband, and he makes me so very happy."

"He stole your legacy while making you fall in love with him. How can that be caring or make you happy?" She turns her head and I see the anger set in her features. Her disregard for the progress we are making is shown in her quick return to the hardest thing I've had to endure this month.

Oof. I take a deep breath through the hurt, knowing that's never going to sit well.

"You're right, I was very unhappy when I found out what he did. But it wasn't just Hayes who took away my legacy. Daddy sold the business to him, like it or not." She shakes her head roughly, so I press on. "It was hard to understand why Hayes would buy the business despite knowing it was my one dream." I swallow the difficult truth and continue. "But... maybe losing the one dream I'd had all my life was what I needed to see there were so many other opportunities out there that needed what I could bring to the table?" It dawns on me as I say it, hope blooming in my chest to replace the ache of losing a legacy. "I was so set on the life I was told I would have that my eyes were never open to the simplest things around me that were beautiful or needed exactly what I have to offer."

"You can't mean that! He took what was rightfully yours and now you will never have the opportunity to lead the Xenios Group or run the hotels."

She doesn't know what Hayes and his brothers did. How could she? I made a grave mistake by not telling her this sooner.

"It's not what I had imagined, but I do have the opportunity to lead something even bigger now. I have a controlling interest and a seat on the board for the hotel group Hayes created that Xenios and The Mansion are now a part of." I tilt my head against Mama's again, trying to help her see this revelation with me.

"He gave you controlling interest in the hotels?" Mama asks, her eyes dropping to her hand on the pearls, where her fingers continue to smooth over the beads one by one, like she's reciting the rosary.

"Yes. I'm an equal with Hayes and his brothers in that endeavor. What they created is something incredible. It's the largest luxury boutique hotel group in the country. It's bigger than Xenios ever aspired to be, and I have a big part in how it operates and what direction it goes."

"You're not devastated about losing out on your legacy?"

"Oh, I was, don't get me wrong."

I shake my head. That's a pain that likely will take much longer to heal, and there will always be a part of me that longs for the simplicity of knowing exactly where I would be in ten years' time.

"It took a while to let that sink in and probably will always be a bit of a sore spot, despite having the role I do now." I tuck my hair behind my ear as I admit this. "It took having that door closed for me to turn and find a hallway of doors now open that I otherwise never would have looked for."

Mama abandons the pearls and takes my hands in hers, her red-rimmed eyes locked on mine. "I always thought I would see you at the helm of your daddy's company."

"Sure, that was the future that was always set out for me to aspire to. But aside from my board position with the Olympus Hotel Group, Hayes gave me my own company to run. I love what he did with Underworld Spirits, and to be handed the reins on that project shows a huge amount of trust on his part. I have a lot of ideas, and already the brand is rising in popularity despite just launching. I get to be creative and take it to new places while learning a new branch of business that will be another tool in my belt for anything that comes along in the future. But, beyond those things, we have also started a foundation to help people that I get to pour my heart and soul into. I can use your family's rich history in agriculture to give back to the community. It's an opportunity to shift my sole focus from the day-to-day of business, that I never seem to pull my head away from, to see that others are in need." My enthusiasm and excitement has worked into my tone, and I finish nearly vibrating with the potential that is now in front of me thanks to one door closing.

"You may be right, that is a new way of looking at things. You might just get the experience we hoped for you, and more this way." Mama's begrudging tone and the words she speaks are unfamiliar, but I latch onto them anyway.

"I'm sorry, did you just admit I was right about some-thing?" I ask in confusion. Am I delirious? Did Hayes screw me silly last night and I woke up in another time-line?

Mama straightens and rolls her eyes at me. "Don't be glib, young lady."

"I'm not being glib, I'm deadly serious Mama, I think that may be the first time you've ever said I was right about something, and I kind of want to savor this mo-ment for posterity."

"I will never say it again if this is how you react. It's not becoming of a proper lady to gloat." Despite her words, there is a small smile playing on her lips and I can feel her mood lighten.

I pull her into an embrace and put my chin on her shoulder. I will savor this moment, even if I have to do it silently. "Thank you, Mama."

"Oh, stop it or I'll start crying again. Who knew all you needed was to be told you were doing something right to get you falling all over yourself to hug and thank me."

I let her go and laugh. "Just goes to show you how little it takes to make me happy. Now, why don't we go terrorize your assistants downstairs? I have a ceremony I need some help with, and you brought all the creative help Savannah has to offer to this very house."

I know this is a turning point in our relationship. We've finally found even ground to stand on as partners, rather than adversaries, and I'm determined to maintain it going forward. There is no going back to the wilting wallflower she usually turns me into now that I know what I want. My happiness has to come first, now. And that happiness is with Hayes.

Twenty-Five

Hayes

I stand at the large factory-style windows of the Elysium Garden overlooking Savannah at The Abyss, nursing a glass of Underworld Spirits bourbon. Paige is off somewhere down there having her bridal portraits taken in preparation for the giant wedding her mother is insistent on throwing, and I'm here wondering how the last month could have changed me so irrevocably.

A month ago, I wouldn't have thought twice about what a gorgeous twenty-one-year-old woman was doing somewhere in this city.

A month ago, I wouldn't have been anxious to get home—to an actual home here in Savannah rather than the small flat I have here in the nightclub—so I can hear about her day.

A month ago, all I cared about was getting my hands on the hotel chain of a prominent family here in town. A family that I now belong to, for better or for worse.

A month ago, I wasn't planning to get married—let alone do it again—two days from now.

A month ago, I hadn't met the sweetest woman who would irreparably turn my life upside down and have me begging for more.

I must be feeling particularly sentimental to be having these thoughts, and a part of me wants to shut it all down and feel *less*. Yet, I'm willingly recounting each of the weeks since I met Paige right here in this garden, thinking about what it will be like to see her walk through it again when she's coming to recite wedding vows to me, in front of our closest friends and family members this time.

I take a sip of bourbon and let the fiery liquor roll over my tongue before swallowing. I turn to the tree next to me and reach into the boughs, finding the leathery skin of a ripe pomegranate and plucking it from the branch. I'll take this home and feed it to Paige, aril by aril, until she's coated in the sticky sweet-tart juice, then I'll lick it off her skin and turn her into the same burning need that I have become because of her.

I am infatuated with the woman. She haunts every thought, bewitches me with every word, beguiles me with a single look. I am obsessed with her, and my desire is fathomless. I want to wrap myself around her, worship her body, and claim her soul. I want her to know every aching need I have for her, and for her to make me feel even more in turn. I have an unhealthy fixation with my wife, and I'm damn pleased about it.

Heavy, pulsing beats of music reverberate against my feet, letting me know that the club has opened for the evening, and it's time to leave The Abyss in order to find my wife.

As I turn toward the private door to my office and flat, I hear the main door to the garden open, and I pause. For a moment, I wonder if it's Paige come to find me, but that thought is quickly doused and my smile slips from my lips when I hear a masculine voice call out.

"I know you're up here. Where are you hiding, Hayes?"

Tavi. No, Tavi was your friend. This is Rex, your rival in all things, I correct myself.

I step out onto the path that winds through the greenhouse and slowly walk toward Octavius Rex, who stands at the French doors separating the green-house from the elevator vestibule that leads to the main floors of the club.

"What do you want now?"

"I heard you own this place and thought we could have a chat. I saw your pretty little wife was busy having photos taken at The Mansion, so you had to be available."

I tighten my grip on the tumbler in my hand. I have to remind myself to keep a loose grip on the pomegranate in the other so as not to crush it, despite wanting to do just that.

"I told you to stop following my wife, Rex." The growl in my words carries a warning. I'm one wrong word away from carrying out the threat.

"I'm staying at The Mansion, so technically she came to me," he says, hands in his pockets and shoulders scrunching up in a shrug. "I just happened to see her walking the property with a photographer and knew she was busy. Can't fault me for taking the opportunity when it was handed to me like that."

I can and I will. I don't like him anywhere near Paige. I don't trust his motives, and know he has plenty of reason to want to hurt me. Obviously, Paige is my soft spot, and someone like him, with an axe to grind, would want to hit me right where he knows it would hurt most.

"Stay away from her. If she shows up somewhere you are, turn the other fucking way and get the hell out."

Rex *tsks* and shakes his head. "See, you can't dictate what others do in real life, Hayes. That's some weird billionaire bullshit you've got going on there." He takes a hand out of his pocket and gestures around the greenhouse garden. "Speaking of which, this is some place you got here. Never took you for a plant lover, but I can certainly see the appeal." Rex changes tack and I grit my teeth.

"What are you doing here? I assume you have a reason, so out with it."

"What, I couldn't stop by the most prestigious night-club in town looking to talk to an old friend?"

"We both know your motives aren't that pure. You want something." *We're certainly not friends anymore.*

"Actually, I have a proposition for you. Something that may make your life easier. I know it can't be fun watching your good name and the business you've built get dragged through the mud."

I don't trust Rex as far as I can throw him, and having him clocking in at an inch taller than me, it wouldn't be far at all. There is a catch in whatever game he is playing right now, and it'll likely fuck me over in some fashion. He's a cunning devil. I would know; we were forged into the men we are now through the same gauntlets of our youth.

"What will this proposition of yours cost me?" I lazily take a sip of the remaining bourbon in my tumbler, my eyes not leaving him.

"Certainly not your soul, you don't have one to bargain with." He smiles, and it actually reaches his eyes, something I haven't seen from him in years.

"You're stalling," I drawl. I smell weakness. I feel my lips curling up into my own smile, though it likely will just make my eyes appear hungry instead of happy. "You actually need something from *me*."

Rex stretches his arms to his sides and shrugs in a *you got me* way. "I happen to know who's behind the lawsuit you're facing, and I have exactly the leverage to make them drop it. Think that's enough of a bargaining chip?"

It certainly is, though I doubt he'd give that information to me without demanding far more in return. I still think he has something to do with the lawsuit, and this could be his way of setting me up for more hurt. I tilt my head and study him, seeing the friend he used to be and feeling a pang of loss that my actions and ambitions changed forever. Paige is in my head even now, demanding empathy from me when I need to be more calculating than ever.

"Come with me." I gesture for him to follow and turn, walking to the hidden door to my office. I hear his steps following on the gravel path and know I've won, despite not knowing what he needs in return. I'll figure it out and I'll make him pay to get it. If he thinks I don't have a soul now, it'll be him leaving his behind tonight.

I open the metal door and lead Rex through the short hallway to my office, letting him follow me in, and close the door. I settle myself at the large mahogany desk and gesture for him to take one of the leather chairs facing me across it.

I plant my elbows on the desk and steeple my fingers. "What do you want from me?" I feel a giddiness that only surfaces when something of value is at stake. When it's mine to own if I play my hand well. The risk makes it more enjoyable.

Rex crosses an ankle over his knee and leans back, looking far too comfortable despite what this may cost him. "I have a line on another mine that would replace your holdings in South Africa and make you even more filthy rich."

"We just acquired a handful of mines a month ago. Why would I need more, even if South Africa isn't panning out?"

"You were intentionally sabotaged with South Africa. You need to bring the culprit to justice and cut your losses."

"And what makes you so keen to provide this information, if it's even true?"

"I want a seat on the board." Rex leans forward, elbows on his knees, and levels a calculating look on me. He is deadly serious and thinks whatever information he has is worth putting a fox in the hen house to get it.

I let my hands drop and flatten against the desk, holding Rex's gaze as he seriously asks to be made a part of Olympus, and not just in any old VP or C-suite role, but on the board—the supreme governing body where our company is concerned, and the only thing that could stop me or my brothers from doing as we please with the direction of the company.

"What sort of delusional mindset would have you think we would *ever* consider adding you to the board of any of our holdings?" I ask, pushing the request off onto a subsidiary rather than Olympus, hoping that's the extent of his reach.

Rex leans back and scoffs at me. "Not just on the board of one of your paltry holdings. I want on the Olympus International board."

I scowl at him. The current board of Olympus International is made up of my brothers, me, my father, and two of his colleagues who were given their places when my brothers and I took over the company. It was a way for the older generation of my father's mining operations to still be a part of the company as we charged forward into diversifying and making a name for ourselves on the global stage. They have kept us conservative in certain situations and allowed us to go all out when it benefited the company most. Adding a seventh member to the board could more than disrupt the trajectory of Olympus, and Rex would have more opportunities to stand in our way.

"You can't possibly be that delusional. Why are you asking now?"

"There are plenty of reasons I can give you, but the most important one is that you took the only path I had away from me when you bought Rex, Inc., and you owe me something in return. That, and I can make your current legal issues disappear and make things right in your world again."

"From where I'm sitting it looks like I did you a favor and made your worries disappear when we took over

Rex, Inc. I'm sure your father is enjoying a comfortable retirement, and you've learned how to build an empire of your own off the ruins of something that would have sunk you had you stepped into the role you were slated for." Though I speak with conviction, I have a nagging sense of guilt for the situation I caused and hope I can make him see it the way I've painted it now.

Rex casually waves away my reasoning. "Hayes, Hayes, Hayes. Always looking to be the savior despite your ulterior motives. You didn't actually think you were helping me when you forced your way in and made my father sell. You did it because you were greedy and wanted the company that was built on the back of my family. It wasn't to make my life easier, that's for damn sure, and it's in spite of your actions that I made something of it rather than because of it."

I stand and walk to the bar by the window overlooking a slice of the Savannah River, grabbing the bourbon and pouring two fingers worth into a couple of cut-glass tumblers. I hand one to Rex and lean against my desk in front of him before taking a sip. The fire is clarifying, stinging away the guilt I feel, and the absurdity of what Rex is asking. I need to know his motives, know what's making him reach for this like Icarus for the sun.

Would I do anything differently in his position? The thought surprises me, and it sounds a lot like Paige. I shake my head and huff out a quiet laugh. My wife isn't just my obsession, she's becoming my conscience as well.

"What you're offering still wouldn't make me let you anywhere near Olympus, let alone give you a seat on the board, but I am sorry I let my ambition ruin our friendship." The words are like broken glass in my mouth, hard to swallow but good to get out after all this time.

Rex tilts his head, studying me. "I might actually believe that you are, but it doesn't change what happened."

And this is why apologies are just for the one doing the apologizing. The mere fact that I'm contrite and admit fault can't make him accept the apology or make anything right between us. That's a lesson I've learned only too recently with what I did to Paige.

"No, it doesn't. It doesn't change my motivations in the moment either, despite what I know now. Still, I'm sorry."

"Tell me something, would you still make that move knowing how your ambition fucked up a friendship?" Rex sips the bourbon. "Damn, that's good," he says quietly, holding the glass up to the light and studying the amber liquor while giving me a moment to ponder the question.

Would I? Paige once asked me why Rex's legacy, and not another transportation company. I knew the intimate details of Rex, Inc. because of my friendship with Rex and hearing from him what their struggles were.

I used my insider knowledge to lead the deal, striking where it hurt and making our offer the only option my friend's father, Balthazar, could take. I could very well have targeted another company with similar gains, yet I didn't. Rex is right, I was trying to be a savior, because I went after his company with the mindset that I was doing something for him, despite quite the opposite.

"I possibly would do things differently now," I admit quietly, looking into my own glass of bourbon like it's an oracle that will reveal the perfect response, when it doesn't, I continue. "Why do you want on the board at Olympus?"

He gives me a wry, knowing look. "Hayes, you know why. It's the only thing either of us really wants. Power."

Twenty-Six

The Atlanta Haute List

S potted: Three Billionaire Brothers Taking Over Sleepy Savannah

Hauties in the know have been blowing up our tip line with reports of all three Olsen brothers out and about in the coastal candyland of Savannah today. It looks like Payton and Zander Olsen are in town for the event that is rumored to be happening there shortly for eldest Olsen brother, Hayes, and his wife, Paige Fairchild. The trio was spotted starting out the day at Hayes's gothic nightclub, The Abyss, grabbing lunch at a local seafood restaurant, stopping to pick up garment bags from a local tailor, and doing some shopping. They were busy boys and we love a man who runs his own errands when he has all the money to hire someone else to do it. Billionaires, they're just like us!

The brothers' arrival is a dead giveaway that the rumored event is slated for this weekend, and we're willing to gamble that it will take place on New Year's Eve. There's no better day for revelry to occur than the most hyped party day of the year. Who can blame them when a New Year's kiss is the stuff of legends and most parties are never as good as you expect them to be. We can safely say that won't be the case for Olsen and Fairchild's shindig, not with their wealth and status to ensure they get exactly the results they want.

Whatever is set to take place will likely be a who's who of the business world and billionaires from all over. We're betting the new darling of The Olympus Group, the storied Southern Antebellum home turned hotel of the Fairchild family known as The Mansion, will be a key player in the event. We have our feelers out and are collecting all tips about what exactly could be happening there. What we do know is it won't just be any old New Year's Eve party, and we want an all-access pass. Any news we get we will share with you, so hit Like and Subscribe for all the haute gossip!

Twenty-Seven

Hayes

"**T**his rehearsal will conclude the boring part of our activities," Zander says, gripping my shoulders and pointing me into the Elysium Garden at The Abyss. "Then all hell will break loose downstairs."

"Slow your roll, Zand. Hayes doesn't want anything crazy," Payton says, pulling Zander off my shoulders.

I give him a nod of thanks, rolling my eyes at Zander's one-track mind.

"Hayes doesn't know what he *needs* let alone what he wants. He's only getting married twice, we hope, so this is our chance to let him go wild with the bachelor party."

"Whatever debauchery you have in mind is strictly for you, idiot. I'm having no part in whatever your scheme is." I stop speaking when I see Paige in the garden, her back to me showing off her lush ass in a tight white dress that has her nearly glowing while framed against the green of the plants and the darkening sky seen through the windows behind her. I smile when she looks over her shoulder at our commotion, her own smile lighting up her beautiful face as she turns and comes toward me, her arms already rising to hug me before she's close.

"I missed you," she says, wrapping her arms around my middle and holding me tight as I return the embrace.

"You have no idea, angel." I tilt Paige's chin up with a finger and place a kiss on her lips that promises to evolve as she meets it.

"That's enough of that, you two," Zander breaks in, pulling Paige away and putting his arm around her shoulders. "Hello Paige dearest, please greet your favorite brother-in-law."

She laughs and hugs him, and I fight the knee-jerk reaction to physically remove his arm from her body. I would never trust my brother near my wife, even if I have already threatened severe bodily harm. He's liable to do something just to get a rise out of me, and I don't want that fight to take place here and now.

"Hello, Zander. I'm surprised you were let out for an evening with the big kids. Did you win over Mommy and Daddy so you could stay until ten, or will they be picking you up early?" Paige asks.

I feel the tension ease out of me as she deftly handles his self-assured ways and takes him down a notch while staying entirely platonic and playful.

Having her continue an inside joke she and Zander established at the Underworld Spirits launch party shows me she is more than capable of dealing with my brother. Remembering that night makes me smile. It was the first time I had seen Zander flustered by a woman, and I was proud of Paige for meeting him on an even playing field despite it being the first time they had met. She had him on his heels and it was glorious. Serves him right, for all of the lewd comments he's made to me regarding my relationship with Paige. At least she didn't have to throttle him against a wall like I did when I heard them.

"Ha, ha. The joke's on you, princess. Mommy and Daddy are here tonight so I get to stay out as late as I want."

"I can't wait to meet them!" Paige says, abandoning the playful tone as she scans the vestibule behind us looking for the elusive parents he spoke of. They will be arriving shortly, so she sees nothing and turns back to us.

"Good to see you, Paige," Payton says, taking his turn to hug my wife.

"Payton, looking wonderful as usual," Paige says, straightening his collar after she returns the hug. "No dates for either of you?" she asks my brothers, looking around their shoulders to see if any models are hiding behind them.

"Hater said we couldn't bring a plus one." Zander punches me in the shoulder a bit too hard to be playful.

I fight the urge to rub my shoulder. He's only telling half the truth. I actually told him if he brought one of his skanky one-night stands to my wedding I would bury him under the titan arum in this garden and no one would ever find him because the corpse flower stinks enough to cover up the smell of decomposition.

"That's a truly horrible nickname," Paige says, her eyebrows furrowing. "I guess that makes me glad I never had a sister to be mean to me like that."

"This is nothing. Hayes was the worst big brother. He was always so serious and mean," Zander complains, holding a hand up to his face and whispering behind it like he's sharing some big secret with her.

"I can imagine he kept you in line more than anything." Paige's smile is radiant, and I feel like a lucky sonofabitch to see that daily.

"Oh, he could be a downer, Zander's not wrong about that. But yeah, I think he meant well," Payton supplies.

"What's this about being a downer? Are we recounting tales of Hayes in his youth?"

I turn to see Mom and Dad entering the garden. Mom's dark hair is down, for once, and she has on a nice navy dress that reminds me of the few times she accompanied Dad to business dinners and galas when we were growing up. She isn't much for getting fancy, so those were few and far between. Dad is wearing a suit he's probably had for a decade despite being able to buy a new one for every day of the year, but it still looks sharp on him. The dark charcoal sets off his thick head of silver hair and twinkling green eyes, which are a little more hazel than my own. Mom's gray-blue eyes are focused on me with smile lines deepening around the edges. Both Payton and Zander got their eye coloring from her, though each favors opposite sides of the spectrum, with Zander being a stormy gray and Payton a vivid blue. We're all dark-headed and share enough of Dad's features that you couldn't miss that we're related when we're all in the same room, like right now.

"About time y'all showed up," I say, holding my hand out for Dad to shake, then turning to capture Mom in a hug. "I was going to send out a search party and see if Dad had insisted on driving after all. Good to see you."

"Hello, dear boy, nice to see you, too. Now, introduce me to your beautiful wife already," Mom says, dismissing me quickly and craning her neck around the garden in search of my bride.

I hold my arm out and Paige moves toward us. "Paige, this is my mother, Rula Mae, and my father, Thatcher. Mom and Dad, this is my wife, Paige."

"It's so wonderful to finally meet you both," Paige says, pulling them into a hug together. Mom's eyes widen in surprise, but she laughs and pats Paige on the back. Dad endures the hug, kissing Paige's head and showing more affection for a stranger than I may have seen from him in the last twenty years. That is certainly the effect Paige has on people, though.

"Honey, ain't Hayes feeding you? You're skinny as a bean pole but twice as pretty." Mom pinches Paige's upper arm between her thumb and forefinger, measuring her against some internal system that assumes I can't take care of the woman I love.

Paige smiles and looks over her shoulder at me. "I like her."

"Wait until she really starts in on you. If you think Zander is bad, you are in for quite a surprise, because that," I say, pointing at Mom, "is where he learned everything."

"Why, thank you, darling," Mom says, flipping the hair off her shoulder.

"Tell me, Paige, how did you manage to turn this one around so spectacularly in such a short time? I never thought he would settle down or let up at work enough to even entertain the idea. You must be something," Dad says, putting his arm protectively around Paige's shoulders and dropping his head toward hers while pointing at me.

"Oh, come on, you make it sound like I was a lost cause."

"You were," Mom says without inflection, causing everyone to laugh.

"I like to think that he was waiting for me," Paige says, sending me a look that reminds me of the heart-eye emojis she's taken to sending in texts. "Or maybe we were both in the right place at the right time, and it was just... fate."

"Now that everyone is here, we can begin the rehearsal," Caroline interrupts, clapping her hands in the air for our attention. "You three, get over there by the judge, and don't make me tell you twice." She gestures for me, Payton, and Zander to stand by the waterfall. "Take your parents with you, boys, you'll be ushering them in first before taking your spots."

"I wouldn't want to see her mad," Mom says under her breath, making Paige and I both laugh.

Zander takes her arm and leads her off to a chair, while Dad and Payton follow, heading toward Judge Whitaker, who will be our officiant, at Paige's request.

"Hayes, get going. Paige, come this way," Caroline continues, gesturing toward the vestibule where Paige will make her entrance and cross through the Elysium Garden to me.

"Ready?" Paige asks quietly, hugging my arm and looking up at me.

"Always." I let her go and watch as she walks through the garden.

I feel a shiver run down my spine in anticipation as I take my place. Despite already being married, and knowing none of this changes anything, I'm still feeling some kind of way about the ordeal, and it has me excited unlike anything else, except for Paige, of course.

The rehearsal goes well enough that Caroline only makes us repeat it twice before releasing us for dinner at a nearby restaurant. Despite seeing it several times, watching Paige walk through the garden gave me chills, and I can't wait to see her do it tomorrow.

After dinner, Paige pulls me into the coat room, feeling a little brazen thanks to a few glasses of wine, and I fuck her against the wall. I have to keep my hand over her mouth when she comes to keep us from being too obvious. The fast and dirty interlude seems to settle both of us, so when we emerge several minutes later, only slightly rumpled and looking no worse for wear, no one says a damn thing.

We say goodnight to both sets of parents and watch as the group dwindles to just my brothers, Alex, Paige, and me.

"Alex wants to go dancing," Paige says, wiping what is sure to be her red lipstick from my lips with her thumb. "Can we join you guys when you go back to The Abyss for a little while before I have to go home to Mama's?"

Fuck. I hate that Payton was right and Caroline is insisting that Paige can't stay with me tonight for some deluded reason. We're already married, so there is no reason we should be separated the night before our nuptials. I'm tempted to keep her with me despite what Hurricane Caroline may want just to get under her skin and show her how little control she has in the new life I have made with Paige.

"I think Zander has something planned there, so if you don't mind whatever he calls fun, we can do that." I pause, scrutinizing Paige. "Do you even like dancing?"

The first night I saw her, she was being presented to society at her debutante ball and had to do her share of dancing in a fluffy white dress, but I've never thought to ask her if she enjoyed that, or maybe something less formal.

Paige purses her lips and tilts her head at me. "I've only really danced for society events, which isn't club dancing, so I don't know. Would you care to teach me?"

"What makes you think I know how to dance?"

"The way you move over and with me in bed tells me you know a thing or two about it."

Damn.

"Is that a good thing?" I growl, pulling her close to me and swaying with her.

"It's a *very* good thing," she purrs, tracing her fingers along the skin on the back of my neck.

"Stop that right now, you two," Zander yells at us from the doorway of the restaurant. "I heard we're all partying, so let's fucking go! You can eye fuck each other all you want, and more, at The Abyss."

Paige laughs and pulls me after her as we head out into the street and walk back to my nightclub. The Savannah night is crisp and cool, with a fine mist in the air that creates halos around the streetlights lining the cobblestone streets. My fingers are laced with Paige's and I'm smiling more than I thought possible. My brothers and Alex sing some song I don't know, not nearly as terribly as they could because Alex can actually sing, holding a clear tenor to my boisterous brothers' meager baritones.

What awaits us at The Abyss is no shock given Zander's predilections. The doors are opened by women in white lingerie and angel wings, while shirtless men in half masks with devil horns breathe fire into the night around us.

"Come in, my king, we've been waiting for you," one of the angels says, beckoning me forward and handing me a jagged black crown that I take despite not wanting anything to do with it.

"What the fuck is this?" I turn to Zander and see his absolute joy at his little joke.

"One last night of raising hell, of course," he replies, taking a mask from a silver tray another angel holds out.

"Payton, he can't be serious." I turn the other direction looking for an ally, but Payton is slipping on his own mask and just smiles wickedly. The bastard was in on it, too.

"And for your lovely bride," Zander says, holding out a smaller black crown ringed in red roses to Paige. "I had a feeling she would end up here tonight, so I planned something you would both enjoy."

"That was very kind of you to include me," Paige says, settling the crown on her hair with a smile. She turns to me and takes the crown from my hands and places it on my head next. "There, now we match."

"We don't have to be here or do any of this. Zander is an asshole."

"It's okay. He just wants to do something nice for you."

"Zander doesn't do nice. He does insane and embarrassing, and I'll likely regret it."

She raises a shoulder in a shrug. "At least we can dance, right?"

I sigh in defeat and take her hand. If Paige wants to dance, who am I to deny her the simple pleasure? We follow my brothers and Alex into The Abyss and enter the strange carnival of debauchery that has descended on my classy nightclub. The stately black decor is lit up with garish red spotlights, hidden machines spewing a roiling carpet of gray fog along the floor around our feet. Women in white sprawl lazily along the balcony above, dropping red rose petals over our heads as we walk by a trio of leather-clad men strapped to St. Andrews crosses, with masked partners teasing them with feathers and leather lashes.

"You better not have turned this whole place into a sex dungeon," I growl at Zander, covering Paige's eyes with my hand. She pulls my hand off her eyes and goes back to covertly glancing at the closest couple utilizing a cross. At least they look quite happy with their arrangement.

"Nah, this is just a taste of the torment of hell. If anyone has sex tonight, it won't be because we created a free-for-all. But before you get to that part, libations fit for the king of the underworld." Zander takes a glass dome full of smoke off of a tray to reveal a tumbler of amber liquid inside. "We smoked that Underworld Spirits bourbon you like so much to make you feel right at home in the hot seat. It's all fire and brimstone, now."

I gratefully take the glass and sip, tasting the variation in my drink of choice from the smoke. Paige reaches for the glass and I let her take it, watching in fascination as she sniffs the cup and takes a delicate sip, rolling the liquor on her tongue before swallowing.

"I'm going to borrow that trick and take it to our next staff meeting," she says, swirling the bourbon in the glass. "See, this night is already proving fruitful."

"You can call it the Zander edition, dear Paige, and I won't make you cut me in on the profits. Happy wedding." Zander salutes her and continues walking us into the belly of the club.

"Lucky me," Paige says and leans into my shoulder with a grin.

Heavy synthesized beats boom out of the speakers coming from the doors to the ballroom, the heart of the club, where we can see snatches of masked revelers who writhe and dance under the strobe lights and lasers. This whole thing feels like Ibiza and Dante's Inferno got together for one fucked up night and created a monster of lust and torment.

"Your den of iniquity awaits," Payton says over his shoulder, pulling open the doors all the way and throwing an arm into the air. A spotlight snaps onto us, and a roar goes up from the crowd inside.

I put a hand up to block the light from my eyes and feel Paige duck her face into my shoulder. "Cut it out, you asshole," I bark at Payton.

A moment later the spotlight moves away, but it takes a few more seconds for my eyes to adjust. When they do, I see chunks of thick marble columns topped with stripper poles placed throughout the dancefloor at varying heights with burlesque dancers perched on them, feathers and fringe decorating their bodies as they undulate.

"There he is!" I turn toward the voice and catch Diego lifting his eye mask to his head, with two familiar men trailing behind him. "This is some party."

I shake my head in annoyance. It's a spectacle. I step to the side so Paige can meet the guys. "Paige, this is Diego, Javier, and Luca," I say, indicating each. "They make up the senior vice presidents of their respective divisions at Olympus. Gentlemen, this is my beautiful wife, Paige."

They each shake her hand in turn, leaning close to say their pleasantries over the music.

"Now that introductions are over, you have a job to do tonight, both of you," Zander says, coming up behind me and Paige and clapping his hands on our shoulders. He forces us into the ballroom and over to a raised dais with an antique black velvet settee he moved in here from the lounge. "The best is yet to begin."

Twenty-Eight

Paige

We're judging a contest. A very wicked, very sexy contest.

Zander managed to find every appealing contortionist, dancer, and sleight-of-hand trickster this side of the Mississippi for his impromptu talent competition, and it is up to Hayes and me to decide if the performers pass muster. *I think.*

The contest began with groups of people performing all at once, and in lulls of the music, Zander holds his hands over various heads and we must provide our judgment via a thumbs up or down, Roman Emperor style. Now, we are down to a pair of dancers in leather straps and bits of cloth covering their private parts who move like water together, and a group of dancers in devil masks who break dance in a fashion that looks like they don't have the limitation of joints or bones.

I'm quite amused by the whole thing, and as long as I'm having a good time, Hayes seems to be content to go along with his brother's schemes.

"Who wins this round?" Zander hollers at us from the dancefloor, his hands over the two groups of dancers, chests heaving and waiting on us to crown a victor.

I look at Hayes, who gives me an indulgent smile. "I don't think I can pick just one. Can't we say they both win?"

"You can make anything you want happen, angel."

I smile and hold out my arm, thumb cocked sideways and wait for Hayes to join me. I nod and we flip our thumbs up.

"They both win," I shout at Zander, rising from my perch on Hayes's lap to make myself heard. I stand and clap along with the roaring spectators as both groups take a bow and dance away into the crowd. I spot Alex off in a group, having found people to dance with while I judge, and I smile. He's always been good at finding friends, whereas I haven't. But I do have Hayes.

"Ready to dance now?" Hayes asks, standing behind me and pulling my behind back into his hips, grinding into me.

"Maybe not up here where we're kind of on display, I'll make a fool of myself," I say, feeling self-conscious as the crowd looks on.

Hayes spins me in his arms, pulling me close to his chest as he drags his hand down my side and hitches my leg up to his hip in one fluid movement, the clingy skirt of my dress rising up my thighs. I gasp as he dips me backward and I throw up a hand to keep the crown from falling off my head. But Hayes isn't done, much to the delight of the crowd around us who are catcalling and whistling as he guides my body around and back up to finish tight to his.

"Never let what anyone else thinks stop you from having the time of your life."

"Easier said than done," I say, my voice breathy with relief and a little thrilled by his maneuver. "See, I knew you could dance."

His chuckle vibrates in the space between our chests.

The strobe lights and lasers flash with the return of the throbbing dance music, casting the dancefloor back into the maddened crush of bodies once more. Hayes steps off the dais and helps me down with a steady hand until I'm pressed tight against him again. In his crown made of jagged stones and his all-black suit, he truly looks like the king of the underworld. It's easy to get caught up in the dramatics of this party Zander pulled together, which is a fascinating combination of a bachelor party and a debauched festival.

I can't keep my eyes off the bodies that twine together, moving seamlessly and with unfettered passion both on the dancefloor and seen in glimpses in the alcoves that ring the ballroom, and I can't help thinking about the crosses we passed on our way through the club. There were looks of pure joy from the people strapped spread eagle to the wood timbers being teased with leather lashes by their partners. I don't know where anyone gets that kind of exhibitionism, but I admired their bravery and commitment to Zander's vision. And I liked watching it. Hayes may be right; I might just have some voyeuristic tendencies after all.

Hayes walks us through the mass of people on the dancefloor to the edge of the crowd, and out of the ballroom where the music isn't quite so loud. He leads me to the bar and gets another tumbler of bourbon, allowing me to sip it first, wiping the pad of his thumb across my bottom lip and following it with his mouth a moment later. His kiss holds an urgency I didn't expect, and I get a feeling he's as affected by this night as I am. I press up on my toes, letting my body slide along his as I meet the urgency.

A throat clearing next to my shoulder breaks our connection, our lips lingering for a moment before I break off from the kiss. I pull away and gasp when I find a face that has haunted me for the last few weeks. It's Hayes's old friend, Octavius Rex, leaning back against the bar and observing the floor at his feet while twirling a black mask between his hands.

He still gives me the creeps despite knowing he was following me because of my connection to Hayes. I don't think he wants to hurt me—he had several opportunities to do so if that were the case—but he has a knack for turning up when I'm alone and freaking me out. Seeing him here tonight doesn't feel safe, even when I'm still in the protective cocoon of Hayes's arms. When he confronted us after the Christmas Eve dinner, I had a feeling he wanted something from Hayes, so that is where I think his actual focus is, rather than on me specifically.

"What do you want, Rex?" Hayes asks, shifting me over so he stands between us. Gone is the playful tone, or the heat of moments before. Now he's all business and protective posturing.

"Relax, I come with only good intentions." Octavius turns and sets the mask on the bar. "Get your brothers. We need to talk."

"Not the time. Not the place," Hayes growls.

"I think it is. You're being played right this moment, and if you don't act immediately, you're going to be facing another industrial *accident* that's sure to bring Olympus down. Ready to take me seriously, yet?" His tone is harsher than he used before, and he's not employing the easy-going affectation any longer. He means business and wants Hayes's attention right now.

I look between these former friends turned bitter rivals and wonder what they could be talking about. How would Octavius know anything about some potential industrial accident that could hurt Olympus? Does this have anything to do with the South African mining accident? I have so many questions, but Hayes is too intent on staring daggers at Octavius for me to expect answers.

"Fuck," Hayes exhales in a harsh whisper, looking down at the bar where he twists his tumbler of bourbon. He faces me. "Do you want to go up to the flat while we handle this?" His question is gentle, providing me a release from whatever is about to go down with Octavius. My curiosity is piqued, though, and if there is an option to finally get to the bottom of why Octavius has been following us and wanting back into Hayes's life, I would like to take it.

I shake my head. "I'd rather stay with you unless you don't want me to be a part of this discussion."

Hayes looks torn, his obvious instinct to keep me far away from Octavius and anything to do with Olympus is warring with his desire to keep me close and give me anything I ask. Finally, he nods tightly. "Let's get Zander and Payton."

The three of us move back to the crowded ballroom, scanning the area for the elusive brothers. It doesn't take long to find them, though, as they are heading our way, heads bent together.

"A little angel told me we had a visitor that wasn't on the guestlist," Zander says when they get to us. He lifts his eye mask off his face and pockets it. "Bribing the doorman gets you in, but not for long." He aims that last sentence at Octavius.

"We need to go upstairs, now." Hayes's words are final, leaving no room to argue. Both Zander and Payton look at Hayes for a moment, then nod. He keeps me tucked against his side as we make our way back to the lobby and the elevator vestibule. Hayes uses his keycard to call the private car and take us up to the third floor where his office is situated.

"You've been busy these last few years. What brings you to our little slice of hell tonight?" Payton asks Octavius amiably as the elevator ascends. He removes his mask, but his face is carefully neutral, while his cerulean eyes remain shrewd.

"Saving your asses, it would seem."

"Oh, this is going to be good. What can you possibly do that would be considered saving our asses?" Zander asks with an air of dismissal.

Before Octavius can answer, the elevator stops, doors opening on the hallway that leads to Hayes's flat and office. We file out of the elevator and Hayes opens the office door, letting us into the spacious room with large windows showing off the Savannah skyline. I stare at the desk where just a few days ago, Hayes had me bent over the top and was asking to have my behind for the first time. My cheeks grow warm, and I look away, settling myself in a corner of the tufted Chesterfield sofa to be out of the way. Hayes sits next to me, his hand resting heavily on my thigh, his thumb brushing over my skin absently. Payton takes the chair by the desk, and Zander leans against the opposite end of the sofa.

Octavius takes the remaining chair in front of the desk, his face hard. "The South African mine was sabotaged. It wasn't an accident at all, and you boys took the blame for it because someone has it out for you. Round two is about to happen and I'm allowing you to make sure it doesn't go down like that again." He cuts to the chase without preamble and I am left shocked by what he says.

"More like you're behind the collapse and playing us," Zander accuses. "We know you've had it out for Olympus since we bought Rex, Inc.; it's no surprise you would stoop low enough to put innocent people in danger."

My eyes grow wide, and I swallow the gasp that wants to make its way out. Could Octavius Rex have really orchestrated the mine collapse? Would he have enough of a vendetta against the Olsens to not care about the resulting casualties? I grip Hayes's arm and hope it's not true for many reasons, but mainly for the loss of life that the collapse caused.

"Why the fuck would I be here now, telling you about the potential devastation of your holdings if I was behind it in the first place? You're not that big of a player in my long game, Zander, no matter how highly you think of yourself."

"What's in it for you? What do you want in exchange for this supposed warning?" Payton asks, lounging back in his chair. "You haven't given us anything concrete to go on other than some doom and gloom accusations and rumors."

"He wants a seat on the board at Olympus," Hayes says from my side, and my eyes snap up to his face, which is deadly.

"You can't be serious," Zander says with a laugh.

"You couldn't possibly expect that we would grant you that kind of access and control with what you've said so far," Payton says, his tone more diplomatic than Zander's outright humor over the situation.

"I have everything you need to make sure what's already set in motion doesn't happen and you can hold the responsible party accountable for what has already taken place."

"Despite wanting to use your likely ill-gotten information to prevent another casualty and secure yourself a position of influence, why tell us anything at all? Why not just let it play out and watch us suffer, since we probably deserve it in your eyes?" Hayes asks, voice low.

Is that what Hayes would do if he were on the other side of the situation? He *is* ruthless, but I would hate to imagine he would let others unduly suffer.

"Not even I would want to see the devastation that is set to happen just because I don't like that you took something from me. I can see past my own personal feelings. After all, it's just business."

Zander scoffs and Payton leans forward, forearms on his knees, eying Octavius speculatively.

"So why don't you blow the whistle on whatever is happening yourself?" I ask, unable to hold back my curiosity. "Why bring it to Olympus first when you could just as easily play the hero?"

Octavius slides his gaze my way and Hayes's hand tenses on my thigh.

"That would likely get me killed, sweet Paige, and I value my life a little too highly to play that game."

"Doesn't being anywhere near us, and telling us this information now put you at the same risk?" Hayes asks, understanding something I don't yet see.

"Yes and no," Octavius says tilting his head back and forth. "Because of our former friendship, I was tasked with keeping an eye on you and letting my partners know if you were following the breadcrumbs they left or if you were getting too close to the actual source. That gossip site has been quite helpful in supporting my reports that you are far too caught up in your own lives to have any inkling of what's really going on, despite what I've told you already."

"So, you're a double agent in some weird corporate espionage scenario? What is this, a B-list movie plot you've come up with?" Zander asks. Despite the mocking tone and the derisive smile, he appears far from jovial.

Octavius glowers at Zander. "You've made a lot of enemies in the years since you took over Olympus. I'm not the only one you fucked out of a legacy or ruined with your quest to diversify and take over everything you can. Who do you think I partnered with over the last few years to raise Rex Omnia from the ashes of my father's company? There are plenty of powerful people wanting a chance to take you down."

"That's a fair assessment, and our own data supports his claims," Payton agrees. "We've made enemies in our quest for industry domination, so who is it that has their hand in this particular revenge plot?"

"I need your assurance that the information I give you will never lead back to me. I'm putting myself at considerable risk to save your asses, and I expect to get this favor repaid in kind as soon as the dust settles."

The silence that stretches out after his request grows heavy. The brothers look at one another, communicating silently. I've never seen them this serious, and this in sync.

Hayes turns to Octavius, his green eyes so dark they look black. "There will be many conditions on any sort of repayment you ask for. Nothing is set in stone, but you have our word we won't let you risk everything for nothing."

Octavius glowers back but nods. "Fine. Do Donner Investments, Kilowen Industries, and Gage Geological ring any bells?"

"Venture capital, industrial production, and precious metals mining," Payton says without missing a beat. "We bought them out, what, three or four years ago?"

"What's special about those companies?" Zander muses. "We've operated in that exact capacity on many more investments than those three."

"We obliterated them," Hayes replies. "We didn't keep much from the sale. Maybe the technology or the infrastructure, but pretty much everything was melted down for scrap once we got what we wanted."

"Bingo. And they were all family companies. You fucked them over and they aren't as forgiving as your lovely wife seems to be," Octavius says, nodding at me.

"Don't talk about my wife in any capacity, Rex," Hayes growls. I risk a quick glance up at his face and catch the steely look he levels at Octavius.

"Fine, fine. Touchy subject, much?"

"Careful, Hayes doesn't need much incentive to throttle you when you bring up his wife. I know that for a fact." Zander rubs his neck. I look at Hayes again and the grim set of his mouth confirms that he likely did as Zander says. He really is that protective of me.

"Get to the point of all this drama, Rex. You said it was time-sensitive and dire that we deal with this tonight. You're drawing this out and I'm starting to think you're just wasting our time when we have better things to do." Hayes leans back against the couch and drapes an arm over my shoulder, drawing me against him. "We're supposed to have a wedding tomorrow and the last thing I want is to spend the night before in this office talking about business."

"They want to act tomorrow, so they can pin another accident on you when it will be common knowledge that everyone was focused on the wedding and not on the safety and security of another mine." Octavius leans forward, his words coming out in a rush. "It would be more bad press and put you under a microscope more so than you have been."

"And what is this big plan of theirs?" Zander asks, toying with the mask he's pulled out of his pocket.

"They've targeted your mines here in Georgia."

Everything stops all at once. Hands still, backs go straight, and breath is held as we collectively realize the scope of what this shadowy plan could mean.

"This isn't a new mine we've acquired across the world without the due diligence needed. He's talking about the mining operations that Olympus was founded on, right here in our home state. The industry our father built for himself and nurtured until we took over. These are federally regulated mines, with highly paid American workers operating them at the top of the standard for anything we do. An accident would look very bad indeed. If they're able to make this look like an accident, and plant evidence of our negligence, we could go down for good," Hayes says, his arm heavy across my shoulders.

My eyes bounce between the brothers and Octavius. This sounds incredibly bad.

"That's not possible," Payton says slowly, his brows furrowed as his mind races through all of the data. "We have every inspection documented since the beginning. We don't cut corners. There's no way this could happen right here."

"They've been infiltrating the operation for months. Plenty of people who run your mines are on two payrolls, and they've made all the documentation necessary to make you look like punk ass bitches."

"Fuck you, Tavi," Hayes says, the nickname slipping out as easily as the curse, it seems.

Octavius looks up at Hayes then, and I see a moment pass between them that hints at their former friendship before Hayes chose to ruin things.

"How do we stop whatever this is from happening?" Zander asks, looking between them.

"You said you had everything we needed to prevent this and hold them accountable. How do you expect us to root out every rat that's been funneled into place over several months in the span of one night?" Hayes asks.

I feel the enormity of the situation settle on his shoulders and wish I could remove it. That's a burden no one needs to carry alone.

Octavius reaches into his suit pocket and pulls out a thumb drive, looking at it for a moment before holding it out to Payton, who is closest to him.

"I have every email, text, recorded phone conversation, and in-person meeting saved on that. I also have details of the explicit plan of attack and how it was orchestrated to look like an accident but could be peeled back to reveal all the ways you were negligent with the slightest digging. It's all there, and I know who you can take it to who will actually act on it without four years of investigations needed."

"How did you get all of that? Were you in on it from the beginning?" Zander asks, his gray eyes looking steely and accusing, the set of his mouth hard.

"I was brought in after the mine collapse in South Africa. I was just a partner on some other investments and projects, but they wanted me to get close to you. I didn't know what was happening before that, but they gave me access to the information. I needed some context for what was going on, and they were very accommodating. I would never have gone along with what they did, no matter my feelings."

Payton stands from his chair and rounds Hayes's desk, pulling out a laptop and plugging in the thumb drive. "This better not be some elaborate way to infect our network with a virus," he grumbles. He taps the keyboard a few times, his hands deftly moving through commands and pulling up documents from the drive while his face is bathed in the light from the laptop screen. "There's enough information on here to take the four years you estimated to go through it all. Shit."

"Won't you be implicated in this right along with your partners?" I ask, worry lacing my words.

"I have plans in place for that inevitability, but I have to go down with the orchestrators or it will look like I was the leak all along. Even if the main conspirators go down, it doesn't mean I would be safe with that target on my back. It's a necessary means to an end and gets me out of this fucked up partnership." There is relief laced in his words, and his willingness to both come clean to avoid this catastrophe and go down with those who put this plot together feels very truthful.

"And that's where we come in for you, is it?" Hayes says. "You want to secure your future before you get raided by the FBI and your career options become extremely limited."

"The best thing you can do is plan for every possibility, right? Why stay shortsighted when I can take my future in hand now?"

"You're complicit to the atrocity that already took place in South Africa. Why stop now when you could see us taken down for good?" Hayes asks, removing his arm from my shoulders and leaning forward.

"I never wanted anyone to get hurt." Octavius leans back into the chair and scrubs his hands across his face. "I'll do anything to make sure they don't get to repeat the loss of life and destruction, including letting you assholes know about it with enough time to step in and keep it from happening, even if it means I'll be dragged down with them."

"What exactly is planned for tomorrow at the Georgia mines? Are they going to blow something up, or is it more insidious than that?" Zander asks, not bothering to address Octavius's comments.

"There will be a few steps skipped in the safety processes, a few charges left in opportune places, and a coordinated attack to shut down the systems in place at the mines. It would be complete devastation if they were successful, both in shutting down your operations here stateside and in drawing a big spotlight onto every operation you hold the world over. Two industrial accidents in the span of a few weeks isn't a coincidence."

"He's actually downplaying the scope of what is really planned," Payton says absently from the desk. He's scrolling furiously, the light of the screen playing across his face in waves as his eyes skate back and forth taking in the details. "There are several layers of plans if this one fails to bring about the outcome they want, each escalating in severity."

"And all they have to do is turn over that information to the right authorities and it will be stopped before anyone can get hurt?" I ask, my hands clenched around Hayes's arm. The last thing I want is for them to act too slowly and see innocent people hurt. Again.

"You probably want to send some trusted people to the operations as soon as you can to make sure every last interloper is removed and do a top-to-bottom systems check to ensure nothing was left behind as a sneaky surprise. The planted workers came from Gage Geological and were unceremoniously let go when you acquired the company, so there were plenty of hard feelings toward you that didn't need to be coaxed out. There should be an exhaustive list of every person that was placed at one of your holdings."

"Found that and already emailed it to the right people at headquarters to have their access cut off and start the removal process tonight," Payton says.

I look out the window at the black night dotted with city lights. It's nearly midnight and they have more than their share of work to do before sunrise to ensure whatever is planned can be stopped. I'm exhausted, but I don't want to leave Hayes's side. The mere thought causes me to yawn, which I try to hide by covering my mouth.

"Let's get you to bed, angel," Hayes says quietly. "You have a full day ahead of you and don't have to sit through this mess."

"I don't want to go home, or to Mama's," I whisper back, while Payton tells Zander more of what he's finding on the thumb drive.

"We'll sleep here tonight. I don't want you too far away, either."

"I'm so sorry this is happening."

"You don't have anything to apologize for, it's me who should be begging you to forgive me for putting business before you tonight. I'm sorry, angel."

I shake my head. "Don't be. There's no way you could have anticipated this. And some things just need your attention right then and there, no matter what else you have going on."

Despite the stress of the situation, he manages to smile for me now. "Let's get you to bed."

Twenty-Nine

Hayes

I t took all night, but we managed to use Rex's information to stop another accident.

Now we wait to see if there are any surprises he didn't know about that could still fuck us over. We shut down the mines, pulled all personnel, and created a buffer zone just to be on the safe side. Zander and Payton brought in the SVPs while I was making sure Paige was comfortable, and then we went to work. We contacted the FBI and the police in the areas where our mines are located, shared all we knew, and pulled every trusted Olympus employee out of bed in the middle of the night to work on our own housekeeping. We'll be dealing with this situation for a long time but having the ball rolling to ensure we don't have rats within our organization, chewing holes in our holdings and making trouble, is a good start.

Payton and Zander only left a few minutes ago. Now, as I watch through the windows at the top of my club as the city comes to life in the cold sunshine of a new winter day, I'm exhausted yet exhilarated. Knowing a tragedy was stopped goes a long way in getting you through a sleepless night. If only that same adrenaline could propel me through the force that is at work thanks to Hurricane Caroline, I'd be much obliged.

"You look like you need a shower and about eight cups of coffee." I turn toward the feminine voice full of sharpness at the entrance to the garden.

"Good morning to you, too, Caroline." The acerbic note in my voice should be routine for her by now.

"Where is my daughter? You kept her out all night on purpose because I said you shouldn't see each other and now I'm going to have to invest in every spa service The Mansion offers to get her looking her best for the wedding."

"Paige is still sleeping in our flat. I made sure she went to bed at a reasonable hour, even if I didn't."

"You still defied my requests," she grumbles, stalking closer and holding out a paper cup of coffee.

It must be a peace offering since she's never willingly done anything remotely nice for me before. I take it anyway, hoping it means she's playing nice today.

"What all happened here last night? The cleaning crew downstairs looks haggard and there are feathers everywhere. It better all be set back to rights before the ceremony. I don't want our guests having to traipse through a filthy club just to get up here. Why Paige had to insist on a ceremony here is a mystery," she finishes under her breath, looking around the Elysium Garden.

I take a sip of the coffee and realize just how badly I need it after a night of adrenaline and bourbon. "I'm sure it will be fine. My brothers may have let things get a bit crazy here last night, but they take things seriously when needed."

If all she saw were feathers, it means the crew has removed the most offensive of the decorations and ac-couterments that transformed the club below into a racy hellscape. Who knows what kind of mood she would be in now if she had seen the St. Andrews crosses and the lingerie everywhere.

Caroline turns and levels a glare at me that makes me choke on my sip of coffee. Maybe she did see the crosses after all. This must be where the coffee peace offering ends and she returns to hating me.

"Why did you single her out, really?" she asks, her tone accusing. "I'm sure you could have found any other girl out there to seduce but you picked my little girl. Why?"

"I didn't single her out, I can promise you that." As for seducing her, well, that was an inevitability that both of us wanted to see happen, but I won't address it with Caroline.

"You couldn't just settle with taking our hotels. You had to be greedy and set your sights on taking our daughter away, too."

"I assure you, I had no plans for your daughter before we met. When she asked for my help, I figured I could do that much. I didn't expect to fall in love with her and have my entire world changed. Now, I can't imagine my life any other way. Paige is the best part of it."

"I don't believe you. You're too calculating. You probably factored in what it would cost us to lose her right along with our business so you could inflict the most damage. That's the kind of devil you are."

She's right about me, I am calculating, and I do take into consideration every available opportunity that could turn a situation in my favor, but she's all wrong about this one. Before I can reply, a voice cuts in.

"Mama, please stop."

We both turn at Paige's pleading tone. She's standing barefoot on the path leading from the hidden door, wearing one of my button-down white shirts that falls to her thighs, hands fisted in the overlong sleeves and clutched at her chest. Her hair is sleep-mussed, but she looks stunning. Any other morning seeing her like this would lead to very bad things, but I'm dealing with a furious mother-in-law who insists on fighting me every chance she gets. I would much prefer the first option.

"Young lady, you have defied me once again. You should have come home at a decent time last night," Caroline says, sounding defensive while trying to spin the narrative.

Paige sighs and walks the last few steps to us. "I get to call the shots for my own life, Mama, even if you don't agree with them. I wanted to stay with my *husband* last night, so I did."

"Well, we're running late. Go get dressed so we can get back on schedule."

Paige reaches out and catches Caroline's shoulder as she whirls to leave, keeping her in place. "Before you go, we need to settle this once and for all."

She lets her mother's arm go and laces her fingers in mine, giving me a small smile that radiates strength before turning back to Caroline.

I can feel the slight tremor in her hand that belies her confidence and tells me she's quite worried about this bit of confrontation. I squeeze her hand in reassurance.

"I was the one who went after Hayes. I asked him to take me away from Savannah because I was running from *your* plans for my life." She gives her mother a pointed look before she continues. "He didn't abduct me or take me away from you in any way. In fact, I was probably the one with the bad intentions rather than the other way around, so if you want to stay mad at either of us, it should be me."

Caroline shakes her head, her face pinched. "He forced you to marry him when you barely knew each other. That was most definitely him taking advantage of your naivety and I can't stand it. He's a monster."

"That's completely untrue. Hayes is wonderful and I married him of my own free will because I wanted to. I will choose Hayes, today, and every day ahead. You won't be able to cajole me into denouncing him, and I won't stand for your mean remarks about him or our relationship going forward. So either get on board or hold your peace if you can't."

Caroline gasps and takes a step back as if Paige has slapped her.

I would understand if Paige had told her to shut up about it, but she was much kinder than I would have been, and it didn't warrant that in response.

"Now, let's put this all behind us and focus on the day at hand. We're getting married again today, thanks to *your* insistence. Give me a few minutes and I'll go shower and change so we can get started. I'll meet you in the lobby."

Caroline looks taken aback, her mouth opening and closing like a fish out of water, which is exactly what she is, having seen Paige stand up for herself and drive the conversation as well as issue the commands.

I'm so fucking proud of her and the work she's done to take less shit from her mother.

Finally, Caroline closes her mouth into a tight-lipped smile, fighting for composure.

"Very well. If that's how this is going to be, so be it. I'll be downstairs." She spins on her heel and stalks out of the garden. When the elevator doors have closed, I turn to Paige and stare in wonder.

"That was hot."

She blushes prettily and ducks her head.

"Seriously. I want to march you right back into the flat and fuck you while you tell me what to do next."

Paige looks around the garden, finally looking up at me from under her eyelashes and giving me a demure smile. "What's wrong with fucking me right here, Sir?"

Fuck. The combination of her innate innocence with the dirty word and adding on a *Sir* for good measure? It's my undoing. I don't have it in me to hold back and be civil. I drop to my knees in front of her, my big hands gripping her thighs right where the shirt ends.

"Not one fucking thing, angel. Spread your legs for me so I can taste that sweet pussy." I love it when she swears, and I love that she's not wearing any panties when she widens her stance to give me access.

I grab handfuls of her ass and pull her against my mouth, tasting her sweet-tart tang, and feel my cock grow uncomfortably hard in my pants. It's not a position I can fully explore, so I hook one of her legs over my shoulder to spread her wider. She holds onto my shoulders for balance, her fingers brushing my nape and digging in as I get to work. I lick and suck at her center, teasing her clit and taking in as much of her as I can. Her juices are coating my chin already and I want more. Her fingers slide into my hair, nails gently scratching my scalp and keeping me right where I want to be.

"Oh, Hayes... that's just... wow," she says, voice breathy. Her legs are already starting to tremble against my shoulders.

I plunge two fingers into her slick heat and feel her body tighten around me.

"Just like that," she gasps as I beckon against her.

I roll my tongue around her clit and press harder against her interior walls until she comes apart in my hands.

"Hayes," she hisses, her fingers clenching in my hair as she comes, her pussy tightening on my fingers over and over.

I slide my fingers out of her delicious pussy with a feeling of regret, but it's quickly replaced by my eagerness to fuck her properly. I stare hard at her as I put the fingers that were just inside of her into my mouth and suck them clean of her juices.

She maintains eye contact, but her lashes flutter and she lets out a moan that has me desperate to be deep inside of her again.

I stand, lifting her into my arms and carrying her back to the rock wall that borders the waterfall. I set her down long enough to push my pants and boxers down to free my cock, then I'm lifting her up my body and directing the head into her hot center with a groan. She wraps her legs around my hips and I pin her to the wall with my forceful thrusts.

We're a tangle of limbs and noises, and I kiss her lips as I fuck her hard so she'll know I love her even if it doesn't feel that way with my rough actions. It's a punishing rhythm, and she's jostled into the wall with each hard thrust.

She bites my lip and tugs once before releasing and leaning her head back with a moan. I take the access she provides and nibble along her jaw, my tongue and lips kissing down her neck until I can bite the spot where her neck and shoulder meet.

"Hayes," she hisses my name again.

"Come for me, angel, I want to hear you scream," I demand, feeling my own release on the horizon and needing her to explode around me.

"So close," she pants, her eyes closed tightly, her arms bracing around my shoulders as her nails dig into my back.

I roll my hips into her body, changing my angle of entry and grazing her clit with each rough thrust. Her eyes fly open and a moment later she is gasping, her body clenching and trembling in my arms and she cries out. As her core spasms, I fight my own release for several hard thrusts, my head dropping next to hers against the wall as I pump raggedly into her tightening pussy. Her name is a roar from my lips as I come with her.

I hold her to me tightly as our ragged breathing slows. When I finally set her on her feet, we're both a mess. I can feel the sharp sting along my back where her nails scratched, my pants are at my ankles, and I'm entirely fucking lost to my amazing wife. She looks fucked hard, her hair a tangle of snarls around her face, the white shirt she's wearing missing buttons and falling off her shoulders, and my cum dripping down her thighs. It's fucking perfect.

"We just desecrated our ceremony spot." Her voice is a low whisper but there is humor underlying the serious words.

"That just makes it better. This garden is made for sin." I kiss her hair and tuck a stray strand behind her ear.

"That can't be true. It's such a beautiful place."

"I wanted to fuck you like that the first time you entered this garden," I admit, dipping my head into her neck and breathing the words against her skin. "I thought of your red lipstick leaving a print around my cock, too. I was already imagining all the ways I could corrupt you, even then."

The blush that blooms across her cheeks is gorgeous, and I kiss her face on each pink spot. I pull back and turn her toward the door.

"You told your mom you only needed a few minutes and I'm pretty sure we've already surpassed that. Time to get you dressed and send you back to her."

Paige pouts her kiss-reddened lips but obliges, pulling the door open and heading down the hall to the flat.

"Will you at least shower with me, first?" she calls over her shoulder at me.

I follow her through the door, my long strides quickly overtaking hers.

"As you wish."

I scoop her up into my arms and enter the flat, dead set on making sure she's squeaky clean and ready for her wedding day. And I might as well throw in a little more fucking while I'm at it.

Thirty

The Atlanta Haute List

Billionaires Bring Hell To Sleepy Savannah

My, my, my. Our favorite billionaire brothers sure know how to throw a party that raises hell! In a fête fit for the king of the underworld himself, The Abyss Nightclub became a den of iniquity for the evening. Revelers were treated to sexy mischief, lingerie-clad angels, fire-breathing devils, burlesque performances, and a dance-off judged by none other than Hayes Olsen and his radiant queen, Paige Fairchild, both sporting black crowns for the evening and looking regal as hell.

It seems Payton and Zander had a few tricks up their sleeve to surprise big brother Hayes the night before his reported second wedding ceremony we have been led to expect will take place on New Year's Eve. Partygoers were treated to every last sin and vice they could imagine for a decadent night of indulgence and fun. It is reported that the king and queen of the underworld were only present for a portion of the evening, though. We wouldn't be surprised if they had their own celebrating to indulge in after witnessing all of the delights that hell can supply.

Notably, all three brothers slipped away mid-way through the night, leaving the club a free-for-all to the delight of hedonists in attendance. The photos that were sent in are five chili peppers spicy and we're here for it!

What could have torn the brothers away from the hellish pleasures so soon? Our haute tip line has a few suggestions that we are looking into now, and it's all work and no play, unfortunately.

It looks like Olympus International was at the center of a corporate sabotage plot and narrowly avoided another industrial accident at the thirteenth hour. Our Hautie informants even claim that Olympus International's previous industrial troubles may have also been the work of interlopers dead set on bringing down our favorite billionaire brothers.

We won't stand for that nonsense! The tip line is open and we're intent on clearing the Olsen name for good. Send us your theories, tips, and stories, and we'll start digging. Hit Like and Subscribe for all the haute gossip!

Thirty-One

Hayes

The waterfall is bubbling gently next to me, blending with the sounds of the string quartet set up near the pomegranate tree Paige loves, and I'm shifting from foot to foot like I'm nervous.

Because I fucking am.

Chairs are scattered throughout the garden between paths and plants, each one wreathed in flowers and filled with a family member or friend who made the merciless cuts to the guestlist as someone we absolutely wouldn't want to miss out on having at this ceremony. That said, it's a small crowd. Even Cerberus is here, patiently sitting at my side wearing a bow tie around his massive neck and looking so proud of himself. The only one missing is my beautiful wife, and I know I'll be put out of my misery of waiting up here with all eyes on me in mere moments.

The quartet finishes one song and there is a lull in the music before they start on Paige's ceremony song next. She picked a Taylor Swift song, making me listen to it on repeat for a few days to make sure I liked it, too. I pretended indifference, but Taylor's a true musician and I ended up liking it. I can hear the words to *Wildest Dreams* in my head as the quartet plays and have to keep myself from mouthing along. *This* is the influence Paige has on me. I'm a fucking bona fide Swiftie now.

Movement on the path from the elevator vestibule draws the crowd's attention, and everyone rises as Paige appears on the arm of her father. He is whispering to her and she smiles, beaming up at him as they begin their slow procession through the plants and flowers of the garden.

I swallow the thick lump in my throat as I take her in, once again in a white gown, glowing against the greenery and sunset-streaked sky seen through the lightly fogged windows as she comes toward me. Her dress is fitted, clinging to her shapely body and flaring out at her thighs, made of some soft-looking lace material that trails behind her. The straps are off the shoulder and as she gets closer, I can see they are made to look like vines and leaves. The neckline is low, rounding over the tops of her breasts in a way that is so fucking sexy, yet still manages to be modest, and I fall in love with her all over again.

As my eyes trail up her body, I'm struck dumb when I see her face, a soft smile on her red lips and her bright jade eyes fixed on me. I feel my own mouth raising into a smile as our eyes meet and wipe away the hint of moisture in the corner of my eye. It must be the damn humidity in this greenhouse or something.

When Paige and William make it to the edge of the waterfall's pool we've deemed our altar, they stop and turn to me as the music slowly ends.

"Who gives this woman to be with this man?" Judge Whitaker asks in his genteel voice that booms through the now silent garden.

"Her mother and I do," William responds, taking Paige's hand from his arm and placing it in mine. He turns and takes a seat next to Caroline, who is barely composed, her cheeks already streaked with tears. She's probably regretting ever pushing for this second wedding, or maybe she's wishing she had never insisted on Paige having a debutante party that ended up being here at The Abyss which allowed us to meet in the first place.

No matter what she wishes, I am grateful for this opportunity to marry my beautiful bride again. I turn my attention back to Paige.

Hi, she mouths at me.

I love you, I mouth back.

The ceremony becomes a blur as we listen to the Judge talk about the covenant of marriage and the seriousness of love. Soon enough, he's asking if we will honor and cherish one another, in sickness and in health, in poverty and in wealth, and to be true to each other in all things until death alone shall part us. We both take turns repeating after him with little difficulty. I would promise Paige so much more in this life and into the afterlife as well.

My attention returns when he asks for the rings and it's time for the vows. Paige and I decided to write our own, since we had already read the traditional vows at our Las Vegas elopement, and if we are getting a second chance to do it, we are going to make it personal to our relationship.

"You'll be needing these," Payton says over my shoulder, handing me a black velvet ring box that holds Paige's delicate diamond wedding band and her engagement ring. He smiles and shakes my hand, proud to have this important role in our second wedding. I take the rings and stack them on the end of my pinky for safekeeping before handing the box back to Payton.

I look back and see Paige repeating the actions, taking my thick gold band from Alex and sliding it onto her thumb on her side of our waterfall altar.

"Paige, please place the ring on Hayes's finger and recite your vows."

Paige follows his direction, her small hands shaking as she places the ring on my finger and takes my hands in hers.

Her eyes are misty as she looks up at me, her face framed by her dark waves woven with delicate flowers.

"Hayes, you are a force of nature that changed my life forever, and I couldn't be more grateful that you took a chance on a silly debutante one night not that long ago in this very garden."

She pauses then, her words growing thick. Her eyes shimmer with unshed tears, and I run my thumbs across her knuckles in reassurance. She grips my hands in hers and steadies her voice before continuing.

"You can be unrelenting in the pursuit of what you want, and you take no prisoners along the way. You are demanding because you know your worth. You hold yourself to the highest standards and ask the same from others," she begins.

I smile and nod because it's the truth. But I can't help but wonder if her vows will highlight all my less-than-admirable qualities.

"I hope I can learn to be more like you in that regard because I admire you so much." She smiles and I wonder at my luck to be blessed with a woman like her. "But with me, you have always been kind, compassionate, and generous. Your love is unfathomable, and you make me feel cherished with every action, every *just because* present, and the simple day-to-day activities that you still manage to put me first in."

I can't take my eyes off of her. She is a radiant queen of grace and forgiveness, and listening to her tell our closest friends and family of our love has me enraptured. I am so fucking grateful she gave me a second chance to prove I could put her first, that I could see past my greed and realize how badly I had treated her, and prove that I will never repeat that bullshit again.

"I promise to ask for what I want, even when it's hard. I promise to love you back as fiercely as you love me. I promise to protect you and our life together from anything the outside world may throw at us. I promise to watch silly eighties movies with you and refrain from calling them old or calling you old by extension."

This gets a chuckle from the crowd. I smile right along with them.

"I promise to give you unlimited second chances and show you grace when you need it. I promise to hear you out and stick around when life gets difficult instead of running away from the hard times. I promise to be open to every new possibility with you."

She gives me a sly wink at that, and her smile is one of cheekiness I hope others will overlook as bridal happiness.

"But most of all, I promise to fight with you and for you and for us every day of our lives. I love you with all of my heart and I love this life we are building together."

A tear slides down Paige's cheek and I reach up and gently brush it away, cupping her face in my hand for a moment longer, just soaking in her heartfelt words and hoping I can do her justice with my own.

"Hayes, please place the rings on Paige's finger and recite your vows," the Judge tells me next.

I take Paige's left hand and slide on her rings, holding her hands in mine and looking deeply into her eyes so I can get through this very public display of my very private thoughts.

"Paige, you are goodness and grace incarnate. You are a benevolent goddess walking this mortal plane, and the fact that you somehow saw me and deemed me worthy of your attention despite being wholly undeserving will be my debt to repay forever. You make me better just by allowing me into your stratosphere, and I will never take that for granted."

I hear a few sniffles in the crowd and think they must be left over from Paige's vows because there is no way anyone would have any sort of empathy for the man I was before she entered my life.

"I fell in love with you the moment you walked into this garden, escaping from a society event just like I had."

This time the crowd chuckles for me, and I feel brave enough to continue.

"You started to change me for the better almost instantly. I knew I couldn't be the man I was before meeting you any longer because that man was undeserving of your time, attention, or love. I wanted all of that more than anything else I'd coveted in this life."

I stroke my thumbs across her knuckles again and compose myself for the rest of what I need to say. When I meet her eyes, they are endless wells of love and devotion I do not deserve, but she is giving them to me anyway.

"I promise to put you first and above anything else in this life. I promise to make you ask for what you want until it's second nature and always give you what you need when you can't. I promise to love you with every breath in my body, in this life, and forever after into the next. I would know you in any lifetime, and in any iteration, because you are a part of me that is walking this world outside of my body. I will love you forever, angel."

Paige's shoulders shake with silent sobs, and I take a moment to draw her into my arms and hold her against me, kissing her forehead and ignoring whatever protocol may be needed for a wedding ceremony. The most important thing at this moment isn't following a prescribed series of events, it's ensuring my wife is taken care of. She clings to my tux jacket and sniffles quietly. When she lifts her face, I carefully wipe her tear-stained cheeks and hold her face in my hands until she smiles and shows me she's ready to continue.

Our tender moment affects everyone in the crowd, with many sets of sniffles that can be heard over the bubbling of the waterfall. I look over at Judge Whitaker, and he's wiping his own cheeks, a small smile curving up his full mustache. He nods at me and holds up his leather book once again to continue.

"By the power vested in me by the great state of Georgia, I now pronounce you husband and wife. Hayes, you may now kiss your bride."

I smile widely as I slide my hand into Paige's hair to cradle her head, my other arm snaking around her waist as I dip her back and kiss her silly to cheers and clapping. Her lips press back, her hands coming to my cheeks and keeping my face close. I raise her back up and she's a vision of happy perfection, her smile euphoric as she gazes up at me.

The blur of events that follows is eclipsed by the depth of love, desire, and devotion I feel for my wife, who endures every photo, each hug, and every offer of congratulations with grace. I follow her lead, going where I'm told, posing as instructed, and staying on my absolute best behavior to do her justice. As long as I have her on my arm, I can endure anything. I could be chained to a mountain while an eagle tore out my liver, and as long as I have Paige, it would be worth it.

The only time I allow Paige out of my arms is when she slips away to change into a silky dress, with her hair caught up at the nape of her neck elegantly. It's an intriguing surprise when she spins in front of me and shows that the dress bares her back, stopping just before the curve of her ass. I'm struggling to keep my hands to myself as we finish our obligations at The Abyss, my hands straying to the soft skin as we pose and move through the garden. Thankfully, the planner calls for everyone to begin the trek to The Mansion and finally directs us downstairs and out of the club.

The vintage Rolls Royce that takes us from the club to The Mansion is a nice touch that Caroline arranged, and for once I appreciate her attention to detail.

I cup Paige's radiant face, running my thumb across her cheek. "How are you doing, angel?" I ask once we can relax, finally alone with our thoughts and each other after what feels like the longest day of my life. The nerves and adrenaline are wearing off, and I feel bone tired. I need to rally for what's ahead, which, according to Paige, will be a spectacle.

"I'm indescribably happy."

She turns her face and kisses my palm. When she turns back to me, I let my hand slide down to her neck, feeling her delicate throat muscles work as she speaks through the caress of my fingers against her skin.

"I'm actually really glad we had a chance to do this after all. For as much of a headache my mama has made this week, having that ceremony be exactly what I hoped for and something so personal to us, it almost makes what's coming next bearable."

I massage the back of her neck, wanting to ease some of the tension that flashes across her features. "It's just a few hours, then we have a honeymoon to enjoy."

She perks up at that, tilting her head at me. "But we haven't planned a honeymoon. I certainly wasn't expecting one."

"You don't have to expect it, but you deserve it after everything this month has held. It's about time I took some time off and really relaxed with you. Does a week in Turks and Caicos with white sand beaches and warm, crystal-clear ocean water sound good to you?"

She closes her eyes and shudders in pleasure. "That sounds incredible."

"We'll leave tomorrow."

"Oh, Hayes, you are too good to me." She pulls my head down and kisses me just as the car pulls up to The Mansion.

"Well, Mrs. Olsen, let's go start the rest of our lives together."

Thirty-Two

The Atlanta Haute List

B illionaire And Belle Throw Wedding of the Year

Our favorite newlyweds had quite the shindig down in Savannah for New Year's Eve. Hauties in the know have absolutely flooded our tip line with sightings of the who's who of the business world, photos, and recountings of the ceremony and reception, and we are positively ravenous for every last detail. Aren't you? Don't worry, we'll share all of the juicy details!

Hayes Olsen and Paige Fairchild held an intimate ceremony that took place at sunset in the vaunted rooftop garden known as Elysium at The Abyss Nightclub, with music by a string quartet and vows that had us swooning when we read them. The bride wore a bespoke off-the-shoulder, lace gown from none other than Haute Belle right here in Atlanta, and the groom wore an all-black Brioni tux that looked positively *yummy* on him. Brothers Payton and Zander stood at Hayes's side in their own classic black tuxes, and Alex Whitaker was Paige's man of honor in a deep green, rhinestone-studded, wide-leg suit that would have looked right at home on the likes of Taylor Swift or Harry Styles. We certainly appreciate the apparel choices of this fashionable crowd, blending classic and unexpected choices as fluidly as any fashionista. A giant black dog even joined the couple at the altar in front of a waterfall, on his *goodest boi* behavior as the best dog. Sources say the dog's name is Cerberus and he belongs to Hayes. We love seeing man's best friend featured so prominently in this beautiful ceremony! We want more Cerberus content and hope the happy couple will oblige us with more outings featuring him in the near future.

The bride—who changed into a stunning silk creation, again from Haute Bell—and groom were whisked away from the club in a vintage black Rolls Royce to attend the much larger reception at the Fairchild family's hotel, The Mansion, where a large conservatory ballroom was turned into a fairytale delight of the senses. The reported four hundred guests were made up of family friends, celebrities, Georgia supreme court judges, the mayor of Savannah, and business elites from every sector. Charming signature cocktails—a blackberry gin and tonic for the bride, and a smoked old fashioned for the groom—were made with Fairchild's own Underworld Spirits elderflower gin and double-barrel bourbon. The gourmet plated dinner featured filet mignon, whipped potatoes, and fried okra as a nod to the pair's Georgia heritage. A five-tier wedding cake had something for everyone's taste buds, including the couple's own tier featuring raspberry preserves between layers of chocolate cake, set in bourbon vanilla buttercream, and dusted with edible gold.

Guests were wowed by aerial performances through-out the evening, danced to a live swing band, and had the pleasure of meandering through a fairy garden that would have done Queen Titania herself proud that took up residence in the hotel lobby.

The twice-as-nice newlyweds were sent off at mid-night with sparklers and fireworks that exploded over The Mansion grounds and lit up the Savannah skyline. The revelers who stuck around were provided dessert shooters and bite-size comfort foods at the after-party with famed DJ Apollon playing hit after hit to keep the crowd dancing. Partygoers left in the wee hours of the morning with gift bags featuring Underworld Spirits liquors, Cartier watches or bracelets, and custom gift boxes of Ladurée chocolates and macarons. Are you drooling over these generous parting gifts, because we definitely are.

The couple is reportedly on their honeymoon, hav-ing left on New Year's Day for somewhere tropical and warm, we would hope. We wish them all the best in their lives together and our sincerest congratulations on their nuptials. We can't wait to have them back in Atlanta helping to keep us warm this winter with their fiery love story that continues to evolve and become one for the ages. We really have become the biggest fans of their relationship as they have disproved our doubts and challenged our preconceived notions of their personal lives time and again, which gives us hope for our own happily ever after.

Who knows, maybe the younger Olsen brothers, Payton and Zander, will take notes from big brother Hayes and be looking for their own great romances right here in Georgia. We know plenty of hauties that would be willing to step up to that challenge, right? One could only hope, and we are triple-crossing our fingers and toes to see that happen.

We'll continue to provide you with all the best haute takes and tips on this happy couple as always, so click Like and Subscribe for all the Haute gossip!

Thirty-Three

Epilogue

Hayes

"Happy anniversary, my love." I wrap Paige in my arms and kiss her as she stands in the kitchen, her heels already kicked off as she adjusts to being home from work.

We got here within minutes of each other, but the short wait to see her had me antsy and needing her in my arms. Who knew a year into our marriage I would still be anxious to have her against me, my hands on her body, my mouth on hers?

"Which one are we celebrating, again? The first wedding, or the second?" she grins up at me before rising on her tiptoes to press a kiss against my mouth.

"Both. We'll start now and celebrate through the end of the year. I heard Paris is extra fun for New Year's Eve.

We could leave now and spend the rest of the month there."

"You absolutely would *not* take three weeks off from work just to celebrate our anniversaries. You're a workaholic and would be climbing the walls after three *days*."

"I could find it in me to relax with you for a few weeks straight," I argue just to be contrary.

"Remember our honeymoon? Even the warm ocean and our villa where I spent most of the time naked couldn't keep you away from work the entire week. Besides, we can't jet off to Paris right now; we have Christmas and this one to consider."

My hands travel down her body to rest on the small bump at her front. It's not even big enough to look like she's pregnant, but a fierce love rises up in me every time I caress her belly knowing *we made that*. It keeps dawning on me that she's pregnant like I haven't had two months to digest the news. It's fucking wild that she is carrying our child, so little and precious, and that we will be parents in a few short months.

If I was protective of Paige before she got pregnant, now the urge to keep her safe is on a whole new level. I insisted she go back to driving the G-wagon despite having her own sportscar, and I assigned a security detail for any time she's not at home or with me. I very much want her to stay safe, but part of my abundance of caution is the tiny baby inside who already has me wrapped around their finger. I have the first sonogram picture up in my office and stare at the tiny bean many times throughout the day. It's too early to know the sex of our child, but I'm ready to spoil it rotten either way. But first, I must spoil my wife and my instinct is to convince her that she needs to go away with me right this moment so I can spend the next few days holding her in bed to make sure she gets the rest she needs while thanking fate for putting us together just over a year ago.

"We could work and play."

"Paris is cold right now. Don't you like the mild December we have here in Georgia? We should really just stay and enjoy it."

I pull away and give her a skeptical look. She's working extra hard to dissuade me from taking her on a vacation. *Who does that?* "What are you up to, wife?"

She casts innocent eyes up at me but can't help the twitch of a smile that tugs at her lips—her tell that she is absolutely plotting and scheming in her best Southern belle Machiavellian way. "I don't know what you mean."

"Is this because of the Christmas Eve dinner at The Mansion? We can come back before it or leave after the dinner is over if that is what is holding you up, but you know you don't actually have to be there in person to make sure it runs smoothly."

"You know for a fact I have to be there! I will not let this be the first year without a Fairchild host in over a hundred years. I won't allow that."

Her indignation is cute. She's a board member for the entire Olympus Hotel Group, but she still maintains a soft spot for the hotels that were once her legacy. She took it upon herself to host this tradition and she's grasped the reins as naturally as one would expect from her upbringing and as the daughter of an absolute hurricane of a woman who was intent on planning out every detail of Paige's life.

But this first trimester has been hard on her. She's often sick, and she's always exhausted.

I double down on my resolve.

"I don't like watching you work yourself to the bone each evening after a full day at Underworld Spirits. I'm more inclined to sweep you off to somewhere remote where you will have to rest and relax after all of this."

"Actually, I have a surprise for you here in Atlanta and I can't give it to you just yet, so we have to stay. If you want to leave as early as Christmas Day to go somewhere else, we can, but not before, please." She bats her long lashes at me and gives me a coquettish grin that I can't refuse.

I don't particularly like surprises, but a surprise from Paige has me intrigued. It's usually lingerie or something sexy, but I don't think that's the case for this one. "Just what have you got brewing, angel?"

"Something even you wouldn't have thought to do for yourself." Her smile is radiant and her joy at my lack of knowledge is quite evident in the shiver of anticipation that runs through her.

I'm slightly terrified.

"Is it a Christmas present or a *just because I was thinking of you* gift?" The two are one and the same, but Paige insists they are different and only accepts the latter from me now.

"Can't it be both?"

"Not when we've agreed that lavish presents are not how we do things. If I can't heap them on you, you won't be allowed to do it, either."

"Fine, I have been looking for just the right gift for you for the last year and I finally found it. You spoil me far too regularly to have any leg to stand on now if we're going to argue about it."

With a growl, I scoop her up into my arms and turn toward the stairs. "We are not arguing about this. There are not enough hours left in this day to spend even a few minutes arguing when I could just as easily strip you naked and fuck the surprise right out of you."

"You are an impossible man, and this is why I have such a hard time shopping for you," she grumbles, but she's not actually upset. She leans her head against my chest and lets me carry her up the stairs to our bedroom.

"You love me all the same."

"Of course I do! But I can still be a little vexed at you for making my life harder just by getting yourself everything you've ever wanted without leaving even a little something for me to get for you. Throw me a bone here, Hayes, I want to heap lavish gifts on you, too."

"You are the gift, angel. Every day with you is a gift. Every time you look at me with those impossibly green eyes, or tell me you love me, or wrap me in that adorable fucking hug, is another moment I feel like I'm the luckiest man alive and don't deserve the life I have that is so good because of you. You are the best present I could have ever received, and I'm damn sure not going to look that gift horse in the mouth."

She makes a soft sound and bursts into tears—a not uncommon occurrence these days as her pregnancy hormones run her emotions—and melts against my chest a little more. "That's the sweetest thing you've ever said to me. I am so happy," she sobs. "I shouldn't be crying when I'm happy."

I kiss her head before gently setting her on the bed. I peel away the layers of clothing she is wrapped in, peppering her with kisses as her tears continue. "You can cry any time you want, and I will always be here to kiss them away."

"Say something filthy and demanding right this minute or I will absolutely lose it and never stop crying because of all the sweet things you say," she demands, hiccupping through a sob.

"Spread your legs and let me see that gorgeous pussy right this instant." I'm working the cufflinks off of my shirt sleeves, the buttons already undone.

Her eyes go wide and a pretty pink blush softens the tear tracks on her cheeks. "Well, that's certainly one way to change my mood." She leans back on her elbows and slowly moves her knees apart just as I want.

I toss the shirt on the floor and move to my belt, making quick work of my pants and boxer briefs before I stalk toward where she reclines. "Do you want me to tease you, taste you, or fuck you?"

Her head tips back and her nipples grow tight in front of my eyes as she makes a sound of longing. "All three sound amazing," she says in a throaty whisper that has my cock hardening even more.

I wrap a hand around the base of my cock and kneel on the bed between her legs, parting her pussy and teasing along her slit to her apex. I roll my hips and stroke the shaft through her folds, letting the head play over her clit again and again while she shivers under me.

"I should make you suck your own juices off my cock. Let you taste yourself and how good we are together. Do you want me in your mouth now, or do you want my cock in your greedy little pussy."

I pause my movements just as the head is at her entrance, feeling her body fight to pull me in, but I resist.

She writhes under me, her hips rolling and looking for more while I keep teasing her. Her hands are on her breasts, fingers plucking at her nipples as I rock my hips an infinitesimal amount to breach her opening. She moans softly and I feel my resolve weakening.

I want to thrust into her as hard and fast as I can and rut into that tight pussy over and over until I come.

"Answer me," I growl, my control slipping. My hands find her hips to keep her still so she has to respond.

"Fuck me, Hayes, please! God, if you aren't inside of me in the next second, I will lose my mind."

Before she can complete her sentence, I slide in to the hilt and feel her body tense and tremble around me, her orgasm detonated by the first stroke.

"That's my good girl," I say on a shuddering exhale. Fuck... she feels so good.

I move her ankles up to my shoulders and work in and out of that tight pussy as it grips and releases, watching as Paige comes apart below me.

Her hands are above her head, fisting the duvet as she takes the thrusts, her moans and sighs music to my goddamn ears. I like her in this position, her pussy even tighter than normal, her body compliant to my ministrations, but as her release finishes, I'm already wanting another from her.

"Do you want to come again, my love?" I gently set her legs back down at my hips.

"What kind of question is that?" she mumbles, not quite coherent yet.

I pull out and help her turn over onto her knees before running the length of my cock along her folds and clit again. "Tell me what sort of surprise you have, and I'll let you come again."

She turns to look at me over her shoulder and frowns. "You're not playing fair, Hayes. That is some next-level manipulation right there."

I stroke against her again, watching as her eyes close and her lips part. "Who said I had to play fair? I do what I need to get what I want, and I want you to tell me what you're up to so I can fuck this tight little pussy again and make you shatter around me."

"Fine, you win, but don't expect another surprise—" Her words cut off as I thrust into her pussy, sliding in until our bodies are pressed tightly together, and she's left gasping in pleasure.

"I'll give you anything you want, my love, but I also take my fair share. Tell me what I want to know, and you can come." I rock my hips slowly and feather a soft brush of my fingers against her clit that has her rolling her hips for more.

She groans in frustration and pushes up to all fours. "You really can be a tyrant when you're motivated. No wonder you're so feared in the business world." She forcefully rocks her hips back against me, and I can't help but smile at her impatience to come.

I still my fingers on her clit and give her a light slap over the sensitive bundle of nerves that has her gasping. "That's not the answer I was looking for." *But it's all truth.*

"God, you feel so good," she moans before finally exhaling. "I'm having a drift car built for you."

"And why would you do that?" I ask, stunned at her unexpected answer.

"After going to the American Drift League events over the summer and seeing how much you enjoyed sponsoring the Beast Cave shop and Carter Ramsey this year, I asked him to build you something special."

I go still and look in wonder at the beautiful, thoughtful, amazing woman writhing impatiently under me. "How did I ever get so lucky?"

"I told you, now please, make me come," she moans, rocking against me again.

"As you wish." I circle her clit and drag my length through her tight pussy again and again.

To keep from coming right along with Paige, I allow my mind to wander to the American Drift League season we experienced this year. I was surprised she had enjoyed going to drift events with me. I don't have to attend events, but as the main sponsor for Carter Ramsey's Beast Cave drift team, I wanted to see how he did in the ADL. Paige came along and ended up loving the sport as much as I do, rooting from the stands and deciding she's a Shelby Jensen fan as much as a Carter Ramsey fan is required by default. I can't fault her on that front, Shelby is a force to be reckoned with and Paige liked seeing a woman challenge such a male-dominated sport.

Drift racing isn't refined like Formula 1, or predictable like NASCAR. Drifting is gritty, full of tenacious drivers like Carter who are desperate to prove themselves, pushing their vehicles, their teams, and themselves to the limit every single time they're on the grid. Sponsoring Carter allowed him to move up during his second season in the ADL. He came in second in the championships, behind Griffin McGregor of the Smoke and Mirrors team.

Paige makes a soft sound and her body tenses below me, bringing me back to this moment and making me curse that my mind had drifted away like the tire smoke on the grid after a race. I'm back here, with her, watching as her hips rock and her head tilts back in abandon. I change direction on her clit and feel her inner walls trembling against me. When she comes, it's an explosive squeeze that forces the breath from me. I work through her tight, vise-grip pussy and try to last, but the feel of her sucking me in over and over is too good. I power through one last thrust and pull her hips tight against me as I come with a fierce groan.

Paige's arms shake and she collapses face down into the duvet with a moan of contentment. I pull out of her wet heat and turn her to the side before heading to the bathroom and grabbing a towel to clean her up. When I return, she is still boneless and smiling.

"Worth it to give up your secrets, angel?" I run the towel over her, catching my cum that coats her thighs. If

I were a less civilized man, I would leave it there. I like seeing a bit of me left on her skin, marking her as mine.

She sighs and gives me a look. "I know that I can't even hint at a surprise in the future. I just have to ambush you completely when it's ready if I want to actually give you something nice." She makes a prim face at me that has me wondering at her machinations. "It shouldn't astonish me that you would be true to your word to fuck the information out of me, but I had hoped that I could do something nice and get one over on you this time."

I smile at her casual use of the word fuck outside of sex. She may only be repeating my words to me, but I like hearing her sweet mouth saying naughty things.

"You are doing something incredibly thoughtful, and it is a complete surprise." I place a kiss on her hip and toss the towel on the floor before I crawl into bed and pull her into my arms. "I never expected this, or even imagined this was what you had in mind." I run my hand over her side and gravitate to the tiny belly that my palm still covers.

"I want you to have more hobbies, so you'll be less of a workaholic. Maybe having a drift car will make you take a break on the weekends to put in some seat time on the track. You're so driven in every aspect of your life; I can't imagine learning to drift will be any different and you'll be hooked until you're a pro."

"How dare you," I say in mock outrage. "I have exactly three hobbies and am a very well-rounded person, I'll have you know."

"Oh yeah? What are your hobbies, because all I can think of is work," she sasses back, poking my chest with a finger.

"Of course, work is one hobby. The other two are you and forcing you to watch movies that came out way before you were born to ensure you have a proper cinematic education."

Paige laughs and drops her head to my chest before she can compose herself again. "You just said I was two of your three hobbies because forcing me to watch movies is still a hobby in which I am the main focus. You can't even come up with three hobbies, proving my point that you work too much and need some more fun in your life."

I frown at her just because it feels like the right thing to do when she makes a valid point that I have no intention of confirming. "How about I cook dinner for my beautiful wife and show you another hobby of mine that is of the culinary variety."

"Mmm, yes, please." She rolls away and walks into the closet, coming out in my Vanderbilt sweatshirt and joggers, her feet in thick socks that may also be mine, as they look way too big for her.

I smile in appreciation of her level of cozy and get myself dressed so I can feed her and ensure she puts her feet up tonight. She hasn't complained about swollen ankles yet, but I'm told it's likely to become an issue and I want to take the proper precautions.

She hurriedly starts down the stairs, but the slick wood is no match for her thick socks and her foot goes out from under her. Her startled cry pierces my heart and gets my adrenaline surging, and I manage to grab her around the waist before she tumbles down twenty-plus stairs to the first floor.

"Fuck, Paige, don't scare me like that!" My words come out with the rasp of sandpaper against metal, harsh and rough enough to cut. My heart is hammering in my chest giving downtown construction jackhammers a run for their money, so I yank her back and wrap her against me.

Her arms are trembling as she holds me just as tightly.

"I didn't expect that," she breathes, her words spoken into my chest where her face is pressed.

"No more big socks without something that grips between you and the stairs from now on, hear me?" I demand into her hair.

The idea of her slipping and falling to her ass on one stair is bad, but to have her roll down the entire staircase while pregnant? I shudder at the thought. There are too many dangers in this world that could harm my wife and our unborn child, and now I have to add the fucking stairs in this gorgeous mansion to the list.

I'm selling it. Single-level homes or nothing from here on out as far as I'm concerned. I'll call the realtor in the morning and buy the biggest sprawling one-story in Buckhead by the end of the week. Fucking stairs.

"You are planning the demise of every sock and stair combination in the world right now, aren't you? Ready to exact revenge on the laws of Physics and the coefficient of friction between smooth surfaces. I bet you're planning on selling the house off and putting me in a place where no stairs exist."

I look down into Paige's face, seeing the obvious humor that is quickly replacing the fear that only moments ago had us on our knees as the weight of the possibility of what could have happened played out in our minds.

Before I can refute her very true assumptions, my phone rings. Saved by the bell? I fish it out of my pocket and see Payton's name on the screen. Paige nods when I look at her.

"What?" I ask when I answer the call.

"Looks like our old enemies are back at it. Our network is under attack. We've had fifty attempts to breach our servers in the last half hour and our team is scrambling to keep our firewalls and protections in place."

"Don't we have the best tech systems money can buy? You built it. Why is this even a possibility?"

"Of course we do, which is why I was alerted at the first breach attempt and we know it's happening at all instead of being something covert or insidious that we find out about later after we're fucked. But it seems someone, or maybe multiple entities, would very much like to access our data, likely with a financial motivation. They could hijack the servers and demand a king's ransom to release them, funnel money into different accounts, or just wreak havoc on the system and leave us stranded for who knows how long."

"Is there a way to keep them out, or is this an inevitability?" I don't know the first thing about the tech side of our company, but Payton has his hand in everything at Olympus and runs the tech side of things like the savant he is.

"I've worked with the best white hat hackers to find weaknesses and shore up our systems for just this type of attack, so it's holding right now. Our tech department is working on finding breach points, but we've never encountered something on this magnitude. It's hard to tell if it will continue until they find some weak spot we are unaware of, or if they will change their tactics to target something else. Right now, it's just a full-frontal attack on every access point and if it continues, there is bound to be some sort of faltering."

"What should we do?" I'm fucking out of my element here. I can't hunt down the problem and fix it with brute force or play mind games to get my way, so I don't see the solution. If I had a name or knew even a little about who was doing this, it would be a different story.

"Prepare for something bad and hope for the best. Even if we get through this, I think it's just the beginning. We have too many enemies to think this will be it, and the group that attacked the mines has more than enough motivation to put on something like this, but we can't be sure it's them. It's time to go to war, brother."

This concludes The Bourbon Duet, but the Southern Gods Series will continue! The other Olsen brothers need their own happily ever afters, and I can't wait to share their stories with you. Keep reading for a sneak peek into Zander's story, The Southern Thirst Trap, which is available now!

Thank you for reading The Bourbon Bargain! If you enjoyed this book, I would be grateful if you could leave a review on the platform(s) of your choice. Reviews are so valuable to authors, and each one helps share our stories with others!

Hugs,
Adrian

Zander

I spent two weeks with a woman who changed my life, then made a vow to never see her again.

My first love is business—particularly the one that made me and my brothers billionaires before we even hit thirty. Nurturing an entity to a place of reaping these kinds of rewards requires commitment and skill, so I vowed to put my career and the growth of Olympus International first and foremost in my life. Nothing could come between me and my race to build something bigger and better than what I have. This is what fueled me and kept me going when the sixty-hour work weeks and the stress wrought by the constant state of expansion seemed crushing. I could look at the business, at my bank account, and what all the hard work afforded me—a life I enjoyed, notoriety in the business world, and a never-ending stream of willing women in my bed—and know it was all worth it.

When that's on the table, why settle for repeats? It became a game of conquest and dominion after a certain point. How many beautiful women could I take to bed? The limit does not exist. So I settled on a love-em-and-leave-em mindset, and it's worked for me. I pursued, I conquered, I moved on. It worked with my sense of adventure and pushing the envelope in all things—with women, with work, and with the wild ways I found to chase the adrenaline high in my off time.

I could base jump from a cliff, free dive in the ocean, take a car around a track at two hundred miles per hour, or scale a sheer rock face for time—it would all produce the sense of accomplishment and all-out body taxing push I needed.

So when I pursued the hottest swimsuit model Sports Illustrated had slapped on a cover—a woman whose face graced every billboard in Times Square, and was featured in dozens of beauty and fashion ads in every magazine you could pick up—I knew I was shooting for the pinnacle for who I wanted in my bed. I coveted Harlowe Sorenson, and I would make her mine.

I broke the rules right from the start for her. Gone was the idea of a single night, I needed my fill of this beauty, so I booked a trip to a private island in the Maldives for two weeks of freediving and fucking for sport. I was only a modicum of nervous for the length of time I planned to spend with someone who could be dull as dirt after a day or two. But from the few times I had crossed paths with her, very intentionally, I knew she could at least carry a conversation and had more going on upstairs than a lot of the models I fucked. My skills in the bedroom also meant I never had to suffer a bad lay and could liven up even the most lackluster partner to extremes of ecstasy.

I took her to dinner and when the bill was paid, I looked over and said, "You and me in the Maldives. Two weeks and not a care in the world. You in?"

"I have the next month off, tell me when and what terminal to meet you at," she replied.

"Tomorrow and I'll only need two weeks. Then you have life right back the way you want it. No promises for anything more, and no attachments," I proclaimed.

"No attachments," she agreed.

It was perfect on paper, a match made in my wet dream fantasies. Something straight out of my own best-laid plans.

So, what the fuck happened?

Harlowe Fucking Sorenson happened. She-Who-Must-Not-Be-Named. From the start when she made herself at home on my private jet during the twenty-plus hour flight, to the moment we stepped off the transfer boat at the island, I was lost to her. She captivated me, plain and simple.

"Race you to the reef," she challenged.

"I'll find more unique sea shells than you will," she taunted.

"I'll swallow your cock and have your eyes rolling back in your head," she promised.

And, what was fucking worse, she more than delivered every time a new saucy phrase was uttered in her husky rasp of a voice that sent chills down my spine on many occasions. I was racing to keep up with her boundless energy, her enthusiasm to experience something new each day, and her fearlessness when faced with a reef shark while running out of breath on a dive. I had never been challenged by anyone the way she challenged me in that short time. It was exhilarating. She got to me unlike any other adrenaline-fueled activity I had partaken in, the rush all wrapped up in a knock-out gorgeous five-foot-nine frame of lithe deliciousness.

She even challenged the island's Michelin-starred chef to a *wok off*, producing a meal just as decadent as the ones he created daily, *and* received his blessing to spend as much time as she wanted in his kitchen.

What's the problem, you may be asking. Harlowe was. I couldn't have this vivacious woman stealing more of my attention and keeping me under her spell when I got back to Atlanta. Olympus International was waiting to be groomed and pushed to new heights, demanding my blood, sweat, and every second of my time. I had made a promise to the mistress of industry first and foremost, and no woman, no matter how tempting, would be worth the risk of losing out on my business successes or what I would have to endure to keep them. The moment I knew she was forever material, I started to pull away. I could see diamonds on her fingers, breakfasts in bed, and growing old with her. None of that could happen.

No repeats, no attachments.

I let myself enjoy her, and the person I was with her, until we climbed aboard the jet home. I cut the strings fate had tied to us, crippling a future before it could take root. Stateside, I blocked her number and deleted it from my phone, not trusting myself with the temptation if it stayed. I fell back on years of the same patterns, which made it a little easier to say goodbye and mean it. There would be no repeats with Harlowe Sorenson. Not if I wanted to remain atop the Olympus International Tower in downtown Atlanta. I could have been a drowning man gasping for breath and still wouldn't take the life preserver she threw me knowing what it would cost me.

Each day away from her got easier, and soon, I had almost forgotten the buttery soft feel of her skin under my palm, the plushness of her full lips, and the way she would smile with the Devil himself lighting up her eyes when she climbed into my lap. I bought and sold businesses without so much as a thought of the woman who could have made forever less of a fantasy. I never expected to see her again, not intentionally, at least. She was off my radar the moment I went back to work, and I didn't go looking for anything she would have been attached to.

So imagine my surprise when I slammed right back into her five years later and realized I had made the biggest fucking mistake of my life.

The Southern Thirst Trap is available now and free to read in Kindle Unlimited!

Acknowledgements

To my readers—thank you for reading this book! Your messages, comments, and feedback have meant the world to me. I couldn't have done it without your love and support. I can't wait to share more stories with you!

Many thanks to the many people who took the time to encourage, beta-read, edit, and provide feedback to help me create this novel. You're all the real MVPs!

Billy—Thank you a million times over for being my person and the best dog daddy ever. Your support means the world to me, and your love is my everything. I love you, always.

Sharon – Girl, your friendship keeps me going when life gets hard. Your humor and support are unmatched. I appreciate your keen eye for proofreading and your love of my projects! Thank you for being the first to read everything!

Rebecca—Three-hour tea parties and Monday writing dates are my favorite things about getting back into the writing groove! You continue to inspire me with your effervescence and perseverance. I'm so glad we can share in the highs and lows of writing together!

Karin—Thank you again for taking on this project with me! I appreciate you moving my commas around like a Tetris ninja. You're the best.

Stephanie Higgins—Thank you for your proofreading expertise and for always being willing to weigh in on graphics and covers so I don't drive myself crazy. Your reassurance is so needed and always appreciated <3

The ladies of Bookstagram—Y'all are simply the best at keeping me writing because of your voracious appetite for romance and your unending support. Your gorgeous edits, amazing reviews, and enthusiastic DMs give me life and I am unendingly grateful to have found each and everyone of you.

About the Author

A drian R. Hale is an enthusiastic lover of life who embraces big dreams, for herself and in her books. She writes new adult and contemporary romance featuring strong heroes with secret cinnamon roll sides, and dream-chasing heroines, with a little angst, a lot of swoon, and all the steam lovingly sprinkled in.

Adrian loves fast cars, baking sweet treats, hiking through Texas hill country, and is affectionately known as an agent of chaos to those closest to her. A self-professed caffeine addict, she loves a good vanilla oat latte, and will never turn down a tea party, especially in celebration of little milestones. When she's not writing or reading, Adrian can be found cuddling with her five dogs and husband, watching the 2005 Pride & Prejudice, DIY renovating her home near Austin, Texas, or listening to Taylor Swift.

Website: www.adrianrhale.com

Facebook facebook.com/adrianrhaleauthor

FB Group facebook.com/groups/adrianhaleread-ers/

Instagram: instagram.com/adrianrhale/

TikTok: tiktok.com/@adrianrhale

Goodreads: goodreads.com/adrianrhale

Also by Adrian R. Hale

A Taste of Bliss
Drift Series
Drift Heat
Broken Drift
Southern Gods Series
The Bourbon Bride
The Bourbon Bargain
The Southern Thirst Trap
The Southern Submission

9 798991 871235